## *"Stay away from me, Mark. For your sake as well as mine,"*

Jenny begged.

"Why? Give me one reason," Mark said gently.

She looked down at her hands, fighting threatening tears. Damn it, she hadn't cried in years, and her sudden weakness scared her. She turned on him fiercely. "I don't like macho cops with outsized egos. Is that enough?"

Anger flashed in his eyes. "Not quite," he said, his voice as clipped and hard as his expression. "Just for the record, Jenny Wilson, what is it you're afraid of? Is it me? Or is it the fact that I'm a cop? Or maybe the problem's simply that, for a few moments, the ice cracked and you felt as attracted to me as I am to you?"

Dear Reader,

The hits just keep on coming here at Intimate Moments, so why not curl up on a chilly winter's night with any one of the terrific novels we're publishing this month? American Hero Duke Winters, for example, will walk right off the pages of Doreen Roberts's *In a Stranger's Eyes* and into your heart. This is a man with secrets, with a dark past and a dangerous future. In short—this is a man to love.

The rest of the month is just as wonderful. In *Diamond Willow* one of your favorite authors, Kathleen Eagle, brings back one of your favorite characters. John Tiger first appeared in *To Each His Own* as a troubled teenager. Now he's back, a man this time, and still fighting the inner demons that only Teri Nordstrom, his first love, can tame. Terese Ramin's *Winter Beach* is also a sequel, in this case to her first book, *Water From the Moon*. Readers were moved by the power of that earlier novel, and I predict equal success for this one. Two more of your favorites, Sibylle Garrett and Marilyn Tracy, check in with, respectively, *Desperate Choices* and *The Fundamental Things Apply*. Sibylle's book is a compelling look at an all-too-common situation: a woman on the run from her abusive ex-husband seeks only safety. In this case, though, she is also lucky enough to find love. Marilyn's book is something altogether different. A merger of past and present when a scientific experiment goes wrong introduces two people who never should have met, then cruelly limits the time they will have together, unless . . . You'll have to read the book to see how this one turns out. Finally, welcome new author Elley Crain, whose *Deep in the Heart* is a roller-coaster ride of a story featuring a divorced couple who still have an emotional tie they would like to deny, but can't.

In coming months look for more great reading here at Silhouette Intimate Moments, with books by Paula Detmer Riggs, Rachel Lee (the next of her Conard County series), Marilyn Pappano and Ann Williams coming up in the next two months alone. When it comes to romance, it just doesn't get any better than this!

Leslie Wainger
Senior Editor and Editorial Coordinator

# DESPERATE CHOICES

## Sibylle Garrett

Silhouette® INTIMATE MOMENTS®

Published by Silhouette Books New York

America's Publisher of Contemporary Romance

SILHOUETTE BOOKS
300 East 42nd St., New York, N.Y. 10017

DESPERATE CHOICES

Copyright © 1993 by Sibylle Garrett

ISBN: 0-373-07476-X

First Silhouette Books printing February 1993

All the characters in this book have no existence outside the
imagination of the author and have no relation whatsoever to
anyone bearing the same name or names. They are not even
distantly inspired by any individual known or unknown to the
author, and all incidents are pure invention.

®: Trademark used under license and registered in the United
States Patent and Trademark Office and in other countries.

Printed in the U.S.A.

**Books by Silbylle Garrett**

Silhouette Intimate Moments

*September Rainbow* #184
*Surrender to a Stranger* #211
*Rebel's Return* #271
*Sullivan's Challenge* #301
*The Twilight Prince* #366
*Desperate Choices* #476

## SIBYLLE GARRETT

is a world traveler who finally settled down on Long Island with her husband of twenty-two years and their two children. Her love of books, vivid imagination and a desire to share her many personal adventures eventually propelled her toward a career in writing. Writing romances satisfies the dreamer as well as the realist in her.

Evi, this one's for you
Love, Mom

# Chapter 1

"Jamie isn't here!"

For a moment, Jenny Wilson thought she'd misheard. The wind was loud, howling like a pack of wolves at a full moon, and the storm door she held open was weaving and groaning under the onslaught. Bright Happy Birthday balloons tied to the glowing brass lantern by the open door beat a wild tattoo against the house. The blowing rain slashed at the concrete stoop, soaking Jenny's legs and back. Shivering, she grasped the hood of her black trench coat more tightly about her and took a small step toward the slender, dark-haired woman hovering in the doorway.

Only when Chris's mother didn't invite her into the house did the words truly sink in.

Jenny stared at Camille DiNigro disbelievingly. "What do you mean Jamie isn't here? Did your husband take the kids to a movie or the store? I know I'm a little early—"

Her voice faltered when Camille shook her head. "Jamie must have left some time ago," she explained in her strident voice. "The last time I remember seeing him was when

Chris cut his birthday cake. That was more than an hour ago," she added, not quite meeting Jenny's eyes. "I have fifteen children here today. It's a little difficult to keep track of them all."

The excuse rang a little hollow. Children didn't just disappear! Jenny, a high school teacher, had an average of twenty-five wily juniors in her classrooms and she managed to keep track of them. And Jamie wasn't a cocky sixteen-year-old with a need to prove his independence. He was only ten. A very insecure ten. And he was afraid of storms. "Are you sure? Have you checked all the rooms?" she asked hoarsely, fear tightening her throat. Maybe her son had broken some heirloom or spilled a soda on the carpet and was hiding in some corner of the big colonial style house.

But even that small hope died when Camille shook her head. "We looked everywhere. His coat is gone, too," she complained, as if more irritated by Jamie's thoughtless behavior than concerned for his safety.

Something snapped inside Jenny and her voice rose angrily. "You behave as if Jamie lives just down the block. It's a five mile walk to our house, for God's sake."

A gust of wind almost drowned out her words. Camille took a step back and closed the door a little more. Brushing some raindrops off her blue silk blouse, she glared at Jenny. "It isn't my fault that Jamie decided to leave. Don't blame me for your son's disappearance."

Jenny huddled a little deeper into her coat. She should never have allowed Jamie to accept the invitation, not on such short acquaintance. But he'd been so eager to go, and he'd known so little laughter in his young life. She had seen no good reason to spoil his fun. The few times she'd talked to Camille at the karate school, where their sons had met, she'd found her a little pushy and self-righteous. Now she added callous to the list. She took a steadying breath. Accusing the woman wouldn't help her find her son. "Are any of the other children missing? Maybe he went next door to play?'' Then another thought occurred to her. What if—? "Could, maybe, someone else have picked him up or given him a ride?'' she asked with hoarse urgency.

Camille shrugged. "I wouldn't think so. All the other kids are still here.''

From inside party sounds drifted out into the cold wet— music, a mixture of adult and children's voices and the occasional squeal. Jenny felt her throat tighten with fear. Didn't anyone care that her son was missing? That he was somewhere out in this storm?

She spun around and stared at the long rows of cars parked on the street. Life had taught her some tough lessons. She'd learned the hard way that while most people would sympathize, few wanted to become involved. She glanced at her cranky Grand Am, standing in the driveway with the motor still running. Branches dipped and leaped, knocking on its white roof like ghost fingers in a shadow play. If Jamie was sheltered nearby, he would recognize their car.

But no boy dressed in a bright orange, turquoise and blue jacket came running toward it. To get back home Jamie would have to cross a busy four-lane highway and a rather seedy area around the railroad tracks—if he remembered the way back to their house.

"What happened?'' Jenny swung back to face Camille angrily. "Don't tell me that Jamie just decided to leave. He wouldn't have, not in this storm. And not without calling me first! We've only lived here a year and he doesn't know the area very well!''

Camille shifted uncomfortably. "He—''

"Camille, close the door. You're letting in the cold!'' A stocky man with wavy brown hair, olive skin and a classic Roman face shouldered his wife aside. With a nod of polite recognition, he told Jenny, "I'm sure my wife already explained that your son left about an hour ago.''

Eyes narrowed, Jenny glared from one expressionless face to the other. "So I've been told. What I want to know is why!"

Rich DiNigro leaned against the doorjamb, sliding his hands into the pockets of his brown dress slacks. "Jamie had a fight with Chris. I won't allow any brawling in my house, so I told him to wait outside for you."

A fight? That didn't sound like Jamie at all. She'd never heard of him hitting anyone before. Her son turned white when someone even yelled at him. He backed away from confrontations, which was why she'd enrolled him in karate school. Jenny stared from one dispassionate face to the other. "You told Jamie to leave because he had an argument with your son? What kind of people are you?" The wind tore the hood from her nerveless hand, cold rain stinging her skin and soaking her hair. Jenny barely noticed it. "Why didn't you call me to pick him up?" When Mr. DiNigro only shrugged, her eyes narrowed suspiciously. "Did you give him a chance to use the phone?"

"Your son didn't ask if he could call." This time there was a defensive note in Camille DiNigro's voice. "And we didn't know he was only ten. He looks more like twelve, and he certainly sounds like it. Jamie has a very nasty mouth on him."

Jenny's eyes raked over the woman standing so self-righteously before her from head to toe, wondering if she was telling the truth. Away from home children often behaved differently. Only she'd never heard any complaints from Jamie's teachers, or from her neighbors. "That still doesn't excuse your behavior. If he was causing problems, you should have called me!" She fixed Mr. DiNigro with an accusing stare. "Especially you. As a lawyer, you shouldn't have to be told how dangerous it is out there."

"Like I said, we thought he was twelve," Camille Di-Nigro repeated, as if twelve were the magic number when children suddenly turned adult. "I'm real disappointed in him. At first I thought he was such a nice, well-mannered boy. Then he stuffed his pockets full of candy—''

She'd heard enough, Jenny decided, meeting the woman's glittering black eyes with scathing contempt. ''May I suggest that you start worrying about the fate of my son instead of a few pieces of candy?''

Richard DiNigro pushed himself away from the doorjamb and protectively placed his muscular body in front of his wife. ''Are you threatening us?''

Jenny watched his beefy hands slowly ball into fists and took an involuntary step back. Three years and a man's anger still made her flinch! Staring at those fists she suddenly understood why Jamie had left without calling her. Her son had been too frightened to open his mouth.

For a moment blood drummed in her ears and she couldn't breathe. The need to run was so strong that she found herself turning away from the threat. Then the cold rain stung her face again and her panic receded, fury replacing fear. No one would intimidate her son and get away with it. Spinning around, she faced the bully. ''Yes, Mr. DiNigro,'' she said determinedly, her shaky voice growing firmer with each word, ''I am threatening you. So you better start praying that nothing has happened to my son.''

The lawyer merely shrugged, unconcerned. ''You want to sue me? Go ahead. There isn't a chance in hell that you'll win. I didn't throw your son out, I merely told him to cool off outside. It's my word against that of a ten-year-old kid. Who do you think the court will believe?''

Jenny's mouth twisted bitterly. She had no illusions about the legal system. Justice was a second-rate word these days. Like any other commodity, it could be bartered to the highest bidder. That was another little lesson life had taught her, but one she still found difficult to accept. Without another word Jenny turned away, racing across the leaf-covered lawn to her car.

The five mile trip back home that night would haunt Jenny for years. The country road was long and narrow, without sidewalks and with few streetlights. Big puddles flooded the pavement. Jenny circled them, uncertain of their depth, fearful her car would stall otherwise. Rain pelted the windshield so hard that she could barely see the road. Driving slowly, she probed the darkness, scanning tree trunks, gardens and open fields, stopping at every shadow, every movement. And with each mile her fear grew. How long did it take a fifth grader to walk five miles in a storm? What if he had lost his way? Or was hit by a car?

Maybe she should call the police.

Jenny dragged a shaky hand through her wet hair and shook her head. Involving cops was a risk she'd only consider as a last resort. First she planned to stop at every store on the way home. With luck Jamie had sought shelter in one of them.

But at the back of her mind lurked her constant fear. What if Burke had found him and had taken her son away?

Detective Sergeant Mark Lawton was wrapping his son's birthday present and making a mess of it. Around him the hardwood floor was littered with bright scraps of red paper, wadded up balls and wrinkled tape. Carefully he spread the last sheet out on the white kitchen counter, smoothing the creases out with the ball of his hand. Placing the unwieldy cardboard box in the center, he measured and cut the paper with the same precision and dogged persistence he used to solve a homicide.

The scabs on his knuckles made his movements awkward and his bruised ribs complained every time he bent over too far. Dropping the scissors on the counter, he slowly straightened to his full height of six foot four.

Perhaps he should have sent his son the money to buy the video game machine out in California, he thought, reaching for a can of beer. But getting a check in the mail wasn't nearly as exciting as receiving a package. His hard face softened. At eight Tim was still young enough to look for surprises. Besides, Carolyn would insist on putting the money in the bank, arguing that Tim didn't need another toy. Maybe he didn't, but with three thousand miles separating them, Mark rarely had the chance to spoil his son these days.

Money—or the lack of it—had been one of his ex-wife's constant gripes during their marriage. Suffolk County cops were among the highest paid in the country, but after paying the bills and Carolyn's college fees, they'd barely managed to stay in the black. Mark grimaced. He hadn't minded the sacrifice or the long hours of overtime. He loved his job, and his wife's engineering classes had kept her busy. But she'd hated his work, and when the offer from Silicon Valley had come soon after her graduation, she'd jumped at it.

Their divorce, Mark thought with a grim twist of his mouth, had come almost as a relief. He missed Tim, though, more and more with each passing month. Seeing his son for only six weeks out of a year wasn't nearly enough. They were slowly drifting apart.

He took a long drag of beer, but the smooth cold drink didn't quell the bitter taste in his mouth. Lately, he'd wondered if the job was worth all the abuse and frustration, the loss of his son.

With a sigh, he turned his attention back to the box. This time he was careful not to stretch the paper too tightly as he folded it at the corners. Holding down the flaps, he tore a piece of tape from the dispenser. The plastic strip stretched, snapped and curled around his thumb. "Damn!"

Frustrated, he straightened and peeled off the tape. Maybe he should leave it until tomorrow. The stitches on his forehead itched worse than mosquito bites and his head was pounding like a loose shutter banging against the house. The last thought brought a grim smile to his face. Perhaps there was a screw loose in his head. Who in his right mind would take two bullets, have his nose rearranged, have some kids attack him with crowbars and still want to go back for more?

Kids. They'd been little more than kids and arresting them should have been little more than a formality. He'd made a mistake that night, an error of judgment and he never did live well with mistakes. Maybe he was burning out and it was time to quit.

During the past week he'd seriously thought of leaving the department and moving closer to his family. His father, Roy, had been pressuring him for years to join the family construction firm in Queens. A retired cop himself, he'd warned Mark that the job wasn't worth the loss of his son. Mark poured the rest of the beer down his throat and tossed the can into a half-filled plastic bag, where it landed with a rattling hollow sound. Empty, like he felt inside.

For a moment he listened to the rain drum on the roof of the ranch house and wind rattle the windows. Perhaps it was the storm that made him feel his solitude more acutely tonight.

Suddenly the blare of a car horn drew his attention. Squinting through the big bay window into the dark night, he watched a black pickup charge down the road, cutting through the big puddles like a powerboat. Even from here he could see how water sheered off, splashing high against the windshield. Apparently blinded, the driver veered toward the side of the road, headlights leaping over a telephone pole, bushes and a brick wall.

Tensing, Mark cursed. Any moment the fool was going to wrap his truck around one of the old maple trees, or worse, drive up Mrs. Wilkins's lawn and land in her living room. But at the last second the driver pulled sharply to the left and cut across the road, making straight for Mark's property.

The headlights picked up a bright spot of color right at the bottom of the lawn. For an instant the small figure didn't move, trapped like a wild animal in the beam of light. Then it leaped aside, diving out of harm's way.

Swearing steadily, Mark strode into the foyer. By the time he opened the front door, the kid had already scrambled back to his feet, staring after the fading red lights.

"Are you all right?" Mark raised his voice over the whine of the wind.

Abruptly the child turned and took a few steps forward into the circle of floodlights. The bright, multicolored jacket was glistening with water, its hood tightly drawn around his face. "That truck almost ran me over," he shouted, brushing a shaky hand over his eyes.

It was a weary gesture, at odds with the anger in his voice. Mark wondered just how long the kid had been out in the storm. He was a little over five feet tall, slender and no more than eleven or twelve years old. Too young to wander the streets after dark, especially on a night like this. With a grimace at his white cotton socks, Mark stepped onto the damp concrete of the covered porch. "I guess he didn't see you until it was too late. Want to come in and dry off?"

Eagerly the boy took another few steps forward. Then, as if remembering that he wasn't supposed to talk to strangers, he stopped beneath a pine tree. "I'm almost home."

"Where do you live?" Mark asked, shivering as the wind bit through his old sweatshirt and jeans.

"Dogwood Lane."

"That's still a good twenty minute walk from here. If you give me a moment to put on my shoes, I'll drive you home."

"Thanks, but I can walk." The boy straightened and turned away.

Mark frowned. To let the kid wade home through the puddles was too damn dangerous. If he didn't get hit by a car, he'd drown or catch pneumonia. "Stop right there," he shouted firmly, hoping that the boy would respond to the voice of authority. He wasn't in the mood to chase after him, not in his socks and with his ribs stabbing at his lungs with each deep breath. And the cold wind was beginning to make his head throb with renewed intensity. "There's no reason to be scared of me. I'm a police officer."

The boy yelled something back, but the wind tossed his words out into the night. For a second Mark wondered if he didn't like cops, but that was ridiculous. The kid didn't seem the kind to be in trouble with the law. He was too polite and too well behaved. With a sigh, Mark walked to the edge of the concrete slab, wincing as cold moisture seeped through his socks. "It's wet out here. Come inside while I get my coat."

A strong gust of wind almost bent the pine tree in half. Watching it, Mark held his breath. He should have cut it down when it started to lose its needles in August. But the tree was the first one he'd planted when he'd bought the house and he'd decided to wait and give it a fighting chance. An ominous crack followed. The boy jumped, turned and raced toward him. His eyes were the size of brown saucers when he gasped, "That tree almost fell on top of me."

Mark watched the trunk straighten, slowly, like a battered man. There was life in it yet, he thought. Grasping the boy's wet sleeve, he asked, "What's your name?"

"Jamie—" The boy had been watching the tree, too. Now he turned, glanced at the hand clamped down on his arm and stuck out his chin. "My name is James Wilson. I'm ten years old and I'm not afraid of storms."

Mark felt a grin tug at his mouth. Gravely, he said, "My name is Mark Lawton, I'm thirty-seven years old and for a moment back there I was scared."

"Really?"

"Really. Do you still want to walk home?"

Jamie wiped water off his face, hesitating. "You don't look like a cop. Where's your ID?"

Someone had done a hell of a job raising him, Mark thought. "Inside. Want me to get it?"

This time there was no hesitation. "Yes."

Grinning fully now, Mark went into the house, opened the coat closet, took the shield from his leather jacket and walked back outside. Flipping it open, he said, "It's called a tin. A gold tin."

Jamie stared at it with awed fascination. "It looks real. Are you a good cop?"

The question startled Mark. Sliding the shield into the back pocket of his faded denims, he wondered how he was supposed to answer that. A week ago he would have laughed and teased Jamie about watching too many shows on TV. Now he found himself wondering, hesitating. "I try to be," he finally said with a glance at his wet socks. "Look, I have to put on shoes and a coat and find my car keys. That will take a while. You can either stay out here in the cold or come inside." Without waiting for an answer, Mark opened the storm door.

After a moment's hesitation Jamie followed him.

Inside the foyer Jamie drew a handkerchief from his zippered pocket and wiped his face while water pooled around his muddy boots. When he looked up he got his first good look at Mark and his movements froze. For long seconds he probed Mark's battered face with eyes that were too old and wary for a ten-year-old boy. "What happened to you?"

"An accident." Mark met the searching gaze steadily. He had seen looks like that before. And suddenly he realized that Jamie's question "Are you a good cop?" wasn't just a remark from a boy who was watching too much fantasy on television. Somewhere Jamie had lost his belief in justice. There were times, especially lately, when Mark felt the same way about the system: frustrated, let down, fed up. But it still hurt to see his own feelings reflected in the eyes of a ten year old.

"What kind of accident?" Jamie asked, caution changing to curiosity. "Are you an undercover cop?"

Mark guessed he looked the part of a tough rogue cop with a heart of gold and a total disregard for the law. Gri-

macing, he ran a finger over his throbbing scar. He might
stretch the rules a little when it suited him, but never enough
to give a perpetrator the chance to get off on a technicality.
"No, I'm just an ordinary detective," he said, leading the
way into the kitchen.

Following at a slower pace, Jamie stopped just inside the
door, a startled look crossing his face. "What a mess!" he
exclaimed. Then, remembering his manners, he gnawed his
bottom lip, "I mean—I'm sorry—"

"That's all right." Mark's glance skimmed over the pots
and plates stacked in the sink, the dirty glasses and two
empty pizza cartons. A week's supply of newspapers and
mail were scattered over the counters. He wasn't a fanatic
about neatness. A little mess here and there gave the empty
house a lived-in look, but he rarely let things get this bad.
He ran a hand over his two-day-old whiskers and grimaced. "It is a mess, isn't it?"

"Yeah." Grinning, Jamie kicked a paper ball. "Who's
the present for?"

"For my son." Mark stopped the missile with his foot,
sent it up in the air, caught it with his hands and tossed it
into the trash. The small action jolted memories of similar
little games he used to play with Tim. "His birthday is still
two weeks away, but he lives in California, so I have to send
it early."

Jamie's grin vanished, his eyes narrowed and he went very
still, like an animal sensing a threat. "California is a long
way away. Don't you like your son?"

Uneasiness rippled down Mark's spine. The boy's clothes
were well made, expensive, matching the address Jamie had
given him. Young children from upper middle class families didn't roam the streets at night, especially not in a storm.

Unless they were afraid to go home.

Mark saw no bruises or scratches on Jamie's face or his
hands, but that didn't mean a damn thing. There were many
ways to hurt a child without leaving marks. "My wife and I

are divorced," he explained quietly. "Tim moved to California because that's where his mother works. He's spending Christmas with me this year. Maybe your mother will allow you to play with him. He doesn't have any friends around here."

Jamie nodded and his smile slowly reappeared. "He can come to my house. I have lots of toys. And my mom won't mind. She's a teacher and she likes kids."

Mark felt his suspicion ease. "What were you doing out in the storm?" Taking a dish towel from a drawer, he tossed it across.

Jamie caught it deftly, wiped his face and hands then untied his hood. Pushing it back, he ran a hand through his damp blond waves. "I went to a birthday party and they threw me out."

With his hip propped against the counter, Mark balanced on his right leg, trying to strip off his left sock, a tricky, painful business. At the boy's flat statement, he looked up. "What did you do? Start a fight?"

Jamie shook his head. "I didn't. Honest. Chris punched me first. When he called me a sissy, I hit him back. I tried to explain to his dad, but he wouldn't listen and told me to get out."

Mark straightened, twisting his socks into a ball. "Why didn't you call your parents?"

"I was too scared to ask if I could use the phone," Jamie admitted honestly. "I thought I could make it home before my mother left the house. I didn't want her to get yelled at, too."

"What about your father?"

"He's...dead."

Slight though it was, Mark caught the hesitation and his eyes narrowed fractionally. There were many reasons why a child would deny his father's existence. After his own divorce two years ago, Tim had gone through a stage of rejection, refusing to talk to Mark for weeks. But there was no anger or pain in Jamie's voice, just the flat statement that his father had died.

Mark turned to the sink and squeezed water out of his socks. He didn't like the picture that was slowly evolving. As a cop he'd seen enough cases of abuse to recognize the signs. As to why Jamie lied about the bastard's existence, Mark could only guess. Maybe because it was easier to deal with a dead monster. Dead men posed no threat.

"How far did you walk?" Mark asked quietly, deliberately changing the subject.

Jamie looked at the kitchen clock. "I don't know. Maybe an hour and a half."

Mark squeezed the socks so tightly water dripped down his hand, wishing it was the bully's neck. None of his anger showed in his voice, though, when he suggested firmly, "Your mother must be scared by now. Why don't you call her and let her know that you're safe."

Jamie laid the wet towel on the kitchen table. "I don't think she's home yet. She was supposed to pick me up at seven and it's barely seven-thirty now."

Wiping his hands, Mark walked to the wall phone. "Do you have an answering machine?" At Jamie's nod Mark picked up the receiver and held it out to him. "If your mother isn't back, leave a message and my phone number." He pointed at the number displayed beneath a clear plastic strip and waited until Jamie began punching buttons before walking down the hall.

In his bedroom he made straight for the bottle of aspirin on his nightstand and shook out three, then stepped into the adjoining bathroom. Filling a glass with cold water, he swallowed the pills, avoiding a look into the mirror above the sink. He didn't care much for what he saw these days.

Jamie's voice drifted through the silent house. "Mom, don't worry. No, honestly, I'm fine."

With a grimace of impatience, Mark walked back into his bedroom, searching for clean matching socks in the laundry basket and eased himself down on the foot of his unmade bed. Apparently the mother was home after all and, judging from Jamie's soothing tone, she was crying. Mark had little patience with the "hand wringing" type of women. Tears were mostly an act of self-indulgence, or manipulation, anyway. Granted, Jamie's mother had spent some anxious minutes. Still, he resented that it was Jamie who comforted and assured when the roles should be reversed.

Or maybe he resented the woman because she reminded him too much of his ex-wife.

"Mark, my mom wants to talk to you."

"I'll take it in here." Frowning, Mark reached for the bedside phone, bracing himself for a flood of tears. The trick in dealing with women like his ex-wife was to remain firm, professional, and not allow them a word in edgewise. "Mrs. Wilson? This is Detective Lawton with the Suffolk County Police Department. Jamie is fine. A little wet, but there's not a scratch on him."

"Detective, I don't know how to thank you," Jenny tried to interrupt him shakily. The phone had started to ring just as she'd climbed the porch steps and she still couldn't quite grasp that Jamie was safe. She would have hugged the devil himself for rescuing her son. But, damn it, did the man have to be a cop?

"What Jamie needs is a—"

As he went on, she leaned against the center island in her kitchen and listened. He had a nice voice, deep, calm and reassuring. Jenny felt her world stop spinning and her tension ease.

"—hot bath, warm food and dry clothes. I'm about to leave the house and in this weather it will—"

Jenny gripped the receiver tightly and straightened, tension flowing back into her. She'd stopped believing in 'Blue Knights' long ago and she didn't want him in her house. "Detective! There's no need to bother you," she raised her voice. At the sound of agitation, Mush, her German shepherd, left his position at the kitchen door, trotted toward her and nudged her hand. Jenny stroked the dog's soft fur, waiting for the cop to run out of steam.

But the deep firm voice never faltered, "—take me at least ten minutes to get to your house, so don't get nervous if it takes a minute longer."

Nervous? She was getting frustrated and irritated, Jenny thought, dragging a hand through her damp waves. What the panic specialist didn't understand was that she wasn't going to faint. She was shaken, yes, and also a little weak with relief, but she'd faced worse storms without falling apart. "Detective, will you just—"

"The roads are flooded and I may have to backtrack—"

He was driving her up the wall! Switching to the speaker phone, Jenny walked to the refrigerator and took a container of chicken soup from the freezer section, then placed it in the microwave. The man carried the motto To Protect and To Serve to extremes, and while she was grateful for Jamie's rescue, she couldn't stand overbearing macho males.

She stabbed at the panel, setting the microwave to defrost, reproaching herself for her lack of gratitude. Without the detective, Jamie would still be wandering the streets and she truly appreciated everything he'd done for her son.

Mark frowned when he heard the electronic beeps and stopped abruptly. "Mrs. Wilson? Are you listening?"

"Yes. I heard every word. Detective, I know what it's like outside. I've been driving around in the storm for over an hour—" Jenny finished setting the timer, pushed the Start button and continued "—I appreciate your kindness, but there's no need to bother you. I still have my coat on, I'm already wet and my car's still warm. If you give me your address, I'll leave right away."

Maybe he'd misjudged the woman, Mark decided with a rueful grin. Still, he wasn't going to take the risk of her getting stuck on her way over here. "Cops get paid to be bothered, Mrs. Wilson. I'll wrap Jamie in a blanket while—"

"—while I heat the soup?" Jenny asked tartly, her glance sliding over the cherry wood cabinets and white tile countertops, looking for something else to do. But the counters were shiny and the dark wood gleamed. Even Mush's water bowl was filled to the brim. She took a steadying breath and continued, "The chicken soup's already in the microwave. Jamie has plenty of dry clothes and the house has a new heating and plumbing system. Hot water at the flick of a wrist."

She sounded tough, organized and well able to take care of herself. Mark hesitated, slanting a longing look at his rumpled pillow. He felt like hell. The pounding in his head was getting worse. If he didn't have to drive he could take the stronger stuff that knocked him out cold.

Only he'd been a cop too long. He remembered Jamie's protectiveness toward his mother too well to fall for her tough talk. "Then I suggest that you make use of the hot water yourself, Mrs. Wilson. You have ten minutes to take a shower and change into dry clothes."

Jenny glared at the receiver, opened her mouth to tell him to mind his own business, then shut it again. She wasn't going to waste time arguing with a brick wall. Also, her resistance might make him curious, even suspicious. "If you insist," she agreed briskly. "But before you hang up, I want your address and badge number. I only have your word that you're a cop."

A slow, appreciative grin spread over Mark's face. He gave her the information, allowing her time to write it down. When she thanked him, still in that brisk, controlled voice, he couldn't help but bait her a little. "Want my phone number, too?"

"Jamie already gave it to me," Jenny said, refusing to allow him to irritate her again. For a moment she listened to the wind rattle the shutters and rain slash against the win-

dows. Suddenly she felt very tired and relieved that she
didn't have to face the storm again, alone. Her voice softened, wavered. "Detective?"

"Yeah?"

"Thanks. And be careful. It's hell out there."

Not so tough after all, Mark decided, his voice softening
at the signs of weariness. "Don't worry, Mrs. Wilson. I'll
get Jamie safely back to you."

His sudden gentleness brought a lump to her throat.
Swiftly, before she could make a fool of herself, she thanked
him and hung up. Then she leaned against the wall, closed
her eyes and let relief wash over her. Jamie was safe and
well.

*But for how long?*

Despite the warmth filling the house, she felt cold, but it
was a cold that came from within. For a moment the cozy
kitchen retreated and she stood once again in the freezing
wind on the steps of the yellow brick courthouse in Dark
Water, Oklahoma, the divorce decree clutched in her hand,
staring at the tall, slender, brown-haired man blocking her
way....

"This isn't the end," he said in the soft, gentle drawl that
always made her want to cringe. "Sooner or later, you'll
come back to me."

"Never!" Her hand closed convulsively over the papers,
crushing them, trying not to show how much Burke still had
the power to frighten her. She wanted to stand up to him,
yell at him, spit at him in the face, the way she had done
four months ago.

The day he had hurt Jamie.

The day Aunt Alys had unexpectedly visited her and had
helped her to escape. But it was too soon. The terrible
memories were only beginning to fade. She licked her dry
lips and took a step back, hating herself for her weakness.

Burke's white manicured hand shot out, cupping her chin.
No one looking at him would guess at the strength hidden

beneath the elegant gray suit or the cruelty of his grip. "Never is a long time, little lady," he said, forcing her chin up so she would have to meet his eyes.

*Lady*—cold, stuck-up and rich. God, how she hated that name.

"Both you and Jamie belong to me. If you plan to run, I'll always be a step behind you, breathing fire down your neck. And when I find you—"

His grasp tightened like screws, pressing her soft flesh against her teeth. Sharp pain shot into her head, making her reel. Briefly she looked into his eyes, those hypnotic eyes that could change from pale green ice to blazing green fury without warning. The threat she read in them was unmistakable. No matter how fast she ran and how far she traveled, he would eventually find her.

Dimly she felt her hand open and the divorce papers drop from her nerveless hand. The wind lifted and blew them down the steps. The fluttery movement caught Burke's attention and distracted him. His grip eased. Sobbing, Jenny twisted free and kicked his shin so hard he howled in pain. And then she ran....

Sensing her distress, Mush licked her hand. Slowly Jenny's eyes slid back into focus and she looked around the cozy kitchen. For close to two years she and Jamie had continued to run, hiding in furnished apartments, changing names with each move. At first there had been some close calls. But Burke was too ambitious to neglect his work for long. A few weeks after that day at the courthouse, he had returned to his job with Global Airlines, while Jenny had drifted farther north.

That's how it would happen, she thought uneasily. There would be no premonition, no warning. One of these days she would look up, and Burke would be there.

And the nightmares would start all over again.

With a sigh, she pushed herself away from the wall. In the last fifteen months, the sharp fear had begun to dull. Until tonight, she'd almost believed in safety and a normal life for Jamie and herself. She'd become careless, almost complacent. Maybe it was time to move on.

She'd think about it later.

Right now, she had other things to do. Working always had a calming effect on her. She had to fill the tub with hot water, warm Jamie's pajamas—

And think of a way to get rid of one pushy, macho cop.

## Chapter 2

Driving conditions were much worse than Mark had expected. The rain was coming down in sheets, and the pavement was littered with downed power lines and torn branches. In some spots the water was so high, Mark's Blazer occasionally sputtered, threatening to stall. If he hadn't known the area even better than the contents of his closets, he would have driven right past Jamie's street. Even so, he almost missed the turnoff. Swearing, he braked, and backed up a few yards.

Turning into the narrow winding road, he checked on Jamie. The boy had fallen asleep the moment he'd pulled out of the driveway, and hadn't stirred since. Mark's face softened. After his long walk the kid was beat. Gently, he pulled the thick soft blanket over the boy's shoulder and tucked it beneath his chin.

Mark grimaced. He'd like to teach that bully a lesson he would remember. Maybe slap him with charges of child abuse and endangering the life of a minor. He knew that the charges probably wouldn't stick. But he'd get great satisfaction out of slapping handcuffs on the guy, then making him stand outside the cruiser long enough for his neighbors to see him. Sometimes the humiliation and a stiff lawyer's fee were enough to make a man think twice before showing another kid the door.

But without a complaint from Jenny Wilson, he couldn't do a damn thing.

Mark swerved to avoid a garbage can rolling down the road. He wondered why she hadn't called 9-1-1. Maybe, like her son, she wasn't too fond of cops. Still, even crooks asked for assistance in weather like this. Only three months ago, when Hurricane Bob had brushed past the Island, his partner, Jay, had literally stumbled over a cache of weapons in the rubble of a beach house while trying to rescue the dealer and his family from their flooded home.

Mark's eyes narrowed. Mrs. Wilson's insistence to pick up her son was, if not suspicious, at least odd. The house, when he caught a glimpse of it moments later, made him even more uneasy. It sat way back from the road, tall rhododendrons and evergreens shielding it from the casual eye. Not exactly a safe place for a single woman with a young child to live in these days.

Cautiously, he eased his car up the steep, leaf-covered driveway, wincing as low-hanging branches scraped the roof. Then floodlights came on, giving him an unobstructed view of a white two-story building with tall narrow windows, dark shutters and beautiful latticework. Pots of bright yellow mums flanked the front door, and on the wide covered porch a swing rocked in the wind. The sight made him think of hot chocolate and roasting marshmallows in a fireplace. Even in the midst of the storm, the sturdy, enduring structure seemed like a tranquil haven.

The tranquillity was shattered moments later when the front door flew open and a big dog charged down the porch, barking furiously. A slender woman followed him, her head bent low into the wind. She leaped down the steps and raced down the walkway, the hood of her black trench coat clasped tightly around her face.

A bundle of condensed, nervous energy, she didn't wait for the Blazer to pull up next to her white Grand Am under the carport, but ran alongside it as if afraid to lose sight of her son again.

The moment Mark stopped the car, she jerked on the handle to the passenger's side so hard that he winced. When the door flew open, the German shepherd jumped up and, with large muddy paws streaking the seat, bared his big white teeth and growled. A deep, ugly scar ran from his left ear across his eye, then down his long black-and-tan snout, giving him an even more ferocious look. Mark braced himself for the impact. He was definitely getting the feeling that he wasn't welcome here.

Then Jamie stirred. He blinked and patted the dog's head. "Hi, Mush," he muttered drowsily.

Abruptly the beast's growl changed to a whine. He would have leaped onto the boy's lap if his mistress hadn't grabbed the choke chain and pulled him back. "Down, Mush! Behave yourself," she ordered with a firm tug at the collar.

Mark counted three more tugs before the dog finally obeyed and got down. But then he immediately trotted around the car and took up a stance beside the driver's door, his watchful gaze steadily fixed on Mark. Mark felt an off-balance sensation steal over him. Dogs had been sicced on him before, but never a battle-scarred warrior with a name like Mush! With a gleam in his eye, Mark settled back against the door, wondering what other surprises were waiting for him.

Apparently, though, Mrs. Wilson had run out of surprises. She tossed an apologetic smile in his direction and said, "I'm sorry about the dog." Then she ducked her head into the car and hugged her son fiercely. There were no questions, no recriminations or tears. But the raw silent intensity of the embrace made Mark's stomach twist. An icy conviction began to crawl up his spine. These two had known fear before, terrors much worse than the storm they'd weathered tonight. Only people who'd been through hell could release such depth of feeling without resorting to words or tears.

Jamie wriggled uncomfortably and muttered, "I told you I was all right."

With a tender smile Jenny released him, but her hand slid inside his damp coat. The sweater he wore beneath it felt dry and the skin at his neck was warm. With luck, he'd brush through this without a cold. "So you did," she said huskily, feeling the tight fist of fear in her chest open.

"I need new sneakers, Mom. Mark says mine have had it." Jamie giggled. "I'm wearing his socks. You should see how big they are. They go all the way past my knees."

"That was kind of you, Officer," she said faintly. The cop's thoughtfulness made Jenny want to squirm. Reaching for the seat belt, she flashed him a brief smile. She was too embarrassed to look at him. Letting Mush outside had seemed a good idea during her long anxious minutes of waiting. The dog didn't bite, but his battered appearance and his ferocious bark had served to discourage the mailman when he'd started to become a little too friendly. She'd been quite relieved then, but now, with this man who had been so kind to her son, she felt small and mean. In an embarrassed rush, she said, "The alarm inside the house went off when the floodlights came on. The dog slipped out before I could catch him."

But she hadn't called off the dog, Mark thought with a quick glance over his shoulder. The beast was still guarding his door. And she was as nervous as hell. Her slender fingers fumbled with the seat belt lock, tugging and pulling. "Here, let me do that," he said, firmly pushing her fingers aside.

Jenny snatched her hands away, took a step back and called Mush to her side. She had thought to send him back to the house, but spotting the scabs on the cop's hand, she swiftly changed her mind. What did she know about him except that he apparently took his duties seriously and was as doggedly persistent as Mush?

Hardly reassuring traits, she thought grimly. Besides, it was his job to serve and protect. A few words of gratitude was all he expected anyway. "I don't know how to thank you, Officer," she said, finally forcing herself to look at him.

He was bigger than her brief previous glimpses had revealed. His tousled black hair almost touched the roof of the car. His leather-clad shoulders were so broad they filled her vision. He looked tough. His firm jaw was covered by black stubble, and his nose had been broken at least once. His skin stretched tautly over high cheekbones, giving him a lean, hungry look. Then she spotted the bright angry scar and the swelling surrounding it and her eyes widened with shock. She'd felt small before; now she felt positively beastly. Angry with herself, she glared at him accusingly. "Why didn't you tell me that you were hurt? I offered to pick up Jamie. There was no need to bother you."

"Cops get paid to be bothered," Mark reminded calmly. She looked about as resilient as the pine tree outside his house. Wisps of honey blond curls peeked from beneath her hood, framing a heart-shaped face. She was all eyes, big brown eyes that were still dark with fear. Her soft mouth was curved into a lopsided smile, as if she weren't quite certain if he was enemy or friend. Mark felt it tug at some rusty heartstrings. Quietly, he said, "I'll carry Jamie inside." And then he'd get the hell out of here. Frightening Mrs. Wilson had not been his intention. She'd had enough shocks for one day.

Jenny shook her head firmly. "You're in no shape to carry a ninety-pound boy." The kindest thing she could do for him was to send him back home, she soothed her nagging conscience. "Jamie can walk the few steps. Can't you?" she asked with a sideways look at her son.

Jamie nodded, a huge yawn splitting his face. "I've got to put my sneakers back on. But I don't know where they are. Mark carried me to the car so my feet wouldn't get wet again."

"They're in the back seat. I'll get them for you." Cautiously Mark twisted around and reached behind him, wincing slightly as his ribs complained.

Jenny's eyes narrowed at the awkward movement. As he stretched, his jacket rode up, revealing the edge of a white bandage wrapped around his ribs. She bit her lip, wishing the ground would open up. The words, "Mush doesn't bite," tumbled out before she could stop herself.

Slowly Mark straightened, humor glinting in his eyes. "The dog won't turn into mush, no matter how often you call him by that ridiculous name," he said dryly, handing her the plastic bag containing the sodden sneakers.

Jamie chuckled and rubbed his eyes. "Mom calls him that, because he'll do anything for a hug. His real name is Siegfried. At least that's what his tag said when we found him."

Siegfried, slayer of dragons and rescuer of damsels in distress. "That sounds more like it," Mark said thoughtfully.

"He won't come to you if you call him that," Jamie warned.

Mark looked at the dog sitting at his mistress's feet with his teeth slightly bared and said dryly, "What a relief!"

Jenny listened to the banter with growing amazement. It was rare for her son to open up to strangers. She had enrolled him in karate classes to help him overcome his fears and, in the last few weeks, she had noticed a gradual change in him. But until tonight there had always been a cautious reserve, a guarded, watchful look that told her he hadn't overcome the past.

At Jamie's chuckle she grinned. "I can see why Jamie called you a 'good cop,'" she said lightly. "What you did was certainly above and beyond."

It was the first natural smile she'd given him and its effect was devastating. Mark felt the connection as if he'd touched a live wire. Jenny, he realized, didn't seem aware of the electrical charge. Calmly she took out a sneaker, grimaced at its soggy state, then pulled it over the foot Jamie was holding out to her. When both sneakers were tied, she took the blanket and folded it neatly, handing it to Mark. "I'll send Jamie around with the socks."

Jamie scrambled to the ground, frowning at his mother. "But what about Mark? He's coming inside, isn't he?" Before Jenny could intervene he'd turned to Mark and said, "Mom makes great hot chocolate."

Frustrated, Jenny compressed her lips. She didn't want him in her house. It wasn't that she had kept any reminders of the terrible years. She'd changed her name. She'd sold her car, had even given her rings to some charity on the West Coast. All her personal possessions were stored in Alys's basement for safekeeping. She'd arrived in Port Jefferson with three suitcases and a trunk full of books. There was nothing suspicious in her house, nothing that would make him want to check her out.

Still, lying had never been easy for her, and the fact that she had something to hide was making her nervous. As a cop he was bound to ask questions. She'd schooled Jamie well, but he was no match for a man trained to trick hardened criminals into confessing their guilt. "Maybe some other time," Jenny said gently but firmly. "You have to get out of those wet clothes and soak in the tub. And Detective Lawton still has to drive back home. You don't want him to get stuck, do you?"

Jamie shook his head, but his mouth drooped and tears glinted in his eyes. Jenny felt the last of her resistance crumble. She had almost lost him tonight and the fear was still too close. Nervously, she ran a hand through her hair, hoping she wouldn't regret giving in to her son. "I made coffee," she said offhandedly, and giving into impulse, added, "And there's the chicken soup."

Mark grimaced. Chicken soup was his mother's favorite remedy to cure all ills, and he detested the stuff. "Coffee sounds fine," he said firmly, getting out of the car before she could change her mind. As Mark rounded the back of the truck, the German shepherd began to growl.

Jenny grabbed the choke chain. "I'll go first and put Mush in his crate. Be careful on the steps. They're slick."

Appearances were so deceptive, she thought, as she rushed up the walkway. No one had suspected that the smooth, controlled Burke Williams had been capable of violence, least of all Jenny herself. The detective looked like a brawler, but something told her that he only used his strength in self-defense. *He reminds me a little of you, Mush,* she thought, looking down at the dog trotting at her side. *A little rough around the edges. A fighter who doesn't know his own limits.*

Still, when she opened the screen door, she felt a desperate need to close it in his face. Too late, she thought with a growing sense of inevitability. It was as if the storm had unleashed forces beyond her control, a tidal wave of events inexorably heading toward her shore whether she wanted them or not. With a small shiver, she went inside, holding the door open until Jamie and the cop had stepped in. Then she made for the empty dining room and locked Mush in his crate.

Helping Jamie out of his coat, Mark cast a swift, curious look around. The house was warm and smelled faintly of lemon polish, some floral scent and freshly brewed coffee. The living room to his left was sparsely furnished with white love seats grouped around a fireplace. Lithographs of old Long Island landmarks hung on the walls and a jungle of plants grew in the windows.

On a table in the foyer he spotted a bunch of bright paper flowers in a pottery vase, the kind kids made in school for Mother's Day. It was the only personal touch so far as he could see. "Nice place," he said quietly, draping Jamie's wet coat over the newel post. "How long have you lived here?"

"Fifteen months." Jamie sat down on the steps at the back of the foyer and took off his sneakers, his face glowing with pride. "You should have seen the house when we moved in. It was a mess. We did all the painting and staining by ourselves. I chose the color in my room. It's yellow and the carpet is brown." Dropping the shoes on the floor, he ran up the steps. Halfway up, he stopped. "Want to see my toys? Then you can tell Tim all about them."

Closing the French door to the dining room, Jenny heard the words and frowned. She'd agreed to a cup of coffee, not a tour of the house, she thought, irritated. On the other hand, she didn't want to leave the cop walking around the downstairs rooms while she helped Jamie out of his clothes. She steeled herself to meet his sharp gray eyes and said lightly, "I don't mind."

They didn't build houses like this anymore, Mark thought, as he followed her up the carpeted steps. The railing was carved out of mahogany, smooth and sturdy beneath his grasp. The high walls had been painted a creamy white, offsetting beautiful old moldings in stark relief. Large animal posters hung on the walls, all of them on the endangered species list. Mark slanted a look at a panda bear and a gorilla and wondered at their significance. Did she contribute to some Save the Wildlife fund, or did she feel hunted herself?

When she opened the door at the end of the hall, he stopped short.

She had given her son the master bedroom.

And he needed it, every square inch of it, Mark decided as he stepped inside. The rest of the house might seem almost empty but this big room was bursting at the seams with furnishings. Apart from the modern oak bedroom set, there was a computer, a game system like the one he'd just bought for Tim, a stereo and a TV. Books and board games were neatly stacked on shelves. Fantasy posters of wizards and dragon slayers filled the bright yellow walls and the desk was littered with what looked like Dungeons and Dragons books.

"It's a mess," Jenny apologized, picking up a big tiger on her way to the bed. "I know I spoil Jamie, but he's responsible for keeping his room neat."

Mark glanced at several video cartridges tossed carelessly on the brown carpet. "So it is," he agreed with a teasing grin at Jamie.

"Not as bad as your kitchen," Jamie defended his clutter.

"Thanks a lot, pal." Mark raked his wet hair back and wiped a hand across his damp face.

Jenny handed him one of the towels she'd laid out on the bed. The harsh planes of his face had softened to an intriguing gentleness and the firm mouth was twisted into a wry grin, forming slashes on his lean cheeks. Jenny felt something stir. Compassion, she told herself firmly. "Would someone explain what that means?"

"Nothing," Mark said quickly, sending Jamie a warning look.

The warning came too late. With relish, Jamie explained, "Mark was wrapping his son's birthday present and there was paper everywhere. And pizza cartons—"

"That's enough, Jamie," Jenny interrupted him swiftly. There was something curiously touching about this big, tough man struggling with flimsy paper and she didn't want to embarrass him. "How old is your son?"

"Eight—"

"He lives all the way in California, so Mark has to send the present early," Jamie chimed in.

"Jamie, don't interrupt." Gently but firmly, Jenny turned him toward the bathroom door and gave him a little shove. "Get out of your wet clothes and into the tub. If you need help, call."

"I'm no baby," Jamie muttered. Pleadingly, he looked at Mark. "I won't take long. If you drink your coffee slowly—"

"I want you to soak in the water," Jenny said firmly, her heart twisting at the look in his eyes. She had tried to give him all the security he needed so badly, but tonight she'd failed him miserably. Tonight he had realized that the safe haven she'd created for him was only an illusion, a temporary shelter to gather strength and confidence. And now he was desperately trying to cling to this big, scarred stranger to keep his world from crumbling. She wanted to reassure him, but with the cop watching them, she had to watch every word. She laid a hand on his thin shoulder. "Mark has to get back home. Say good-night and thank him for his kindness, sweetheart."

Jamie swallowed. "Thank you," he said with a mulish set to his chin. Then his eyes brightened with eagerness. "What about Tim? I promised I would play with him when he visits Mark over Christmas."

Jenny felt a hint of panic at these words. Suppressing it, she said sternly, "If you get sick you won't be playing with anyone. So scoot."

"Do what your mother tells you, Jamie," Mark added quietly, ruffling the boy's hair. "I'll see you when you return my socks." He couldn't have cared less about a pair of socks, but something was very wrong here. Jamie was clearly upset and Jenny wasn't too calm, either, though she tried to hide it. And it wasn't his appearance, Mark thought. She had gotten past that hurdle before she'd invited him inside.

At Mark's words Jamie's face brightened. "All right!" he said and went into the bathroom without another objection.

Jenny watched him close the door with a mixture of irritation and relief. "I don't know what's got into him. He's usually so quiet around strangers," she said, turning back to Mark.

"Don't worry about it," Mark said gently, running the towel over his face. "He's a little shaken, that's all."

Jenny slanted him a troubled look. "You're a nice man, Detective Lawton. And I want to thank you for what you did for Jamie," she said quietly. She didn't quite know how to tell him that she didn't want his son in her house. If he'd been anything but a cop, she would have welcomed the boy with open arms. She loved children. But Jamie's safety came first. She watched him run the towel over his hair, waiting until she had his whole attention. The motion made his sweatshirt ride up, revealing his lean waist.

Jenny stared at the play of muscles sliding smoothly beneath his skin, feeling a tightness in her throat. Suddenly she realized that this was the first time she'd been alone with a man for years, and a stranger at that. Abruptly, she raised her eyes to his face and found him watching her.

Then their eyes locked...and held. For a moment the air hummed between them. Her pulse began to race and she forgot to breathe.

She seemed surprised by the sudden sexual charge, almost shocked. Mark wondered just how long it had been since she'd been kissed, held, loved. Not for a very long time, he guessed from the stunned look on her face. Then she blinked, almost snatched the towel from his hand and said briskly, "Why don't we go downstairs."

Mark cast a last glance around the room before he followed her. Everything appeared to be new. The carpet, the furniture, even the stuffed animals looked as if they'd been recently bought. No photos, either, he noticed with growing unease. None of Jamie's father, nor of family. It was as if a fire had purged this place of memories. Yet he could have sworn that Jenny Wilson was the type of mother who saved a baby's first shoes, the one-eyed teddy bears, and every finger painting her son had ever drawn.

The dog began to bark again as they walked downstairs. "He's not used to being locked up," she explained with a troubled look at the French doors leading into the dining room.

Leaning against the counter in the kitchen, Mark slanted her a sharp look from beneath lowered lashes. "If you want to let him out, go ahead."

Jenny shook her head. She didn't want to be constantly distracted by Mush. Reaching for the coffeepot, she said, "How do you like your coffee?"

"Black." Mark watched her take out two mugs. The inside of the cabinet was as neat and clean as the rest of the house and only half filled with dishes.

All these empty spaces nagged at him. A woman with a nesting instinct and the money to indulge it would have filled up this place in no time flat. Jenny Wilson had the instinct. She also had to have some money besides her salary. Old houses like this weren't cheap and cost a fortune to maintain, even if she was doing some of the work herself. Maybe she had so little because she was giving it all to her son. He wondered what her bedroom looked like. Probably sparsely furnished like the rest of the house.

The problem, Mark suspected, was the man whose existence Jamie denied. He wished he'd stumbled over something as simple as a cache of weapons. Instead, he seemed to have come up against a flesh-and-blood ghost.

"Careful, it's hot." Jenny handed him the mug. She'd been prepared to field questions, but those light gray eyes didn't miss much, she thought nervously, reaching into the refrigerator for a carton of milk. She felt awkward, like a desperate criminal, and she resented the quiet, patient gaze with which he seemed to watch her every move. Finally she couldn't take the silence anymore. "Did Jamie tell you what happened?"

"Some. Mainly that he got into a fight with a boy named Chris and that the father told him to leave."

His voice was detached, as if he didn't want to become involved. That suited her just fine, Jenny thought, sipping her coffee. She would have to talk to Jamie about the reason for the fight. What amazed her was why Jamie hadn't taken one look at the detective and decided to run. Maybe it was Mark's eyes that inspired such confidence, or the quiet kind of strength he exuded. They must have appealed very much to a boy lost in a storm. "How did you find him?"

"He was walking across my lawn when I looked out the window and spotted him." It wasn't the complete story, but Mark didn't think she could handle much more tonight. "Why didn't you call 9-1-1?"

So the questions were beginning. She took anther sip and leaned against the center island. "I doubt I would have been allowed to use the phone at Chris's house," she said quietly. "Besides, if I'd called the cops, I would have been told to go home and wait. I teach eleventh grade, Detective Lawton. I know the routine. You don't start looking for missing children until twenty-four hours have passed."

Mark noticed the bitterness she tried to hide. Sometimes he, too, felt frustrated by rules and regulations. "Jamie is a minor, and he didn't just disappear. From what he told me, he was kicked out into the storm without a chance to call home." Come on, Brown Eyes, give me a reason to get involved, he urged silently. Ethics stopped him from telling her outright what to do.

Jenny's lips tightened. "I was given a different version. That he was sent outside to cool off. That he didn't ask for the use of the phone. I know that's not true. But I can't prove it. It's the word of an adult against a ten-year-old kid." Jenny put down her mug and looked at him, her eyes filling with a bitterness she didn't bother to hide this time around. "This may not be a wise thing to tell a cop, but in my opinion the law stinks."

Mark's suspicions returned full force. "Sometimes," he agreed quietly, while his stomach slowly tightened into knots. The more he saw and heard, the more certain he grew that these two were in trouble, hiding from a man Jamie feared so much that he denied his very existence. Dead men posed no threats. Mark had seen his share of battered women and children, and the sight never ceased to make him sick. Fear of a brutal husband frequently trapped a wife in a hellish marriage and kept her from fighting back and seeking help. Some women, the strong ones and those with caring families, eventually managed to escape. Unfortunately, all too often the nightmares didn't stop with the divorce. Abuse was a vicious cycle; in many cases mistreated children became abusers themselves and ex-husbands continued to harass and terrorize their ex-wives.

His voice was gentle when he said, "I know the system has flaws, and it often frustrates the hell out of me, too. But, sooner or later, the bad guys *are* caught."

Jenny's mouth twisted in disbelief. Tell that to Jamie, she wanted to fling at him. *Explain to my son why his father didn't get punished for beating him. Explain to me why we have to live in constant fear.* She looked at him, struggling to express the bitterness and despair she'd fought for so long. He had such calm eyes, weary eyes, she thought. Eyes that had seen a lot, but somehow had learned to accept. She wished she could do the same. "Police work sounds like a lousy job. Why do you do it?"

"Why do you teach?" Mark countered softly, setting down his untouched coffee. "Facing a class of youngsters day in, day out, isn't exactly a picnic, either."

Her eyes narrowed and she bristled slightly. "My juniors are great kids, I'll have you know."

Mark thought of the kids he'd surprised stripping a BMW a week ago and his brows rose skeptically. "Yeah. And your Brutus is a lapdog."

"Mush," Jenny corrected lightly. "If you keep insulting him, he will turn into a brute."

Mark looked at her soberly. Her strategy might work in a classroom setting, but out in the real world, kindness was usually seen as a sign of weakness, especially by bullies. Setting aside the untouched mug of coffee, he advised, "Keep Jamie away from his friend, Chris. If the father gives you any more trouble, give me a call."

"Thanks," Jenny said lightly, watching him open the door and walk outside. For a moment her eyes rested on his broad shoulders and she felt an irrational need to call him back. She was losing her mind, she thought uneasily, running a hand through her damp waves. He was a cop, for God's sake, and an honest one at that. She felt certain that he couldn't be bribed or tempted to look the other way.

When she entered Jamie's room a few minutes later, balancing a bowl of hot chicken soup in one hand, her son was curled up in bed with the covers pulled up to his chin.

Jamie opened his eyes and looked at the tray. "I'm not hungry. Did Mark leave?"

"Yes." She didn't want to talk about Detective Lawton. He was gone from their lives and not a moment too soon. She'd been aware of his looks and probing glances, and they worried her. Placing the tray on the nightstand, she sat down on the edge of the bed, hugging Jamie tightly. "Tell me what happened at the DiNigro's tonight."

"Chris called me a sissy." He looked at Jenny accusingly. "I don't like to fight. But the kids laugh at me when I don't."

Gently Jenny brushed his damp hair from his face. "I know it's tough. So you punched Chris?"

Jamie nodded. "But he punched me first. Then his dad came and told me to get out. At first I was going to wait for you. But I didn't want Mr. DiNigro to scream at you."

Jenny shook her head in exasperation. "Jamie, I can take care of myself. I was much more worried when I couldn't find you. Why didn't you stop at one of the stores and call me? I taught you how to make a collect call."

"I wanted to go home. And I didn't get lost." He hugged his pillow tightly, then added, his voice slurring, "I didn't tell Mark anything. But I like him, Mom. And he's big and strong."

With a tender smile, Jenny pulled the covers up to his chin. She turned the lamp off but left the night-light burning. Mush, released from his crate a short while ago, had followed her into the room and now settled down on the carpet next to the bed.

With a last look at her son, Jenny carried the tray downstairs. She wasn't the scared little rabbit on the court steps anymore, she thought. Time had healed some wounds and had dulled the fear. Or maybe the fact that she had eluded Burke for so long had given her confidence. He didn't seem like a big omnipotent monster any longer. He was just a man. A dangerous, obsessed man, yes—she should never forget that—but he had weaknesses, just like everyone else.

One of his weaknesses had been his tendency to underestimate her, Jenny thought as she poured the remaining soup into Mush's bowl. He hadn't believed that a woman who had been cosseted all her life could elude him for very long. And in the beginning, she *had* made mistakes, she admitted to herself, rinsing the dishes before putting them into the dishwasher.

Like the old Buick she'd bought at a used car dealer in Seattle shortly after she had spotted Burke. That rattletrap had gone up in smoke only thirty miles down the road. And then there had been the credit card she'd accidentally tossed into a Salvation Army collection box in Miami along with their winter clothes. She still didn't know for certain if it had been the credit card that had brought Burke to Miami or if it had just been a freak accident. That time, it had taken her three days to shake him off her trail, she recalled.

It was the last time she'd seen him.

She sighed. Living with constant fear took its toll, though, especially on Jamie. For a year after the Miami incident Jamie had been afraid to let her get out of his sight. During the following six months, while they'd hidden in Chicago, they'd both gone to therapy and that had helped some, though the nightmares Jamie had begun having had continued—until recently.

Quietly she moved through the house, turning off lights and resetting the alarm. She'd known the risks of buying a house. Putting down roots left a paper trail that was much easier to follow than rental receipts. But after nearly two years of running and hiding, the need for a nest of their own had been so great that it had far outweighed the risks. And when the real-estate agent had shown her this century-old house, she'd fallen in love with it instantly.

So far they'd been lucky, she thought, walking up the steps. But she'd taken a lot of precautions to ensure their safety. Port Jefferson offered easy escape routes by land and sea. She'd even adopted her grandmother's maiden name. She sighed. So many precautions and lies. And in one careless moment she'd almost lost the one person she'd gone to so much trouble to protect.

Later, just before midnight, Jenny heard a high, piercing scream. Leaping out of bed, she raced into the adjoining master bedroom. Jamie was kicking and screaming, his eyes wide open and dark with fear. "He's going to get me. He's going to get me. I can see his green eyes. Stay away from me, you monster! Mo-o-om!"

"I'm here, Jamie. It's just a dream." Jenny grabbed his flailing arms and held his shaking body tightly against hers, calling his name over and over again. Finally he stopped screaming, sobbing quietly into her shoulder.

Jenny kept holding him, tears in her eyes. "He's never going to hurt you again," she promised him.

"It was bad, Mom," he whispered. "This time the dragon almost got me. He was so close I could see his green eyes. And the music. I can still hear the music."

"What music?" Jenny asked, frowning down at him. He had never mentioned hearing music before.

Jamie didn't answer her, he had already fallen back to sleep.

## Chapter 3

The following morning the storm had blown out to sea. Gray clouds still dominated the sky, but here and there the sun peeked through. By noon, Jenny thought as she raked leaves out of a flower bed, all signs of the storm would be gone. Bending down, she picked up an armful of leaves and stuffed them into a plastic bag, wishing she could dismiss last night from her mind just as easily.

Jamie's shrieks of laughter and the dog's excited bark drifted to her from the backyard. Wiping her hands on her scruffy jeans, Jenny walked to the white picket fence, watching Jamie chase Mush across the lawn. Jamie hadn't mentioned the nightmare at all this morning; he was bursting with energy, his face was flushed, and twigs stuck out of his ruffled hair. With a tug and a twist he wrestled a stick from the German shepherd's mouth and held it up triumphantly. Yelping, the big dog leaped up and pushed Jamie off-balance.

Jenny chuckled as boy and dog landed on the soft damp ground in a tangle of limbs. This was what she'd hoped for when she'd caught her first glimpse of the house. Peace, laughter, contentment. A place to hide and to heal, a home to raise her son in and watch him grow healthy and strong.

Suddenly Jamie spotted her, a guilty look crossing his face. He wiped his hands on his dirt-streaked jeans. "Mom?"

"You were supposed to collect branches, not play with them," Jenny said dryly.

With a mischievous grin he pointed at the dog, who'd picked up the stick. "Mush won't let me."

"Mush already had his meal. Since we're not leaving until the garden is cleaned up, I guess we'll miss ours."

"No way!" Jamie protested breathlessly, scrambling to his feet. Grabbing the branch from Mush, he quickly tossed it into the wheelbarrow. Going out for brunch on Saturday morning was a family tradition Jamie enjoyed as much as Jenny herself had as a child. No matter how busy her father had been, he'd emerged from his study around noon to take the family out. Even during the dark days when she'd been waiting for her divorce to become final, she had clung to this ritual. It was like an anchor in a life otherwise out of control.

With a pensive smile Jenny watched Jamie run to broken twigs and fallen branches, piling them up in his arms as Mush danced around him. With only the two of them, it was hard to keep family traditions going. Jenny's parents had died in her senior year in college, and her aunts, uncles and cousins were spread all over the States. Except for Aunt Alys, her mother's sister, contact had long ago dwindled to the occasional birthday and Christmas card. Since her divorce, even those had stopped.

For Jennifer McKenzie and James Daniel Williams didn't exist anymore.

With an angry swipe of her rake Jenny tossed leaves high in the air. Adopting her grandmother's maiden name had been an act of desperation, and after three years she should have become used to it. But while the name didn't make her a different person, sometimes she felt as if she'd not only lost her name, but her youth and her memories as well.

Moving with swift, jerky movements, Jenny continued raking. She didn't want to think of the past and the mistakes she'd made. But bagging leaves required little concentration, and her heart was heavy with guilt and shame. Why had she stayed with Burke? Why hadn't she left him the first time he'd slapped her? If she'd divorced him then, Jamie would have been spared. When she looked back on those years, she saw a stranger, someone who had nothing in common with the young girl who had dreamed of conquering the world.

A branch of gold button mums got caught between the teeth of the rake. Jenny dropped to her knees and gently freed the blossoms. Like the blossoms, she'd felt trapped, helpless, with no place to go. As a troubleshooter for Global Airlines, Burke had moved from city to city, never staying longer in one location than a year. For Jennifer, who'd grown up in the same house, been surrounded by the same faces all her life, it had been disorienting and lonely. Burke had been her sole anchor, her entire family. Later she'd been so wrapped up in Jamie and making a home for them that she hadn't become aware of the gradual erosion in her self-confidence, or the change in her relationship with her husband. Until it had been too late.

Jenny gently touched the soft small petals, so easily bruised, then carefully removed the leaves. For a moment she stared at the new strong growth peeking through the earth, wondering if she'd be here to see them bloom. She'd known the risk of staying in any one place too long, but, like the mums, she needed roots to gather strength.

"Mom, I'm finished," Jamie shouted, running toward her with the dog at his heels. "Boy, you're slow today. Want any help?"

Jenny rose to her feet, forcing a smile. "What's it going to cost me?" she asked cautiously.

"A trip to the movies?" Jamie flashed her a hopeful grin. "I want to see *Robin Hood*. Mike says it's really great."

Mike Sherman, the boy next door, was a year older than Jamie and her son's authority on most things. "I don't suppose you'd wait until it comes out on video?" Jenny asked hopefully. There was a stack of papers to be graded, and the laundry basket was filled to the brim.

A mutinous expression crossed Jamie's face and he stuck out his chin. "That's not the same. I don't want to wait. I like going places now that Burke has stopped looking for us."

Jenny's smile froze. Jamie refused to call Burke his father, in fact he rarely mentioned him and that he did so now, alarmed her. Anxiously, she probed his flushed, dirt-streaked face, but saw no fear. Defiance, and a stubborn determination to get his way, yes. "Temper, temper," she warned, lightly flicking his jutting jaw.

Abruptly, Jamie changed tactics, flashing her a grin. "Please?"

Jenny felt herself weaken. She never could resist his smiles. Unfolding a plastic bag, she opened it and handed it to him. "All right, I'll take you this afternoon. Now hold onto the edges and don't let go."

"Not this afternoon," Jamie protested. "Did you forget that I have karate at two?"

She hadn't forgotten, but she'd hoped that Jamie had decided to miss class today. Mark Lawton's warnings were still ringing in her ears. "I don't think you should go today. Mr. DiNigro takes Chris to the dojo on Saturdays and I don't want any more unpleasantness."

"But I want to go! Sensei Luke is teaching today and his classes are always fun. And if Mr. DiNigro starts yelling at us, I'll call Mark."

"No, you won't." Sternly, Jenny faced him over the leaf bag. "Mr. Lawton was very kind to you, but he is a stranger and I don't want you to pester him."

Jamie slanted her a belligerent look. "He's not a stranger. He's my friend!"

Jenny brushed a few strands of hair behind her ear. She understood her son's need for a hero, but did he have to pick a cop? "Sweetheart—" she began, choosing her words carefully. She didn't want to hurt his feelings, didn't want him to withdraw back into his shell "—isn't Mark a little bit too old to be your friend?"

"Don't you like him?" Jamie's eyes narrowed anxiously.

Jenny sighed. That was part of the problem. She wasn't quite certain how she felt about the man. Like the storm, he had unsettled her in some elemental way. "Yes, I like him. How could I not after all he did for you? But Mark is a policeman and you know how I feel about them."

The nightmare last night showed that deep down her son also felt threatened, Jenny thought. The walls of the little nest she'd built for them had been battered somewhat yesterday, and Jamie was looking for someone to fix the damage. Only the battle-scarred giant he was looking to for help was the wrong man. "Before he left, Mark also mentioned that it would be a good idea to avoid the DiNigros."

"But why? I haven't done anything!" Jamie cried, sudden tears shimmering in his eyes. "If I promise to be very polite can I go?"

Jenny hugged him tightly. She'd tried to make a normal life for Jamie and herself. But last night had reminded her that their safety was, at best, temporary. Life for them wasn't normal, would never be normal until Jamie reached adulthood, or he was strong enough to stand up to Burke.

Yet how was he to conquer his fear if she insisted on wrapping him in cotton wool? Besides, all she had were a handful of vague premonitions that might never amount to anything. She took a deep breath, then said, "All right."

An hour later Jenny pulled into a large parking lot in downtown Port Jefferson. The restaurant where they would be having brunch was nestled into the side of a steep hill, about halfway up. Climbing out of the car, she turned her face into the stiff breeze blowing from the sound. The wind whipped her long hair across her face and she brushed it back. From where she stood she could see the top of the ferry that ran between here and Bridgeport, Connecticut. Sea gulls squawked and the noon sun warmed her skin. She took a deep breath and filled her lungs with salt air.

She loved the sea. Even as a child the ocean had lured her with its wild beauty and indomitable strength. Some of her most precious memories were of days spent walking with her parents along the beach, fishing on her father's boat, or whale watching in the Atlantic. Those happy memories had drawn her back to Long Island, despite the threat that this was one place Burke would almost certainly search. But Long Island was big, over one-hundred miles long, with a fast-growing population that already exceeded two million people.

"Mom, want to race me to the steps?" Slamming the car door, Jamie zipped up his denim jacket and slanted her a bright, challenging look.

Jenny grimaced, wishing for some of his boundless energy. She'd slept fitfully last night, checking on her son at regular intervals, and her lack of rest was beginning to tell. A good run might ease her tension. "All right. But watch out for cars."

"Sure. See you at the steps." With a wave and a grin, Jamie dashed between the parked vehicles toward the row of houses rising up the hill.

Jenny gave him a few seconds' head start, then set out after him, cutting diagonally through the crowded lot. At the rate Jamie was growing, she wouldn't be able to catch him in another year, she thought, skirting a sea gull pecking at a piece of bread. She weaved past a yellow Jeep, then sharply rounded a white panel truck. Jamie was no more than fifteen feet in front of her now. She always let him win, though she never made it easy for him. She surged forward to close the gap a little more—and ran full tilt into a large man rounding the truck from the other side.

Strong hands shot out to steady her. Slightly breathless and a little embarrassed, Jenny looked up—straight into Mark Lawton's face. Damn! Why did it have to be him? was her first thought. Then she saw him wince slightly, as if the impact had jarred him, and her annoyance changed to concern. "Are you all right?"

Mark slowly released the breath he'd been holding and looked down at the glowing woman in his arms. Gone were the signs of strain. Her delicate skin was flushed, her eyes sparkled and her hair was tangled from the wind. His hands itched to brush the waves back from her face, wondering if they'd feel as soft as they looked. "I'm fine. You pack quite a punch for a midget," he teased, a slow grin creasing his lean face.

Jenny could feel herself blushing, and suddenly her heartbeat doubled. Her voice sounded oddly breathless when she explained, "I was racing Jamie to the steps."

Glancing over his shoulder, Mark spotted the boy streaking past a blue Corvette near the end of the parking lot. "Looks like you've lost this one."

"I know. And I'll never hear the end of it. It's getting tougher every day to keep up with him," she admitted, shifting uneasily from one foot to the other while she studied his averted face.

He looked different this morning, clean shaven, more rested. Male. Even the scar looked less angry, and the taut lines around his mouth had softened. She felt a strong sexual pull—a quick, unexpected flash of desire that stunned her. Suddenly his touch seemed to burn through her gray tweed jacket and sweater, heating her skin. Swiftly, she retreated a step. "Soon I'll be the one asking for head starts."

"I'll give him another year." Mark slowly released her, then slid his hands into his pockets. He hadn't been able to get her off his mind. Long after he'd finished wrapping Tim's present and had straightened out the house, her lopsided smile had haunted him. He imagined a man of his own size and strength knocking her and Jamie around and tasted grit. "Jamie must get his build from his father," he commented casually.

"No! He doesn't resemble him at all!" Jenny denied with sudden fierceness. Although Burke was tall, her ex-husband was lanky and fine-boned. And while logic told her that Jamie had inherited half of his father's genes, Jenny preferred not to dwell on that fact. "He's the spitting image of my dad. Dad was blond, big-boned and over six feet tall."

Mark's eyes narrowed at the first part of her comment. He prompted quietly, "Jamie told me that his father was dead, too, but perhaps I misunderstood." He watched her hesitate, slant a glance at her son as if weighing the risks. He held his breath.

Jenny watched Jamie stop at the steps, breathing hard from his run. They'd both denied Burke's existence so often the lie should have come easily. But for some reason, the moment she met Mark's compelling eyes the lie seemed to stick in her throat. Uncomfortably, she shifted from one leg to the other. "Both my parents died in a plane crash twelve years ago."

Mark released his breath, frustration making his hands curl in his pockets. Her reply, which pretty much ignored his question, told him clearly that it was still too soon. All she saw was the cop. Once they got past that hurdle she might open up to him. "That must have been tough for you," he said gently. She couldn't have been more than twenty at the time of her parents' death, and a young, sheltered twenty at that.

She turned toward the view of the sea, watching the wind rustle through the bright yellow leaves of a maple tree nearby. Twelve years had dulled the pain of loss, but she felt as if she'd been adrift ever since. "It was unreal at the time. I was away at college. My parents took a trip to Spain and Italy...and never returned. Their plane went down over the Mediterranean and for weeks afterward I kept hoping that somehow they'd survived, that maybe a fishing boat had picked them up."

She'd met Burke, a troubleshooter for Global Airlines, when he'd brought her the news of the disaster, and for a long while after that, she'd called him every day. He'd been so kind then, so supportive. He'd even taken a week of vacation when her grandmother had died, to be at Jenny's side. She sighed. Granny's death three months later had been much more real. Jenny had been able to say goodbye to her; she had watched her being laid to rest. In a way she'd buried them all on that day.

And a month later, two days after her graduation, she had married the man who had helped her through the most difficult time of her life.

Mark's glance rested on her rigid shoulders. They seemed too slender to carry the burden fate had placed on her. "Do you have any brothers or sisters?"

Jenny shook her head. "My parents were the kind of people who should have had more kids, but they were already in their late thirties when I came along." They'd always wanted a large family. When her mother had become pregnant, they'd sold their apartment in Manhattan and had bought a rambling old house in Sands Point, hoping for at least one more child.

Instead, over the years, her mother had filled the vacant rooms with a collection of musical instruments. They were in storage now, together with so many other memories. Waiting. Would she ever feel safe enough to take them out? Would she still be able to play the flute or the piano? She hadn't touched an instrument in twelve years. Now longing stirred in her, like the first breathless, haunting note of a flute. Abruptly, she turned her attention back to Mark, a wary look in her eyes. What was it about this man that made her want to confide in him, to trust him? Swiftly, she changed the subject. "What about you? How many brothers and sisters do you have?"

"There's six of us."

"Six?" His answer surprised Jenny. She'd thought of him as a solitary person, a loner. "Do they all live here on Long Island?"

"In Queens and Nassau County."

Less than an hour's drive away. Then what was he doing alone in the house, licking his wounds in private? Jenny wondered. "Are you the oldest?"

"What gave you that idea?"

A slow grin curved her lips. "The oldest siblings of large families tend to be bossy," she teased. But with him in charge, his mother had probably never worried about the safety of her younger children.

"Is that right?" Mark watched three freckles wink at him from the bridge of her nose. "Then I must be the youngest one. I'm very easygoing, amiable—"

"Sure," Jenny scoffed, watching the wind ruffle his black hair and give him a rakish look. "I'll bet you were hell on wheels as a child. Am I right?"

Mark flashed her a white, mocking grin. "You'll have to meet my family and find out for herself." The moment he issued the invitation, he wanted to take it back. Not because he didn't want her to meet his family—to his surprise, he did—but because his words had frozen her smile and made the light vanish from her eyes. Suddenly the cautious, wary look he was beginning to hate was back.

"That's very kind of you, Detective. But Jamie and I don't need your pity," Jenny said firmly, her chin tilting with pride.

"My name's Mark." His voice was edged with irritation, though it was mostly directed at himself. He wasn't usually so clumsy or impatient. "Jamie invited my son to play with him over the Christmas holidays. I hope that wasn't pity."

"No, of course not . . . Mark. Tim is welcome any time." Jenny raked her fingers through her hair. Things were moving too fast, she thought with a hint of panic. She'd known him less than a day, less than an hour really, and already they were talking about Christmas and meeting his family.

She might not even be here in seven weeks! Dear God, where would they hide next? she wondered wearily. She looked for Jamie, saw him leaning over the railing, searching the parking lot for her. Waving until he spotted her, she turned back to Mark. "I have to run, before Jamie gets impatient and wanders off." *And before he can invite you to tag along.*

"Walking might be safer."

Jenny's eyes flashed with annoyance. "I don't make a habit of running into things. I didn't see you because of the panel truck."

"That's all right. I'm easily overlooked."

"About as easily as a six-foot-two wall," she commented dryly. With his rangy build, he almost filled the space between the two cars completely. Before she could resist the urge, her gaze flicked over the strong column of his neck and the wide arrogant spread of his shoulders. He wore a faded denim jacket this morning, a light blue chambray shirt and soft worn jeans. The breeze molded the clothes to his broad chest and powerful legs. Her throat suddenly felt tight and her lips dry. Swallowing, she added, "A wall that's blocking my way, I'd like to point out."

Mark caught the brief flare of her nostrils and the movement in her long slender throat. The protective shell was beginning to crack. And if shrinking him by two inches in her mind made her feel less threatened, he wasn't going to correct her. With a teasing grin, he pointed to the small gap between him and the white panel truck. "There's plenty of room for midgets to squeeze through."

Jenny's eyes narrowed fractionally. Her students played those silly games constantly, testing, challenging one another. There had once been a time—the time before Burke—when she wouldn't have backed away from a dare. Still, she felt an almost irresistible urge to shove him out of the way. Airily, she said, "I'm a little too old to play silly games."

Not too old to race your son across the parking lot, though, Mark thought. "Coward," he taunted softly, enjoying the sparks flashing in her eyes. She was losing her temper, and with it her caution. How long would it take to peel away the protective layers, he wondered, watching her face flush. She had a passionate mouth, he thought. "But you weren't above siccing your dog on me last night."

Jenny tossed her head. "I didn't sic Mush on you." His answer was a disbelieving lift of his brows, and with a half laugh, she amended, "I just didn't call him off. There's a difference."

"Where? The bottom line is that I was trapped," Mark pointed out dryly.

Tilting her head to one side, she taunted lightly, "I think I like that thought." Mark smiled down at her crookedly. Her laughter slid like warm sunshine over his skin and the sparkle in her eyes made him catch his breath softly. Little did she realize that he *was* trapped—by three dancing freckles, sparkling big brown eyes and soft taunting lips. "You seem to like the idea of having me at your mercy. Does that mean you're not afraid of me any more?"

"You've got an outsized ego, Mark Lawton. I'm not afraid of you."

"Prove it, Jenny Wilson. Have dinner with me tonight."

The low vibration of his voice washed over her skin like a lover's caress. For a moment she just stood there, mesmerized and holding her breath. He wasn't the first man to ask her out, but before it had always been easy to say no. Now she found herself actually wanting to accept. In her mind she was already going through her closet for something to wear. What could it hurt? But then, at the last moment she drew back. Her fingers curling tightly around the shoulder strap of her purse, she shook her head. "I can't."

"Can't? Or won't?" Mark watched her twist and mangle the black leather strap of her handbag. He wanted to cover her hand, to still her restless movements and tell her that she had nothing to fear from him. But words meant little—she'd probably heard too many such promises in the past—so he kept his hands in his pockets and his voice calm. "Maybe it's my scars that turn you off."

Her eyes flew to the thin red line on his face. They both had scars, though some were more visible than others. Some festered deep inside. He had his share of those, too, she thought. "I think you know better, so I won't even answer that." It was her own emotions she was afraid of. He made her feel again. He made her want. She could afford neither. Slowly, she backed away and said with rough urgency, "Stay away from me, Mark, for your sake as well as mine."

"Why? Give me a reason," he said gently.

His sudden gentleness made her blink. She looked down at her hands, restlessly tugging at her purse strap, fighting threatening tears. Damn it, she hadn't cried in years and her sudden weakness scared her. She turned on him fiercely. "I don't like macho cops with outsized egos. Is that reason enough?"

As a cop Mark was used to not being wanted, and he was arrogant enough not to give a damn. But this was personal, and her words stung. Anger flashed in his eyes. "Not quite," he said, his voice as clipped and hard as his expression. "Just for the record, Jenny Wilson, what is it you're afraid of? Is it me? Or is it the fact that I'm a cop? Or maybe the problem is simply that, for a few moments, the ice cracked and you felt as attracted to me as I am to you?" He could tell that he'd hit a raw nerve with that one. Her face went pale, the look in her eyes changing from one of fury to fear, before becoming carefully blank.

"All three," she shouted, poised to escape. Then she spotted her son running toward them. At the sound of their raised voices, he slowed and the smile froze on his face. For a moment he just stood, his eyes darting from Jenny to Mark and back to Jenny again. "Mom?" he asked, his voice cautious, uncertain. "Are you and Mark fighting?"

"No." Shaking her head, Jenny took a deep steadying breath and forced herself to ask lightly, "Why would I fight with Mark?"

Jamie relaxed slightly and his smile reappeared, but the glance he gave Mark was still wary and faintly accusing. "You were shouting at Mom."

Mark met Jenny's eyes steadily, already regretting his loss of control. He'd set out to annoy her, prod her and push a few buttons. But he hadn't meant to hurt or frighten her. "Your mother and I were arguing and sometimes arguments get noisy," Mark explained calmly, shifting his attention to Jamie. To deny a scene the boy had witnessed would only make him more anxious, not diminish his fears.

"I thought so," Jamie said. To Jenny's surprise he walked up to Mark and asked in a voice that was more curious than anxious, "What was it about?"

Mark shrugged. "That's between your mother and me. Adult stuff."

"Oh." Jamie took a moment to digest the answer, then asked, "Are you angry with my mother because she's letting me go to karate this afternoon? She didn't want me to, because Mr. DiNigro always takes Chris to the dojo on Saturdays. But I promised to be polite to him."

Mark's eyes narrowed at this first mention of the bully's name. "Rich DiNigro, the lawyer? Little guy, with brown hair and a nasty temper?"

Jenny's mouth twisted wryly. "I don't know about 'little'—he's about five-eleven—but the rest seems to fit. You obviously know him."

"I've met him a few times in court." They'd also had a few run-ins out in the hall afterward. "He's little," Mark said firmly. "Mean little mind, little courage, little conscience."

Jenny felt a grin tug at the corners of her mouth. Somehow his words seemed to sum DiNigro up—or scale him down to size—accurately. "If you rate people by their height, I hate to think where I rank," she said lightly.

Mark slanted her a long tantalizing look from beneath lowered lashes that made her breath catch and her heart rate increase all over again. "Have dinner with me and I'll tell you," he promised softly, his voice pitched for her ears alone. "And just to set the record straight, you cut my height by two inches a little while ago."

Jenny's eyes began to sparkle. "I did? You mean you're even bigger than I thought—on stubbornness, persistence and machismo?"

Mark acknowledged the hit with an exaggerated wince. "I've a feeling I'll need every fraction of those two inches at the rate you're chipping away at me." His gaze darkened, becoming intimate, almost caressing her as it settled on her smiling lips.

Jenny suddenly felt cold and hot, all at the same time. Longings, needs she'd thought buried a long time ago, pulsed through her, frightening in their intensity. She wanted to give in to those needs. She wanted to stop running and stand in the bright noon sun without a care in the world. She wanted to turn back the clock and recapture some of that magic power of innocence, fearlessness and love she'd once had. And for a few breathless seconds, with Mark's eyes on her, she could almost feel it, taste it—

Then Jamie asked, "What is machismo, Mom?"

Her longings burst like a soap bubble, leaving nothing but the bitter taste of reality. "Machismo means—" She hesitated as words like virile, sexually competent and potent flashed through her mind. She chanced a glimpse at the prime example of the term and found him watching her with wicked amusement and a blatant challenge that was hard to resist. Her chin came up a notch. "Machismo means gutsiness, the ability to take care of oneself against opposition, self-confidence and—" she added with an impish grin "—a touch of swagger to keep up the image."

Mark chuckled out loud, ignoring the stab in his ribs. For the last week he'd been living in a self-imposed exile, brooding about the mistakes he'd made, and she was drawing him right out of it. It felt good to laugh again, to feel a burst of emotion and life sweeping through him. And then he remembered how this conversation had started and his face sobered. "Which dojo do you belong to, Jamie? The one on Nesconsett highway?"

Jamie nodded, his eyes bright with eagerness. "My class starts at two. Maybe you want to come and watch me? I only have a yellow belt but—"

"Jamie, I'm sure Mark has other plans," Jenny interrupted, firmly gripping his arm.

Calmly, Mark looked down at her. Everything, from the determined look in her eyes to the firm slant of her mouth and angled chin told him that she felt she didn't need, and didn't want, his protection. She didn't know DiNigro as well as he did! The lawyer would sue his own mother if she stepped on his toes. His glance slid to her slender white fingers, now gripping the leather strap of her purse as if it were a life preserver. Or maybe she did.

He ruffled Jamie's hair and said gently, "I'm sorry, but I can't. Your mother's just reminded me that I have a doctor's appointment in fifteen minutes. So I better get going."

It was what she'd wanted, Jenny told herself sternly as he turned away. She didn't want to be protected or defended. She could manage DiNigro on her own.

But it would have been nice to have a dinner companion who was a little more than ten years old. Just once.

## Chapter 4

"It's all your fault. Mark would have come to the dojo, if you'd let him. Why did you have to send him away?" Jamie growled angrily as Jenny pulled into a parking spot in front of the dojo an hour later.

The outburst came out of nowhere, taking Jenny by surprise. During lunch at Jim's Deli, Jamie had been unusually quiet, sulking over his macaroni and cheese. Then he had met a school friend and in typical child fashion had forgotten all about Mark. Now with class about to start, he was a little apprehensive, she guessed. She, too, felt butterflies flutter in her stomach.

With a sigh, she shifted into Park, turned off the engine, and unbuckled her belt. She wanted to drive home and forget about DiNigro. Even as a child she'd disliked confrontations. She had always been the peacemaker among her friends. Her father used to tease her about it, she remembered suddenly. "Little Mother Teresa," he would call her in his deep baritone voice.

Jenny bit her lips to control the aching pain. Big old-fashioned Daniel McKenzie had been a solid rock—like the Scottish mountains that were a part of his heritage, he'd been a buffer between his family and the outside world. He'd taught her to swim, sail and how to invest in stocks. What he hadn't taught her was how to deal with people like DiNigro and Burke.

Turning her head, she watched Jamie reach into the back seat and drag the blue canvas tote into his lap. She wasn't nearly as tough as she wanted to be, but she had developed some ability to stand up for herself. She'd also learned that ignoring certain problems didn't make them disappear. And the macho cop was becoming a tough, six-foot-four problem she had to deal with before it was too late.

A glance at the clock told her that they were fifteen minutes early. She might as well get the discussion over with. "I know you like Mark," she said gently, searching Jamie's face for signs of the fear or apprehension she suspected was behind the reason for this sudden attachment.

"You do, too." Jamie clutched the tote lightly, but his eyes were bright with accusation. "You were joking with him."

Jenny bit back a groan. It wasn't the first time he'd seen her joke with a man. There had been too many good and decent men in her life before and since Burke to see them all as a potential threat. Yet she had always been casual, even detached with men. Today had been different. There had been nothing casual or detached about her encounter with Mark. The air had sizzled between them like an electrical charge. Jamie, too, had sensed the difference and now he was confused.

"Yes, I was," she admitted, and that fact still irritated her. For years she had believed she was immune to sexual attraction. She'd never been a sensuous woman. Maybe that was why she hadn't anticipated the danger of it, or noticed the warning signs. She snatched the key out of the ignition and tossed it into her purse. She didn't want those feelings, didn't need the complications. Her life was already difficult enough. Closing the bag with a snap, she took a calming breath and turned back to her son.

"I know why you like Mark. He's big and strong and he makes you feel safe." I understand exactly how you feel, she added to herself silently, because he has the same effect on me. For one moment, one long indulgent moment out in the sunshine, she, too, had been tempted to lean on him. She sighed. "Jamie, just because he helped you last night, doesn't mean that he can help us in other ways."

A battered old blue car pulled into the spot next to them and two blond, ponytailed girls in white *gis* scrambled out. Lisa, the taller one, spotted Jamie, and shouted, "Are you coming in?"

"Later," Jamie said. He waited until they had disappeared through the glass door of the red brick building and their ride had left. When he looked at Jenny, his eyes shimmered and his bottom lip was trembling. "Why not? Mom, I don't want to move again. I like my house and my room. Sensei Luke said that if I worked real hard I could test for blue belt after Christmas. And what about Mike, Lisa and Dana and all my other friends? I want to stay here forever! And Mark would help us. I know he would. He's a good cop!"

"Who said anything about moving?" Jenny said lightly. But her heart wrenched and her throat was raw with pain. She swallowed, wanting to soothe him, reassure him, but the words he needed most to hear refused to come. He would have sensed the lie anyway. He was as finely attuned to her moods as a weather vane to the slightest breeze. And the wind had shifted since the storm. The sun was perhaps shining again, but she was still nervous, restless and worried.

She swallowed, clearing her throat. "Why do you call Mark a good cop?" she asked curiously, gently brushing the

tears from his face. "Is it because he was kind to you?"
When Jamie nodded, she said, "Sweetheart, it's his job to
help and protect people. Most policemen feel that way."

But there were other, less dedicated, narrow-minded cops
who weren't interested in justice. Jamie had met some of
them, too.

Jamie pushed her hand away and rubbed his eyes with his
fists. It was a childish gesture, but there was nothing childish in his voice when he said, "Mark believed me when I told
him what happened last night. He didn't say it was all my
fault. He didn't blame me. He's not like Sheriff Reed."

Jenny felt the old bitterness well up again, burning like
acid in her stomach. Sheriff Reed had not believed Jamie's
statement that his father had beaten him, and then kicked
him down the stairs. The Williams's had ranched in Dark
Water, Oklahoma, for generations. The sheriff had known
them all his life. Burke and his parents had insisted that the
"fall" had been an unfortunate accident and that they were
above reproach. Her ex-mother-in-law, Mabel, played the
organ in the Baptist church and Chuck had business deal-
ings with the judge. And everyone in Dark Water knew that
Burke's wife was a stuck-up Yankee who made his life a living hell.

Jenny doubted that she would ever forget what had come
next. Reed had turned to Jamie, lying in the narrow hospital bed with his head bandaged, his face bruised and his
fractured leg in traction, and had warned him not to lie
again. They put little boys in prison if they didn't tell the
truth in court.

Frightened, Jamie had lied and the charges of child abuse
against Burke had been dropped.

No, Mark wasn't like Reed, she thought wearily. He
wouldn't have threatened her son. He would have recognized the terror on Jamie's face every time Burke had come
near him and would have questioned it.

Just as he was already questioning their lies.

Fear coiled in her stomach. Mark had a casual way of extracting information, like a gold panner, picking truth out of slush. How much had she unconsciously told him already? How much had he guessed? she wondered anxiously. Those steady gray eyes saw too much.

"Of course, he believed you," Jenny said, sudden urgency tightening her voice. "Mark is much smarter than Sheriff Reed. That's why it's safer if we don't see him again. I know you can keep a secret, but sometimes we all slip up."

For a moment Jamie bit his lip in indecision. Then a cunning look came into his eyes. "If he's smarter than Sheriff Reed, he's not going to let Burke hurt us. He's going to lock him up. And then we don't have to move again."

Jenny shook her head at his logic. "It's not quite that simple," she warned. There were some things Jamie didn't know and was too young to understand. She could only hope that her words had enough of an impact to make him think. "For right now, let's just be a little more cautious," she said. "And I don't want any more arguments between you and Chris."

The class started smoothly, so smoothly that Jenny began to relax. DiNigro had merely dropped off his son. Other parents had come in briefly, then left.

Now Jenny was the only parent in the small, narrow waiting room. The place was quiet, peaceful. Muted voices drifted in from the karate shop next door. Lainie, a karate student who helped out in the office, played country music in the small room at the end of the hall. Jenny could hear faint groans and grunts from the exercise room a few doors down and laughter and giggles from the dojo itself.

She walked to the windows inserted into the wall that separated the dojo from the waiting room, watching the children clean the parquet floor, scooting around on their knees like busy white ants.

Luke Brown ran the dojo like a family enterprise. The gym area was the meeting place and everyone had to keep it clean. The youngest members buffed the floor, the older, taller ones cleaned mirrors, windows and exercise equipment. Advanced students taught classes and sponsored the beginner students. It was a friendly, nurturing place, and from the beginning Jenny had been impressed by the warmth, respect and discipline.

Until today Chris and Jamie had always worked next to each other. Now they were on opposite sides of the deck, both looking grim. Jenny felt a mixture of relief and regret. The boys had enjoyed each other's company. Left to themselves, they would have gradually sorted out their problems.

Tired, she sat down on the hard wooden bench, leaned her head against the dark paneled wall and willed her body to relax. But Mark Lawton stuck in her mind like a nettle. Nothing could shake him loose. She'd known that he was a man she should keep at a distance. How had he slipped past her defenses? She had never anticipated the strong sexual pull between them, had been stunned by it. Yet that wasn't the reason she had stayed to talk with him.

Perhaps it was the scars. Not the visible ones; they were healing nicely, she thought. It was the ones hidden beneath his macho facade that had called out to her. She couldn't bear to see anyone in pain. She could no more have turned her back on him than she could have left the growling, bleeding German shepherd on the beach last year. She shifted into a more comfortable position and closed her eyes. She shouldn't want to know about his scars. The less she knew about the man, the easier it would be to erase him from her mind.

She must have dozed. When she heard the door open, she felt too lethargic to move. Then a warning tingled down her neck and her eyes flew open. She stared at Mark blankly, then shot to her feet. "You—what are you doing here?"

Mark calmly closed the door. For a moment, while she'd thought herself unobserved, she had looked lonely, tired, vulnerable. Now all the nervous energy was back. And the wariness. He felt a twinge of irritation, wondering if she would ever trust him enough to let down her defenses and welcome him with an open smile. "I got through earlier at the doctor's than I thought."

Jenny watched him stroll into the room as if he owned it, as if he were certain of his welcome. The already narrow space suddenly seemed to shrink to cubbyhole size. His cocky arrogance set her teeth on edge. "I was hoping they'd keep you all afternoon."

"That's downright nasty," Mark said lightly, noticing that he checked him over with a swift, but thorough glance through the veil of her long lashes. He was getting to know Jenny Wilson, her weaknesses as well as her strengths. She was fiercely protective of her son and for some reason—he intended to find out what it was sooner or later—she considered him a threat. "Don't you want to know the doc's verdict or when I go back to work?"

She did, but she wasn't going to weaken. He was dogging her footsteps, crowding her, cornering her. A simple no hadn't worked with him. She had even pleaded with him to leave her alone. He'd ignored that, too. He was stubborn and bullheaded, and far too perceptive. She had to make a firm stand now. The trouble was, when she was with him, she didn't fear the dragon breathing down her neck nearly as much. It was a dangerous illusion, though. "No," she said firmly, "I didn't want you to come here and you knew it."

Mark stopped right in front of her. "Didn't you?" he asked lazily, raising one black brow questioningly. "You send out conflicting messages, Jenny. Maybe that's why we got our lines crossed."

And she still did. Her eyes were shooting darts at him and her small chin was angled defiantly. His glance dropped lower, down the slender column of her throat to the pulse that fluttered erratically. She might not be aware of it, but a part of her was glad to see him. "How come you're all alone here? Didn't DiNigro show up?"

"He only dropped Chris off." She cleared her throat and added more forcefully, "There's no reason for you to stick around."

"He's coming back for his son, I assume."

"Not necessarily. His wife may decide to pick Chris up." Jenny's eyes narrowed with exasperation. He stood with his feet firmly planted apart, unmoving. The message he was sending was loud and clear. He planned to stay and nothing she said was going to make him change his mind.

Mark's mouth twisted cynically. "I doubt it. But it'll suit my purpose just as well."

"What purpose?" Jenny asked, irritated. She didn't need more aggravation. All she wanted was to be left alone! She glanced at the scabs on his knuckles and snapped, "If you want a boxing match with DiNigro, choose a different arena. Just leave me out of it."

The bungled arrest still haunted him and her pointed glance reminded him that a boy was in the hospital because of his mistake. Guilt washed through him. His jaw tightened, but his voice was mild when he said, "I'm trying to smooth things over, not start a fight. DiNigro may hate my guts, but he isn't a fool. If word of last night gets out it won't do his reputation any good. He specializes in civil complaints against the police department and cases of alleged brutality. No one wants to deal with a man who threatens women and children. Even crooks get squeamish on the subject."

Jenny bit her lip. She didn't really believe that he was a man who would start a fight. He was too calm and too controlled. But he wouldn't back away from one, either. Was that how he'd been injured? Trying to defend someone? Something must have gone wrong she suspected, because he was sensitive about those scars. "I'm sorry. I didn't mean—" Agitated, she stuffed her hands in her pockets and started pacing. Three steps to the wall and three steps back. "It has nothing to do with you."

Unconsciously, she placed a hand on his arm, trying to soothe the pain she'd inflicted. "I just don't like threats or violence. I know you're trying to prevent another confrontation, and I'm grateful. But I can handle it." Jenny knew she should move away. She was so close to him that she could see his eyes darken, soften and slowly fill with sensual heat. So close that she could sense the warmth of his big body reach out to her and seep beneath her clothes. Her fingers began to tingle and something shimmered to life deep within. Something precious, something she wanted to grasp and hold on to.

Then he blinked, and Jenny snatched her hand away. Walking to the window, she stared blindly into the gym. What was she doing? She had to keep him at a distance; she couldn't allow herself to forget that. But something strong and, oh, so compelling drew her to him, and she was proving unable to resist it. Her lips tightened with sudden anger. There were other reasons she had to stay away from Mark. Hadn't she learned that she wasn't a woman men found attractive? She'd been told often enough by Burke that all her warmth was on the surface. Beneath it she was as cold as ice.

She stuffed her hands into her pockets. Of course she realized that Burke had used those words as a justification for his anger toward her, to excuse the womanizing and the physical abuse, but there was some truth to it. Even in the early days of her marriage she hadn't felt any desire for sex.

Frowning, Mark stared at her straight back, uneasiness coiling in his stomach. "I know you're in trouble. I've been a cop too long not to recognize the signs." Through the reflection of her in the window's glass, he could see her already large eyes widen even more, and the angry flush bleached from her skin, leaving it white and translucent.

"Don't do this," she whispered through stiff lips, raising her hand as if to ward him off. "Please, stop and leave. Forget that you ever saw us."

So his suspicions had been correct, Mark thought, feeling his gut tighten into knots. She was on the run from her husband, hiding from him. Mark's hands slowly clenched at his sides, trying to control the rage welling up in him. "Get a lawyer," he said harshly, "divorce the bastard and—"

"Divorce him?" Stunned, Jenny stared at him. Whatever she had expected or feared, this wasn't it. Relief washed over her and the words tumbled out before she could hold them back. "I've been divorced for three years."

Three years! Mark studied her face with narrowed eyes, but she looked straight back at him, the truth clearly visible on her expressive face. "If you are divorced, why didn't you ask for protection for Jamie and yourself?"

"Protection?" Jenny stared at him. Yes, he probably believed in the system he had sworn to uphold. Otherwise his work, and his life, would have no meaning. But her own life and Jamie's would be pure hell if they dared to share those beliefs. "What good would it do? Would you park a patrol car outside my house twenty-four hours a day, forever?" she asked, challenging him.

Mark shrugged. "It's a huge precinct. We don't have the manpower to protect everyone." He was as aware of the limitations as she was, more so because he was confronted with the restrictions they posed on upholding law and order daily. Last year, alone, he had investigated three homicides where women had been murdered by their ex-husbands. They had asked for protection, had received threats from their ex-spouses, but with no proof, the department had had their hands tied. The thought sent a chill down his back and he said with sudden urgency, "Talk to me, Jenny. Give me a reason to become involved."

Jamie's good cop coming to the rescue, she thought. Touched, one corner of her mouth lifted, but then it dropped again. Her lips compressed and she hardened her heart against temptation. "Sorry, Mark, you'll have to find something else to fill those empty hours until you go back to work."

Mark's hands curled slowly in frustration. Perhaps, initially, he'd welcomed Jenny and her son as a sort of distraction, but her lopsided smile had changed it all. He'd kill that bastard if he ever hurt her again, he thought grimly. Outwardly calm, he said, "I go back to work the day after tomorrow. How about dinner Monday night?"

"Damn it, Mark, get out of my life."

The corners of his mouth kicked up. So the lady could swear. He was finally making a dent in the fastidious, organized image she projected to cover the mess in her life. Be content with it for the moment, he told himself. Easing off, he slanted a quick look around.

The place reeked of sweat, and the odor drifting from some twenty pairs of sneakers neatly lined up on a rack wasn't too pleasant, either. Carolyn would have refused to spend five minutes in this place, he thought. Though well kept up, the waiting room, with its brown vinyl tiles and hardwood benches, was strictly utilitarian. In contrast the gym was sunny and bright, with whitewashed walls and skylights. For a moment he watched the children do a combination exercise of a downward block followed by a quick punch. Jamie was in the front row, his face red and beaded with perspiration. "How much longer does the class last?"

"Another thirty minutes," Jenny said after a glance at her watch. She must have dozed longer than she'd thought. Maybe that explained her irrational behavior a few minutes ago. She'd been dazed with sleep. "This is Jamie's favorite class. Sensei Luke owns three other dojos on the Island and only teaches here on weekends.''

Mark judged the instructor with a swift, comprehensive glance. About five-ten, late thirties, twenty pounds overweight, curly brown hair and an easy grin. "He looks like a teddy bear. Not what I expected from a black belt.''

Jenny felt the tension ease. "He's about as cuddly as a grizzly. At the last tournament I saw him step between two adult fighters and send them both flying through the air.'' Wrinkling her nose, she added lightly, "Jamie was very impressed. Is your son into sports?''

"Tim used to be good at soccer and basketball.'' Mark missed taking him to practice and playing with him in the backyard.

"Used to?'' Puzzled, Jenny looked at him. He seemed like a man who would enjoy kicking a ball around with his son, taking him out fishing, all the things a father should do and for which Burke had never had the time. "How often do you see him?''

"Six weeks out of the year. More like four, actually. The other two he spends with my family.'' Sometimes he regretted not putting up a fight when Carolyn had demanded sole custody of their son. But at the time it had seemed better for Tim. His hours were so irregular. He didn't work by the clock. Lately, though, he felt a nagging sense of guilt, as if he had abandoned his son. "It's all the vacation I have.''

Startled, Jenny stared at him. She hadn't expected him to settle for visiting rights, but from the slightly defensive note she guessed that was what he had done. It surprised her. He obviously had a soft spot for kids and he knew how to deal with them. But then again, she guessed a child would have interfered with his job. "I'm sure you pack more into those four weeks than many fathers do in a year,'' she said gently.

"We play video games.''

The wry sound of his voice made her chuckle. "I know what you mean. It's an addiction. Jamie used to spend hours in front of the screen. Until he discovered karate. He's taken to it like a duck to water." She glanced back at her son, punching and blocking in a steady rhythm. Around him, other children began to flag and slide to the floor, but Jamie kept going with dogged determination.

Jenny felt a twinge of uneasiness. Sometimes his restless intensity reminded her too much of Burke. Her ex-husband had pushed himself relentlessly during his daily workouts until his breath had come out in gasps and his muscles had quivered with exertion. Once, sick with the flu, he'd fainted in the middle of a session. His weakness had made him furious.

Mark saw the sudden tension flitting across her expressive face. Damn it, did the woman ever relax? He glanced into the gym, but all he saw was a bunch of tired kids dropping to the floor like flies—until only Jamie and a dark-haired boy with DiNigro's features were left, punching air, glaring at each other, neither willing to concede victory.

He wanted to place a hand on her shoulder to ease the tension, but decided not to push his luck and instead moved a little closer. "Relax, Jenny. Nothing's going to happen, not with the *sensei* keeping an eye on them. Are those two always in such competition with each other?"

How was she supposed to relax with his body almost touching hers and his breath fanning her cheek, Jenny wondered distractedly. "They joined the dojo at the same time, but Chris wasn't nearly as interested as Jamie. If DiNigro hadn't pushed him, he would have dropped out last week when he failed promotion. That's why he still has two yellow tips. DiNigro wasn't too pleased at the time. I guess last night Chris tried to show his father that he was as good as Jamie. And he is. He just lacks the motivation."

Jamie had inherited that trait from his father. As much as she wanted to, she couldn't deny Burke genes. But just because Jamie enjoyed the physical challenge didn't mean that he had inherited Burke's defective fuse. "But this is looking a little dangerous."

"What? Them punching air?" Mark asked, raising one brow in disbelief. "Come on, Jenny, how many fights do you break up in school every day?"

Jenny watched the two boys stop and drop to their knees. Relieved, she tilted her head and looked at Mark, wrinkling her nose. "I told you, my students are angels."

Mark watched the freckles dance, taunting him. He was tempted to run a finger down her pert nose, but he liked the smile curving her lips too much to risk watching it disappear.

"All right, kids. It's *kumite* time. Scramble and get your protective gear." Luke's raised voice drifted into the waiting room.

"Whatever *kumite* is, the kids seem to love it," Mark noted, as twenty-odd white-clad bodies raced into one corner of the gym.

"They sure do. *Kumite,* by the way, means fighting," Jenny explained, as one by one children began to separate from the crowd, sliding mouth pieces between their lips and fastening their padded red gloves. "The *Shorin Ryu* school is one of the least aggressive forms of karate, emphasizing self-defense. Their maxim is, There's No First Attack—"

Abruptly she stopped. Chris, with his gloves still in his hand, had suddenly spun around and kicked Jamie in his stomach. Jamie doubled over for a moment, then his gloved fist shot out, hitting Chris solidly in the face.

Then Luke was there, stepping between them, pulling them apart by the scruffs of their *gis,* sending Jamie to the side of the deck. "Fifty knuckle push-ups," he ordered before turning back to Chris.

Jenny expelled the breath she'd been holding. "So much for punching air," she muttered, throwing Mark an exasperated look. But exasperation suddenly changed to horror when Sensei Luke picked Chris up and carried him off the deck.

Blood was running down the boy's face, soaking into the white *gi*.

Jenny stood frozen in shock for a moment, then moved to open the door. Mark was there before her, asking calmly, "How bad is it?"

"Just a bloody nose," Luke said reassuringly. Brushing past them he made for the office at the end of the hall. Anxiously, Jenny followed him into the small crowded place, watching as he carefully lowered the boy onto the black plastic couch at the end of the room.

Lainie, a psychology major at a nearby university who also worked part time for Luke, jumped to her feet, returning seconds later with a towel, pressing it into Jenny's hand. "I'll get ice and water."

From the door Mark watched Jenny and Luke care for the boy. The place, which had seemed so quiet only moments ago, suddenly became a beehive of activity. Doors opened. Two teenagers, both wearing brown belts, brushed past him and entered the dojo with a bow, intent on continuing the class for Sensei Luke. Parents began to drift in, crowding around the office door. With the ease of a man who had dispersed many a crowd, Mark dealt with them until the petite, black-haired secretary returned with a bowl of ice water. Closing the door behind her, he was making for the entrance so that he could head DiNigro off, when Jamie came charging out of the dojo.

"Is Chris all right?" he asked, clutching Mark's arm. His face was the color of wax, and he swallowed convulsively.

Mark had a sudden, strong urge to bend down and hug him. He remembered his ribs just in time, though, and ruffled the boy's hair instead. "He'll be fine."

Big tears welled up in Jamie's eyes. Embarrassed, he blinked them back. "I didn't start it. Honestly. He kicked me first. But I didn't mean to hurt—" Suddenly he clapped a hand in front of his mouth and dashed down the narrow hall.

With a last look at the parking lot, Mark followed the boy. Fights. Nosebleeds. Nausea. He'd forgotten what it was like being around kids. Taking care of them was a full-time job in itself. It was one of the reasons he'd settled for visiting rights, he reminded himself.

When he entered the bathroom, Jamie was bent over the sink, rinsing out his mouth. "Feel better?"

Nodding, Jamie turned off the water and wiped his mouth with a paper towel. "I'm glad you're here. Mom won't be as mad with you around."

Mark bit back a grin. He had to admire Jamie's candor. "Why should she get mad? You said you didn't start it."

Jamie crumpled the towel. "I didn't. He pushed me when we were getting the gloves. But I did call him a jerk. Mom said I shouldn't talk to him."

Mark propped his shoulder against the wall. Color was slowly seeping back into Jamie's face. "Sounds like good advice to me."

"Yeah. I wish I hadn't said anything." Jamie tossed the crumpled paper ball into the basket. "Now Chris's father is going to yell at Mom. He gets real mad, just like my—" He bit his lip and looked up at Mark anxiously.

Mark pushed himself from the wall, his mouth compressing into a flat line. "No, he won't," he said quietly, reaching for the door. Opening it, he suddenly heard DiNigro's voice. The angry parent was apparently just about to enter Sensei Luke's office.

"This is the second time that brat of yours has hit my son. If you can't control him, I'll sue the pants off you."

Jamie started to push past Mark. "I told you so."

Mark's hand clamped on his shoulder. "Is your class over?"

"No." Jamie's hands balled into fists and his chin stuck out. "But I'm not going back."

Mark swiftly drew him down the hall. The door to the office was still open, although DiNigro had moved into the room. "You don't have to worry about your mother. *Sensei* Luke is with her."

As if on cue, the Sensei intervened, his voice firm but with an edge to it. "I don't know what happened yesterday. But I saw what went on today. When the kids went for their fighting gear, Chris kicked Jamie in the stomach. Jamie hit back. Jamie is not an excessively aggressive child." At that point, though, someone closed the door, shutting whatever was going on inside.

A grin flashed over Jamie's face. "Maybe Sensei Luke's going to send Mr. DiNigro flying," he said hopefully. "Boy, you should have seen him the other day at the tournament."

Mark bit back yet another grin. He, too, would derive immense satisfaction at seeing DiNigro being taken down a notch or two, but a physical confrontation wouldn't solve this problem. "If you don't practice, you'll never be as good as the *sensei.*"

"Someday I will," Jamie vowed, and with a bow disappeared inside the dojo.

Mark quietly let himself into the office. DiNigro stood with his back to the door, yelling at the *sensei,* one hand slicing the air angrily. "I thought *Shorin Ryu* was supposed to discourage brutality and violence. You're supposed to teach your students to defend themselves, not to attack. I'm sure Chris meant no harm. He was only playing. Weren't you, son?"

Chris nodded mutely, his dark eyes frightened, crying out as Jenny pressed a cold towel to his nose. "Ouch!"

"Stop sniveling, Chris," DiNigro snarled, towering over them. He was so close that Jenny could see the cold flecks in his eyes and feel his hot breath near her skin. "God, what a little coward you are. Just wait until I get you home."

Jenny's mouth tightened angrily and her heart went out to Chris. "To do what?" she asked sarcastically. "To beat some courage into him?" She must have chosen the right words, because the man backed off.

"If you're suggesting—"

"I'm not suggesting anything," Jenny interrupted him firmly. "Except that Chris will recover faster if you don't scare him half to death. Maybe it would be better if you waited outside."

"I think that's an excellent suggestion," Mark said from the doorway, as disgusted by DiNigro's behavior as Jenny was. The way he saw it, DiNigro should have been sitting on the couch calming down his son, not frightening the hell out of him.

Heads spun around.

DiNigro's black eyes narrowed with dislike. "Lawton. What the hell are you doing here?" Then he turned back to Luke Brown. "Did you call the cops?"

Ignoring DiNigro, the *sensei* looked at Mark with the swift, assessing glance of one warrior judging another. "I saw you earlier. Are you a cop?"

He must have passed muster, Mark decided, because a gleam of approval came into the hazel eyes. "I'm here as Mrs. Wilson's friend, not in an official capacity."

DiNigro stuffed his hands into the pockets of his jeans and smiled thinly. "So she came running to you last night. I don't know what lies she told you, but I didn't kick her son out. I sent him outside to cool off."

Mark's eyes narrowed fractionally and his quiet voice had an edge of steel. "Jamie almost got run over by a truck last night. Walking, the way he was forced to, he could have taken any number of wrong turns and never made it home. I don't have to tell you that while he was at your house, at your invitation, you were responsible for him. The way I see it, you're looking at charges of neglect, endangering the life of a minor and several other misdemeanors. You might be able to get off, but the newspapers would have a field day, don't you think?" He paused to let the words sink in, and then, in a dangerously soft voice, added, "And if you don't back off, we're talking about harassment, too."

Luke had been listening quietly. Now he threw DiNigro a disgusted look. "Maybe it would be better if Chris joined a different dojo."

"But I don't wanna go someplace else," Chris cried, his voice muffled by the ice pack. He turned pleading black eyes to Jenny. "I'm sorry I kicked Jamie. I won't do it again."

Jenny was pushing the heavy fabric aside to wash away the blood when her hand suddenly stilled. Sharply, she asked, "Where did you get this?" She pointed to a big black bruise about the size of a man's fist just above the pants.

Abruptly DiNigro took the towel away and tossed it into the bowl nearby. Lifting Chris to his feet, he pulled the *gi* back farther. "Jamie did that last night."

Horrified, Jenny stared at the discolored flesh. No, not Jamie, she wanted to cry out. Then she noticed a yellowish tinge at the edges. She breathed a sigh of relief. "This happened at least three days ago," she stated flatly. Then her hands were suddenly shaking, from an unexpected surge of anger. She reached for the towel and wrung it dry, twisting it so tightly that water poured from it in a spurt. Glancing at the boy's nose, which was still bleeding, she put the towel to good use. By the time she wiped Chris's face, her anger was under good control. "How did it happen?" she asked the boy gently.

"Tony, the boy next door, did it," Chris whispered with a frightened look at his father.

Jenny knew it was a lie and so did everyone else in the room. But unless Chris came right out and accused his father, there was nothing anyone could do. Unfortunately the boy was obviously too afraid to tell the truth, and wouldn't, not with his father standing only a foot away. Gravely, she looked at Chris and said, "If Tony does it again, will you tell me about it?"

Chris hesitated, slanted a glance at his father and bit his lip. "Can I stay?"

Jenny looked at Luke, a silent message in her eyes. If Chris left the dojo they would not be able to help him. "It's all right with me, if it's all right with you."

Luke nodded. "But no more fighting."

Mark had kept quiet for several reasons. For one, Jenny and Luke seemed to have the situation well under control. And second, to the boy he was a stranger, a stranger his father didn't like. When Chris left to get his coat a moment later, Mark turned to DiNigro and said with deceptive mildness, "If I were you I'd make damn sure that Tony didn't beat my son again."

DiNigro shot him a look of such hate Jenny felt a shiver run down her spine. "Back off, sarge," he warned coldly as he opened the door. "You're way out of line. *If I were you,* I'd worry about the boys you arrested last week. The last I heard, Pete Houligan was still in the hospital with a wired jaw."

## Chapter 5

Shocked, Jenny's eyes flew to Mark, a protest rising hotly to her lips. He still leaned against the white wall next to the door in a deceptively casual pose, his thumbs hooked into the pockets of his jeans. But she could see tension in his broad shoulders and in the hard set of his jaw. The eyes watching her were without expression, an opaque gray, distant thunderclouds.

"The man's a monster," she said clearly. "He doesn't give a damn whom he hurts. To accuse you of all people—" She dragged a shaky hand through her curls. She might not know Mark very well, but she was certain on two points: Mark was a dedicated cop; and he loved children. Besides, she knew from personal experience just how DiNigro twisted facts. She wouldn't honor his slander by asking Mark what he'd been talking about.

At her outburst, Mark felt some of his anger ease. He hadn't been certain what her reaction would be. Until now she had avoided asking the questions he'd seen reflected in her eyes every time she looked at his scars. He'd wondered if they were one of the reasons she was reluctant to trust him. He'd done her an injustice, he thought. She might dislike cops in general, but her fear of this particular one was fading fast. "He went too far this time." Though quiet, there was a steely edge to his voice.

"He has one hell of a nerve complaining to me about violence!" Luke growled, his strong hands curling around his belt. "I never particularly liked the man, but I never suspected he beat his own kid."

"Don't blame yourself," Jenny said quietly. Luke cared for his students as if they were his own children, his personal responsibility. At the moment he looked as angry as a grizzly ready to defend its cub. "You only saw Chris once a week, and your class is always crowded."

But she herself had no such excuse, Jenny thought, her stomach churning with guilt. Over the last few months she had seen Chris three times a week. He was frequently angry when he first arrived for class and she had often talked to him, even teased him, out of his sullen, argumentative moods. But when DiNigro himself brought Chris, the boy never argued with his father; he always tried to please him, she recalled. The boy never changed at the dojo but always arrived dressed in his *gi*, sometimes even wearing a T-shirt beneath the loose tunic.

How could she have ignored those simple signs? she wondered angrily. She'd assumed that he didn't want to come to class and was angry because he was being forced into it. And she hadn't paid close attention to the boy when his father was around, because she generally avoided men. Jamie might have sensed something, she thought. Perhaps that was why her son had befriended Chris. Children were often more sensitive to threats from adults, because they were so vulnerable and dependent on them.

Tears pricked her eyes. How could she have, even for one second, suspected Jamie of cruelty?

"Don't be so damn hard on yourself," Mark said quietly. He was startled by the fierce protective instincts that were suddenly surging through him.

"That's right. Blaming ourselves won't change anything," Luke agreed. "The question is, what can be done?" He looked at Mark with his brows raised.

Jenny's mouth twisted bitterly. Deep down she felt she knew what Mark's answer would be even before he voiced it, but hope leaped into her eyes anyway. Laws concerning domestic violence changed from state to state. Perhaps in New York the laws were more progressive than in other places.

Mark saw the pleading in her eyes, the small flickering flame of hope. His jaw tightened. He hated to disillusion her. "Not much," he answered Luke. "One bruise is not enough evidence to get the Child Protective Services involved, especially since Chris denies everything. The best we can hope for is that this incident has served as a warning, and that DiNigro will be more cautious from now on."

The small flame in Jenny's eyes died. Frustration sliced through Mark's gut when she turned away from him.

Shivering, Jenny crossed her arms over her chest in an instinctive self-protective gesture and leaned against the desk. Outside the sounds of children suddenly erupted—giggles and the pattering of running feet. A ringing in her ears made her desperate for fresh air. Her glance flew to the small overhead window with the weak late afternoon sunshine pouring in through the open slats of its vertical blinds. The walls of the small room were suddenly closing in on her like a prison cell.

Luke was talking, but she didn't hear his words. Her glance riveted on the bowl of discolored water and the bright red stains on the white towel. A feeling of unreality was stealing over her, the present and the past merging into one. Nightmares began flashing before her eyes like fragments of glaring Technicolor. DiNigro's face, Burke's eyes. She took a deep breath and forced the visions back, rising abruptly to her feet. "Class is over. I'm going to check on Jamie," she said in a perfectly steady voice. Putting one foot methodically in front of the other, her steps quickened as she walked through the door.

Running again, Mark thought, pushing himself away from the wall. Turning to Luke, he said, "If there's any problem, any problem at all, call me at headquarters."

The waiting room was crowded with parents and children, some students leaving, and others arriving for the next class. As always, Jamie was one of the last students to leave the deck. He was hovering near the door to the gym.

Spotting her, he pushed his way through the crowd, his protective gear clutched in his hands. "Mom, are you angry?" he asked, his eyes anxious and his face pale. "I didn't mean to hit Chris in the nose. Has it stopped bleeding yet?" He cast a searching look around. "Where is he?"

"No, I'm not angry. And Chris already left." Damp hair curled onto his forehead. Gently Jenny brushed it back. Her hand was trembling and she slid it into her pocket before he noticed her agitation. "Why don't you get your stuff out of the locker room. We'll talk when we get home. I'll wait for you in the car."

Outside, the setting sun brushed the blue sky with a golden glow, but evening shadows were rising in the distance. The wind had picked up again, biting through her jacket and tossing her hair into her face. Shivering, Jenny stopped next to her car. She wanted to go home and close the door on the outside world. Worse, she wanted to cry. She took in deep gulps of brisk salt air, exhaling slowly while she searched in her purse for her keys. She didn't notice that Mark had followed her until he said from right behind her, "You're in no shape to drive."

Jenny could hardly hear him for the buzzing in her ears. "I'm fine," she said, brushing her hair out of her eyes. "Or I will be, if you would just leave me alone."

She wasn't going to break down. Not in front of him. If she did, the whole sordid tale of her past would pour out of her like water through a broken dam. The scene in the office had brought it all back vividly, so clearly that she could almost feel Burke's controlled, cold menace. It was much more terrifying and dangerous than DiNigro's rage.

Mark saw her shiver in the breeze, and her hands shake like the red leaves on the oak tree a short distance away. "Not a chance," he growled.

Jenny glared at him. "Now listen. Being a cop doesn't give you the right to push me around."

"Wanna bet? I can confiscate your keys, if I think the situation warrants it." Until now he hadn't realized just how furious he was. Anger was smoldering inside him, licking at the edges of his control.

Jenny's chin came up, her eyes narrowed and her fingers closed over her purse protectively. "More threats? I've had more than enough for one day, thank you."

He almost lost it then. His hand cupped her stubborn small chin and tilted it up a fraction more. "I'm trying to eliminate threats, not add to them," he said in a very carefully controlled voice. When he had her startled attention, he covered her mouth with his.

Jenny stiffened, too shocked to protest. Reflexively she raised her hands to push him away. But she hadn't expected his hard, uncompromising mouth to be so gentle, so soft. There was no pressure, no demand, just a light soothing exploration. Surprised, her fingers pressed into the soft denim of his jacket. He tasted of salt air, fresh and cool. Awareness flickered to life, chasing away the chill. She felt the smooth texture of his mouth and the tangy taste seep into her senses, seducing her. Her fingers curled and opened in restless indecision.

Mark could sense her struggle with her emotions, fear against need, and knew he would have to allow time for her trust to grow. Reluctantly he raised his head, eyeing with satisfaction the flush stealing into her cheeks.

"That was—" Agitated, Jenny raked back her hair. She wanted to cover her lips to keep the memory sweet and fresh.

"Nice?" Mark suggested.

Her eyes snapped back into focus and she cast a swift anxious glance over her shoulder. Jamie was nowhere in sight. But his blond-haired friend Lisa was staring at them from a few feet away. With a giggle and a swish of her ponytail, the girl climbed into her car. Furious, Jenny glared at Mark. "Damn you. Haven't you done enough?"

Horrified, she bit her bottom lip and covered her face. She took in a deep breath, exhaling slowly. "I'm sorry. I didn't mean to let it out on you." She took another breath in a deliberate effort to relax and dropped her hands, searching for her car keys once more. "I've got to get control of myself. I don't want Jamie to see me like this."

"Where is Jamie?" Mark took the keys from her the second she found them, opening the door for her. Gently he helped her into the car but kept the keys, taking advantage of her distracted state. By the time he returned with Jamie she would probably have recovered enough to drive, but he wasn't taking any chances.

"Probably still in the locker room. He always takes his time getting dressed."

Mark smiled slightly at the sound of annoyance; it was the sound of recovery. "I'll find him. While I'm gone, think about sitters and where you want to eat tonight."

Did he ever give up? Jenny wondered with a flash of irritation. "Now listen—"

Mark cupped her chin and brushed his thumb over her lips, stopping the words. "Later," he promised calmly. "I want to talk to you, and it may as well be over a meal."

"I don't feel like talking anymore today," Jenny muttered, but she could feel her resistance fading. God, it would be nice to get out in the evening, especially tonight. She didn't want to brood and pace the house. And surely one night out wouldn't hurt, would it?

Mark saw her waver, watched the mixture of emotions flitting across her face. Apprehension followed by doubts and a small light of eagerness. How long had it been since she'd gone out on a date and enjoyed herself? he wondered, a sudden ache in his throat. "We both have to eat and I'm tired of my own company," he said softly. Ignoring his ribs, he bent down and lightly brushed her lips. "No demands. No pressure. Just a friendly meal."

Jenny's thoughts flew back to Jamie's description of his kitchen, the pizza cartons and the sack of empty beer cans. She simply wasn't strong enough to resist the appeal. "I'll try to find a sitter," she agreed.

With a grin Mark closed the door and walked into the school. He had no idea where this crazy relationship was going to lead them or how long it was going to last. It wouldn't be smooth. Of that he was certain. For a moment he wondered if he was losing his mind. Like most cops he was lousy at relationships, and preferred his private life calm and uncomplicated. There had been only one woman since his marriage had ended, another shell-shocked veteran of the divorce courts. Their affair had been safe, comfortable and undemanding. It had ended three months ago when the woman, Susan, a social worker at a psychiatric center, had accepted a promotion at another institution upstate. Mark hadn't been in any hurry to meet someone else. Until now.

Now everything had changed. Jenny was perpetual motion and restless energy. And hell might well freeze over before she trusted him enough to confide in him. A week from now he might find her packing up and closing the house. His mouth kicked up at the corners. She was a challenge and he hadn't felt so alive in years. He hadn't realized that he could still feel such potent need for a woman. He was, he suddenly realized, eager to slay a few live ghosts, and was discovering afresh the simple masculine joy of sexual anticipation.

Jenny watched him until he disappeared into the dojo. He walked with such confidence and power, his head held high. The man was in complete control of himself and that rankled. He had a funny way of removing threats, she thought, trying to hold on to her anger. Yet strangely, today he had done just that, she realized, a reluctant smile curving her lips. It was difficult to dislike the cop, when he had defended her to DiNigro, and at no little cost to himself. In a burst of optimism, she decided that it was especially foolish to fear the man who had kissed her with such gentleness.

"Does Chris ever talk about his father?" Jenny asked Jamie two hours later, keeping him company while he worked his way through two slices of pepperoni pizza. He had already taken a shower and was dressed in yellow sweats. His best friend Mike's older sister had agreed to be his sitter for the evening.

Jamie shook his head. "Only that his dad yells a lot. And sometimes he spanks him," he said, picking a slice of sausage from the top of his pizza and holding it out to Mush.

"Don't feed the dog at the table." Jenny eyed Jamie with exasperation. "Why didn't you tell me about it? I wouldn't have allowed you to go to his house."

Shrugging, Jamie wiped his hand on the napkin. "Mike's father yells at him sometimes, but he stops when I'm there. And it was Chris's birthday."

She couldn't argue with Jamie's childlike logic. Most people did stop quarreling when strangers came into their midst. And she herself had taught him that birthdays were celebrations where no arguments were allowed. The trouble was that Jamie lacked exposure to a normal family life. Families *did* argue on birthdays, and not everyone avoided fights when strangers were around. "Have you ever seen bruises on Chris?" she asked.

Jamie frowned. "Only once. But it wasn't his dad. He had a fight with Tony."

For a moment he eyed her solemnly, then asked the question he'd been wanting to ask since the moment Jenny had told him she planned to have dinner with Mark. "Did you change your mind about Mark? Are you going to tell him about Burke?"

Jenny picked up a glass of water and drank from it. "Not tonight," she said firmly, steeling herself against the look of disappointment darkening his eyes. "It isn't something I can decide overnight," she added, her voice softening. "We only met him yesterday."

"But he puts people in jail all the time. If you wait, maybe Burke will find us first. Are you going out with him on a date?"

The buzzer of the dryer sounded in the basement. Relieved, Jenny pushed back her chair and escaped. "It's not a date. Just a meal between friends," she said, hoping Jamie wouldn't place too much importance on this evening. She hadn't considered his reaction at the time and she didn't want to raise his hopes. "When you're finished with the pizza, clean up your room. I don't want Lizzie to faint."

Lightly she ran down the narrow basement steps. The walls needed another coat of paint, she thought, opening the dryer and taking out a yellow sheet. With a sigh she matched the corners, folding the material neatly before placing it into the wicker basket. Then she reached for a pillow case. When the phone rang, she listened, waiting for Jamie to answer it. He did after the second ring. "Mom, it's Aunt Alys," he shouted.

"You talk to her. I'll be right there." Swiftly, Jenny folded the rest of the clothes, then transferred another load of wash. Running up the stairs, she picked up the extension in the kitchen and listened to Jamie's excited words. " . . . he's real big and I think he likes Mom. They're going out to-night.''

With a sigh of exasperation, Jenny interrupted her son. "Hi, Alys. Jamie, let me talk."

"Oh, all right. I was just telling her all about Mark. Good night, Aunt Alys."

"Good night, son," Alys said. After thirty years of marriage to Ralph Harper, a Texas petroleum engineer, her voice held a distinct Southern drawl. "Jenny, my dear, how are you? I heard all the latest news already. It must have been quite a shock to you. Why didn't you call?"

"If I had you wouldn't have slept a wink last night. Besides, it wasn't an emergency."

Alys sighed with exasperation. "You shouldn't have to go to a pay phone to call me. And I shouldn't have to sneak into Ralph's office to call you. It can't go on like this! It's really getting to me. I'm the only close family you have, Jenny. You're like a daughter to me. When are you going to contact the lawyer I've mentioned before and put a stop to it all?"

Jenny felt tears prick her eyes and swallowed hard. If there had been a way, a safe way to live near her aunt, she would have done so. But Dallas had been the first place Burke had looked for her. For a while he'd even hired someone to watch Aunt Alys's house. "I don't know, Alys," she said, leaning her head against the wall. "Jamie had a nightmare again last night. But he's getting stronger. Soon, I hope."

Alys sighed. "I wish you could come down for Christmas. Jenny, you can't keep this up for much longer. One of these days your luck is going to run out. It's just a question of time. And you must feel more confident or you wouldn't go out at night. Especially not with a cop. Unless—do you think he would help?"

She knew that Alys was right. Sooner or later the inevitable would happen. "It isn't what you think." Jenny tried to explain Mark to her aunt without giving her the wrong impression. Alys firmly believed in marital bliss and had hinted more than once that Jenny should start dating again. "There was trouble at the dojo with DiNigro and Mark just happened to be there," she said evasively. "He sort of railroaded me into going out. I didn't want to make him suspicious." *Liar.* "Besides, he has troubles of his own."

"What kinds of trouble?" Aunt Alys asked sharply. "Can he be bought?"

Aunt Alys's devious mind made Jenny chuckle. "You've lived too many years overseas. In this country, bribing an official is a criminal offense."

Alys snorted inelegantly. "Let's be realistic. There are plenty of cops on the take."

"Mark isn't one of them," Jenny said heatedly. "He believes in the system."

There was a sudden long pause. "So do Ralph and I," Alys finally drawled. "But that didn't stop us from helping you. Jenny, the more I hear about him, the more I like the sound of him. Maybe you should consider telling him the truth and let him decide if he wants to become involved."

*Let Mark decide if he wants to become involved.*

As she took a shower and dried her hair, Aunt Alys's suggestion kept going through Jenny's mind. "It's too dangerous," Jenny told her mirror image while applying bronze eye shadow to her lids. Talking to herself in the mirror was a habit she'd slipped into one night when the walls had started to cave in on her. It helped her see things in perspective. The first time Jamie had seen her do it, he'd looked at her as if she'd lost her marbles, Jenny thought with a sudden grin. But it was difficult to lie to one's mirror image. And she had no one else she could talk things over with. "I met him less than twenty-four hours ago. I don't know him well enough to take the risk."

"Then why are you going out with him? You trust him or you would have said no," her mirror image demanded. "You let him kiss you. Not only once. Twice. The first time took you by surprise. But what about the second time?"

Jenny looked away, not quite ready to answer that, searching in her cosmetics bag for the mascara. "I was upset. It felt good to lean on him, to have someone care," she said defensively as she darkened her long lashes. "Also, I'd just realized that Burke didn't destroy me altogether. I do feel. And to use Jamie's words, I believe he likes me and that feels good, too. I amuse him, and I don't think he's laughed much lately. But going out with him is a one-time event. Those shrewd gray eyes see too much."

"Is that the only reason?"

Jenny capped the mascara and applied a little blush to her cheeks, then applied burnt orange color to her lips. "No. I'm scared. The cop I can handle for one night. But the man—I'm afraid of him. Afraid of what he could come to mean to me. And scared out of my mind at the thought of being rejected again. But is it wrong to want to go out to dinner with a man? Other single women my age do so every Saturday night."

"But other women don't carry fake IDs in their purses."

Jenny compressed her lips. Whatever she had done, she'd done to keep Jamie safe, and she refused to feel guilty about it. So while it wasn't wrong to go out with Mark, it certainly wasn't safe.

With a last look into the mirror Jenny walked into her bedroom and searched through her meager wardrobe, finally choosing a slim black wool skirt. From the plain pine chest, she chose the white angora sweater Aunt Alys had given her for Christmas last year, still in its original plastic bag. Jenny lightly ran her fingers over the pearl embroidery on the shoulders and around the neckline. Perhaps it was too elegant, but for her it was a festive occasion. Her first evening out—and her last one, she reminded herself firmly.

With a sigh, she sat down on the edge of the bed and pulled on black tights. Because Jamie couldn't bear the thought of leaving here, he had, with a child's intuition, latched on to Mark in the hopes that he could help. She couldn't bear the thought of giving up their little nest, either. For a moment she looked around the room with its bare walls and cheap furniture. Except for Jamie's room, the house seemed to be waiting—waiting for a time when she felt safe enough to unlock the doors to the past and get her parents's belongings out of storage.

There was a treasure trove filled with furniture, personal items she hadn't been able to part with, books, music sheets, her father's coin collection, her mother's instruments. In her mind Jenny had already picked out suitable spots for everything. Although where she'd put her mother's concert piano, she had no idea.

Abruptly, she stopped daydreaming, hoping, wishing. Standing up, she pulled the tights over her lace panties, then stepped into her skirt. Her fingers fumbled with the zipper and the button. She was as nervous as some of her students before a test. The attraction for Mark had come out of nowhere, unexpected; and she didn't know how to deal with it. In fact, she hadn't the vaguest idea what to do next.

The button finally slipped through the hole. Jenny reached for the soft, pearl-studded sweater and pulled it over her head. Slipping into low-heeled black pumps she walked into Jamie's room.

Jamie and Lizzie, Mike's sixteen-year-old sister, were sorting through the stack of video games. Lizzie was one of her students, a little cheeky at times but responsible, and with her parents living next door, Jenny knew that Jamie was as safe with her as with an older woman. She was a little taller than Jenny, with a mass of brown curls and hazel eyes that looked her over critically. "You look gorgeous. I've never seen you all dressed up before."

Jenny bit her lip in consternation. Perhaps she had overdressed. The seafood restaurant Mark had suggested looked like an elegant place the few times she'd driven past it and she had dressed accordingly. She tugged at the edge of her sweater. Was she so badly out of touch, she didn't know what to wear anymore? The one thing she had never worried about before was what to wear. "Is it too festive, do you think?"

Lizzie shook her head. "It's a winner."

At that moment Mush began to bark. Jenny hugged Jamie. "You do exactly what Lizzie tells you."

Jamie slanted a mulish glance at his best friend's sister and wrinkled his nose. "Do I have to?"

Jenny's lips twitched, though her voice was firm. "Yes. The good news is that you can stay up until I get back home." She didn't want to chance his waking up with a nightmare and finding her gone. Hearing the door knocker clang, she turned to Lizzie. "I left the phone number of the restaurant next to the phone downstairs. If anything unusual happens, anything at all, *call me.* And don't open the door to anyone except your parents. I have a key."

Lizzie slanted her a cheeky grin. "You're more nervous than I was on my first date with my boyfriend, Frank." When the door knocker banged again, she added, "You want me to answer it?"

Jenny shook her head. By Monday it would be all over class that Mrs. Wilson was as nervous as one of her students on her first date, she thought with a rueful grin as she walked to the door. Downstairs, she grabbed Mush's collar—he was stationed by the front door, growling—and opened the door. It was ridiculous to feel nervous, she told herself sternly. It was ridiculous to suddenly feel shy. At least, she did until Mark asked teasingly, "Are you going to sic the dog on me again?"

"When did you do that?" Jamie asked from the top of the stairs.

"I didn't. It's a joke," Jenny said with a sharp tug at the chain. Mush growled one more time, then settled down at her feet. Releasing the dog, Jenny looked up and steeled herself to meet Mark's mocking glance. The glint in his eyes made her heart skip a beat, then begin to drum furiously. Blood rushed through her, heating her skin, and her voice was husky when she said, "Please, come in."

Mark walked inside and closed the door. For a moment there, while he'd waited for her to answer the door, he'd wondered if she'd changed her mind again. She was as unpredictable as the weather on the island, which could turn from below freezing to warm spring sunshine within a few hours. Come to think of it, her smile was just like the first rays of the spring sun, a little hesitant, a little nervous and shy. His glance went over her, struck again by just how slender she was. The black skirt loosely hugged her gently rounded hips and even the soft fuzzy sweater couldn't hide the fact that she needed to gain at least ten pounds.

Mark felt a vivid bolt of heat flash through him, an emotion much more complex than mere desire or protectiveness. "You look stunning," he said quietly. "Are you ready to leave?"

"Thank you." She wanted to make some polite remark herself, but he looked more formal in charcoal slacks, a gray tweed jacket and white shirt, and somehow the words refused to come. "I just have to get my coat."

Lizzie had joined Jamie at the top of the stairs for a curious peek. Jenny saw her eyes widen with female appreciation and her lips form a silent "Wow." Then Lizzie winked and said, "Have fun. Come on, Jamie, leave your mother and her date alone."

With a wave, Jamie followed her. "Mark's a friend, silly, not a date."

"What do you know about dates? You're just a kid."

Mark looked at Jenny. Her cheeks were flushed but there was an anxious look in her eyes. "Those two seem to get along fine," he said firmly.

Jenny waited a moment, listening. When she didn't hear any real arguing, she relaxed. "I guess so. Lizzie's parents live right next door. If anything should happen—"

"You can call from the restaurant, if you're worried."

Abruptly, Jenny walked to the closet and took out her coat. "You must think I'm crazy."

Mark took the black trench coat from her and helped her into it. "No," he said quietly. She was just plain scared out of her mind. Placing his hands on her shoulders, he slowly turned her around. "What I think is that you need to get out for a few hours. And frankly, so do I. I've been cooped up for over a week, living on pizza. I can do with a nice juicy steak."

"Steak? But I thought we were going to a seafood restaurant."

"They serve steak with lobster tails."

Jenny shook her head. "This is stupid. If you want red meat, let's go to a steak house."

"You said you preferred fish."

"I do, but—"

"Let's argue on the way. I'm starving."

Not until she was sitting in the car did Jenny realize just how neatly he'd gotten her out of the house. "That was a first-class con job, if I ever saw one," she said torn between irritation and amusement.

"What do you know about con jobs?" he asked lazily, enjoying her smile. She didn't do it nearly often enough, he thought, pulling out of the driveway before she found a reason to go back into the house.

Suddenly Mark realized that he'd never heard her laugh openly, with her head thrown back and helpless giggles ripping loose. Not the way she had made him laugh out loud in the parking lot earlier today. The sudden disquieting thought occurred to him that Jenny hadn't enjoyed herself in quite a while. From what he had heard and seen so far, she didn't even seem to have any friends. The phone in her house never rang and no neighbors knocked on her door. Jenny, he guessed, hadn't been wined, dined or flirted with for a long time. She was hiding in her house like a nun in a cloister, sacrificing her life on the altar of motherly love. He watched her look back one last time before the house disappeared behind a curve. "If you want me to, I'll ask a patrol car to drive past your house and keep an eye on it."

Jenny's fingers twisted the poplin of her coat. "That's kind of you. But it's really not necessary." She made an effort to relax and said lightly, "About that con job. Try keeping up with twenty-five juniors."

"I thought they were all little angels."

"Well—sometimes they slip."

"Figures. I didn't think you could control twenty-five little devils. Not when you can't control that brute of a dog." Mark slowed down at the intersection he'd almost missed last night and slanted her a searching look. The battle flags were being raised, he noticed with satisfaction.

Jenny grinned at him wickedly. "Who says I can't train him?"

He was sorely tempted to kiss that saucy mouth. Instead, he taunted her, "Careful what you say, Jenny. Siccing a dog on an officer is against the law."

She knew what he was doing—removing threats again. At the moment she didn't feel even a twinge of apprehension, just a need to best him at this silly game. "I told you my opinion of the law. It stinks."

He raised one arm and held it to his nose, sniffing. "Smells clean to me. Sure hope you teach those little devils of yours a little more respect for the institution."

"Oh, I am," Jenny mocked, flashing him a taunting grin. "In one class I'm talking about the French revolution. Lizzie's learning about Caesar crossing the Rubicon with his armies in direct defiance of orders from Rome.''

"Great! More little anarchists is just what we need. Lady, how about teaching them to obey speed limits—''

Out of the corner of his eye he saw her stiffen. With a quick glance in the rearview mirror he slowed down. When he looked at her again, the lopsided smile was back. Frowning, he wondered what he'd said that had wiped the laughter from her eyes.

"Speed limits isn't my subject. Terry Carlson teaches driver's ed,'' Jenny forced herself to say lightly, trying to recapture the light mood one careless word had dimmed. *Lady.* She reminded herself that this wasn't a date, anyway, no matter how much she wished it were. Nervous, she raised a hand to run it through her hair.

Mark captured it, holding it firmly in his grasp, looking for a safe place to park. The road was narrow and had no shoulder. Then he spotted the elementary school. "I like your hair just the way it is, smooth and unruffled. Lady-like. I'm not taking you to a hamburger joint.''

With a strangled sound Jenny tried to snatch her hand away. He held it easily while steering into the parking lot. "Only words, Jenny,'' he emphasized, guessing the problem was linked to her ex-husband. He kept a tight leash on his fury. He was only now beginning to realize just what that bastard had done to her. He had not only knocked her around, but had terrorized her to such an extent that the mere mention of some word still made her shiver three years later. "I want to know what he did to you.''

She wrenched her hand free. "It's not what he did to me that counts. He nearly killed Jamie.''

"I happen to disagree.'' He parked the car, unsnapped his belt and leaned over her, deliberately crowding her while he unbuckled her. His ribs stabbed sharply at the sudden twist and he braced himself on the door frame, ignoring the pain as he had all day. "I want his name and his address.''

Jenny pushed back the panic welling up in her. "You're spoiling my appetite."

*"His name and address."*

"Damn it, Mark, this is one threat even you can't remove."

"His name and address, Jenny."

"He's not in your jurisdiction. And that's all you're going to get out of me." His face was so close she could feel his breath on her cheek, the scent of shaving cream and soap filling her senses. No cologne. No after-shave, like Burke had used.

Some of the fury went out of him. At least the bastard wasn't an immediate threat. "Cops stick together. I can get all the information I need by phone."

That was what she was afraid of, what she'd tried to avoid. Suddenly desperate, her fingers slid over the door, searching for the handle. Finding it, she opened the door. Her chin shot up, and her hands came up to push him away. "Back off, macho cop. I'm walking back home."

He wasn't about to back off. He had a point to prove, to her and to himself. "Running again? I think you're a coward, not a lady. Ladies don't run."

Her fingers were splayed across his chest. Beneath it she could feel the edge of the bandage and the steady beat of his heart. He made no move to protect himself, but left himself wide open to a shove from her. "Damn it, Mark, you're not playing fair. I'm not a coward. You don't understand!"

# Chapter 6

"Then make me," Mark said softly. Her eyes narrowed at the challenge, glittering like golden topaz flames. He preferred the fire to the glazed look of panic that showed every time she thought of her ex-husband; the ghost he was determined to exorcise out of her life.

"I told you, I don't want to talk about him anymore!" Her hands shifted, moving restlessly over his soft cotton shirt. She could feel his muscles ripple beneath her touch and the strong thudding beat of his heart.

"All right. No more talk. There are other ways to prove that you have courage."

Jenny shot him an angry glance. "I don't have to prove anything to you."

But her hands were still touching him with restless little movements, driving him crazy. "Not to me, Jenny, to yourself." Smiling faintly, he raised one black brow in challenge. "I know you better than you do yourself. Right now you want to touch me, kiss me."

Instant denial rose hotly to her lips. "No!" Then why was she still touching him? Why wasn't she simply telling him to back off? Perhaps it was pride that made her hesitate. Or this burning need to feel whole again, to be with a man, to neck in cars and parking lots if she wanted to, without knots twisting inside her. "I know you're conning me into this," she groaned, "but someone has to take you down a notch." Her arms slid around his neck and she pulled his mouth down to hers, touching it briefly before she pushed him away.

"That was a peck, not a kiss," Mark taunted. "I know you can do better than that."

Angry humiliation ripped through her. "According to *Webster's* a kiss is a gentle contact—"

"Just once forget that you're a mother or a teacher," Mark cut her off. "You're a young and beautiful woman, Jenny." He saw her eyes widen in disbelief. Then pride snapped back into place and she started to push him away. It was more than he could take. Lowering his head, he covered her mouth with his.

A small sound of protest escaped her, then was muffled by the tip of his tongue. This time there was no gentleness, but demand, hot and fierce, as if he had to prove something not only to her but to himself. Reflexively, she stiffened under the assault. "You don't want this," she warned desperately against his lips. "You know nothing about me."

He silenced her protest and continued the seduction, his tongue invading her mouth. He didn't hold her, didn't touch her, enticing her with the hungry pressure of his lips alone.

Needs welled up; deeply buried, long repressed needs suddenly erupted with a quick flash of heat. She wanted nothing more than to be touched by him, held by him, and her body arched to meet his.

Mark had had no intention of drawing out the kiss, but he felt her response—the swiftly erupting eagerness, the small shivers, the heat—and found that he couldn't pull away. He'd known that she would be passionate if he ever managed to slip beneath her defenses, but he hadn't expected it to happen tonight. Her fingers curled into his hair and pulled his head down closer with a desperation that made him ache. *Too soon,* he thought, fighting the need to reach for her. Too soon for both of them.

He framed her face with firm steady hands and lifted his head, reluctant to break all contact. "Ah, Jenny—"

Slowly, reluctantly, Jenny forced her eyes open and looked at him. His face filled her vision. She dragged fresh air into her lungs, but she still saw only him. How had it happened that this man had became so important to her overnight? she wondered frantically. Dear God, what was she going to do?

Swinging her legs out of the car, she leaned her head against the door frame. She needed time and distance to steady her reeling nerves. Perhaps in another minute she could convince herself that nothing earth-shattering had happened. But deep down she knew that the time for running had passed.

"This is crazy," she said finally, when the silence began to grate on her nerves. "I don't want to be attracted to you. I don't ever want to become involved again."

"So you're going to deny it ever happened," Mark said flatly, staring at her back, wondering if she ever planned to turn around and look at him.

"What is there to deny?" she asked fiercely. "It was an experiment, a stupid, crazy test."

Only a kiss.

If she looked into a mirror she would find her clothes unwrinkled, her hair untangled and, except for her lipstick, her makeup would still be fresh. With shaking hands she reached for her purse and searched for the small tube, dragging the creamy, scented balm over her bottom lip as if renewing the color would make what had just happened disappear. It didn't. She could still taste him.

Mark leaned back against his door. "An experiment, maybe. Even crazy, I will admit to. But I draw the line at stupid."

The humor in his voice steadied her. There had been a time when she had buried her head in the sand, when she had lived from day to day telling herself that her life wasn't nearly as terrible as it seemed.

The denial had nearly cost Jamie his life.

And if she kept pretending that the kiss had meant nothing to either of them, she would ruin another life. His. Abruptly she swung her legs back into the car, closed the door and looked at him with serious eyes. "You're wrong. It was plain dumb-stupid," she said. "Only you don't have enough sense to see it. Other men would run from trouble, but you think you're so tough you can handle anything."

"Not everything," Mark said, a small smile playing around his lips. But beneath his lowered lashes his eyes were sharp and watchful.

That faint smile made her furious. Why wasn't he taking her seriously? Somehow she had to get through to him! "Just look at yourself," she said fiercely. "You're all beaten up. This afternoon DiNigro all but threatened to take you to court. You need my troubles like you need another blow to your ribs. What does it take to penetrate that thick skin of yours? I don't want you involved in my life in any way. And that includes the situation involving DiNigro. Luke and I can protect Chris."

Mark pushed himself away from the door and reached for the key. "You can tell me to stay out of your life, Jenny." Though his voice was still mild, there was a steely edge to it. "But don't tell me how to do my job." Shifting into drive, he glanced over his shoulder and eased the Blazer back onto the road. "The restaurant only holds reservations for fifteen minutes. We can discuss everything over a meal."

Food. How could he possibly think about food? Jenny slanted him a resentful, exasperated look. He was like a brick wall, impervious to threat and reason, she thought, jerking the seat belt across her shoulder and watching him do the same. "I want to discuss it now. You just don't get it, do you?" Agitated, she started to run a hand through her hair, stopped, then stuffed the hand into her coat.

Mark smiled faintly. "It's a little difficult without all the facts. Why don't you spell it out for me?" But he understood one thing very clearly. She was trying to protect him. *Him.* A man almost twice her size, with sixteen years of experience on the force. Him, the tough guy even the mob didn't like to mess with. He felt an ache in his chest and it wasn't caused by his ribs.

Jenny's hands curled in her lap. "You won't have a job if he catches up with me."

Mark slowed down at a red light, watching cars zipping by on the highway ahead. So the bastard had power and money, he filled in grimly. That narrowed the field a little and left only a few million suspects, spread all over the country. He had faced better odds. "If that's supposed to scare me off, forget it, Jenny. He wouldn't be the first man to want my badge."

Jenny gripped the bag in her lap tightly, twisting the strap. "I know. DiNigro's going to have a good shot at it first," she said bitterly. "He's going to try to discredit you to save his own skin."

The light changed to green. Mark joined the heavy, fast-moving traffic, heading north, toward the sea. "If you're talking about the kids, Pete Houligan and his three buddies, let me set your mind at rest. Both Internal Affairs and the Civilian Complaint Review Committee have already investigated the case and dismissed it as a regrettable, but unavoidable accident."

Jenny drew in a sharp breath. There had been four of them! DiNigro hadn't mentioned that fact, she thought grimly, turning to look at Mark. In the light from the dashboard, he looked weary, shadows deepening the grooves bracketing his mouth. The committees might have cleared his name, but his conscience was still giving him a hard time, she guessed. "Was it unavoidable?" she asked softly. Even a seasoned veteran like Mark would have trouble controlling four kids.

Wearily, Mark rubbed the back of his neck. "I keep asking myself that question, but I just don't know. I'd had a hell of a day. It was past midnight, and I was on my way home, when I spotted two teenagers stripping a BMW on the side of the road. I stopped, identified myself and told them to freeze. They started to run, but they didn't run very far, just to the edge of the woods behind them. I should have suspected something then. They made it too damn easy for me, gave me no trouble in following them at all." At the time, all he'd been able to think of was that filing this report would mean doubling back to the station. Consequently, it would be too late to drive back home and get a few hours of sleep.

"There were two others with crowbars hiding in the trees," he continued in a flat voice. "When they attacked, I'd already put handcuffs on one of the two I'd chased—Pete. He got caught in the middle and couldn't move out of the way fast enough. Luckily backup arrived within minutes."

Crowbars! Jenny felt sick just trying to picture the scene. He'd been off-duty, on his way home. It should never have happened. But then again, men like Mark were never off-duty. Even injured and weary, he took on other people's problems. Looking at him, she could tell that he was tired, bone-weary tired, the way she sometimes felt in the middle of the night, when past mistakes and failures came back to haunt her. Yet for a confident man like Mark, failure was even tougher to face. He'd made a mistake that night, an error in judgment that could have cost him his life and might still demand Pete's. Mark took none of it lightly. It was obvious the whole matter weighed heavily on his conscience.

Her heart ached for him and she wished she could help. The details of the situations might be different, but basically what it came down to was that they both had made mistakes. Slowly Jenny could feel a bond forming between them. A bond that was tighter than mere physical attraction, she realized, panic welling within her. She would have to cut it, before it could strangle her and destroy him.

"You might have been killed, instead," she pointed out angrily. "You risked your life for a stupid piece of metal. I hope the owner was suitably grateful."

Mark heard the catch in her voice, saw her hands mangle the strap of her purse and a gleam came into his eyes. "The owner is fuming because his car's been impounded. And I didn't risk my life for just a piece of metal. We're talking about grand theft."

"Big deal. All they'll probably get is a slap on the wrist," Jenny shot back, knowing well that they weren't talking about grand theft auto. On a different level, what they were really talking about was principles, rights and needs; her right to live in peace and his need to ensure that she did.

Mark took his eyes off the road and looked at her steadily. "Maybe this time around. The next offense, they won't walk."

It was that simple for him, she suddenly realized. He had a very basic belief in right and wrong and an unshakable confidence in the system—flawed though it was—that made her want to confide in him. Or was it this strong attraction she felt that made her want to trust him? She didn't know. "Don't you ever get tired of risking your neck?" she asked softly.

His hands tightened on the wheel. Carolyn had used those same words like a battering ram, trying to wear down the wall of his resistance and make him quit his job. But even on the occasions when he had felt doubts—and there had been times when he'd been frustrated enough to turn in his badge—he wouldn't have admitted it for a second. She would have used that knowledge against him. But he was more than frustrated now. The mistake he had made scared the hell out of him. "Sometimes," he admitted quietly. "I guess there comes a point in everyone's life when they have to ask themselves 'Is it worth it?'"

Jenny looked out the window and watched the trees fly past, their swaying branches dark silhouettes against the star-studded, moonlit sky. Lights glowed in the houses set back from the street and smoke curled from chimneys. A woman was walking her dog along the sidewalk and two kids were racing into a driveway on the other side of the street. Normal, quiet, peaceful, the way she wanted to live. And this man put his life on the line to make it possible for others to live this way. She touched his hand and said gently, "Yes, I think it is."

And for one night, this one night only, she wanted to pretend that there could be a normal life for her, too.

Candlelight, white table cloths, simple elegance. Soft piano music whispered in the high rafters of the A-frame style house. With a smile of appreciation, Jenny looked around as they followed a waiter to a table next to the wall of glass overlooking Long Island Sound.

It was the kind of place her parents would have loved, Jenny thought, glancing over at the deserted terrace and the empty jetty below. Good mooring, quiet elegance and seafood.

Burke would have hated it. He liked more ostentatious places, with exotic drinks, chrome and glass.

Abruptly, she dismissed the thought. If this was to be her only evening out, she was determined to enjoy it. "I've driven past this place several times," she said, smiling at Mark. "But it isn't the sort of restaurant that serves macaroni and cheese."

The flickering flame burning in the ruby glass on the table cast a rosy glow over her pale skin and reflected off the pearl embroidery of her sweater, drawing his eyes to her small high breasts. He had a sudden vision of making love to her in front of a fireplace, with the glow of the flames dancing over her creamy soft skin. But at her words he looked up, startled. "Are you trying to tell me you never go out without Jamie?"

Jenny nodded. "The only time we're separated is when we're in school. Jamie goes to St. Mary's Elementary. I drop him off on my way to work and pick him up on my way home. Sometimes he sleeps over at his friend Mike's house. But other than that, I don't dare let him out of my sight. I know it's unhealthy, though. He needs to get out more on his own. That was why I allowed him to go to Chris's party." She could read the questions in his eyes, questions he wanted to ask and she couldn't answer. Abruptly, she held out her hand, palm up. "Please don't probe and prod anymore this evening. I want to forget—just for one night."

For a moment he stared at her silently, watching one corner of her mouth tilt up. The cop in him knew that she had reached a breaking point. The cop in him argued that it would be a foolish move to ease the pressure now. One strong squeeze and perhaps he would end this nightmare for her. But tonight he was more man than cop. Slowly, he took her upraised hand and brought it to his lips, lightly brushing his lips over the tips of her fingers. "All right. And I know just the way to take your mind off your problems."

Jenny felt her heart skip a beat and her fingers began to tingle. He had such strong yet gentle hands, hands that made her feel soft, feminine and safe. But her being any of those things was just another illusion, a part of the pretense of this whole evening. She would do well to remember that.

But while she couldn't afford to be soft and she didn't want to lean on anyone ever again, it occurred to her that perhaps it would be possible for them to become friends. Oh, she knew he had something totally different in mind, and that he wasn't easily discouraged, but that didn't worry her. His interest would fade the moment he realized she didn't enjoy sex. He was a very physical man and would expect more from a woman than a few kisses. Gently, she withdrew her hand and picked up the menu, looking at him over the top of the laminated card. "I know. Things always look better on a full stomach."

Mark's mouth twisted dryly. He had agreed not to probe into her past, but he hadn't agreed to let her crawl back into her shell. He reached across the table and lightly tapped the edge of the card. "Just to set the record straight, that's not what I meant. Though feeding you up a little isn't such a bad idea."

Things were going great, Jenny congratulated herself. If he liked his women more robust, that suited her just fine. "It's a hopeless cause. I was always skinny, even as a child. Grandmother McKenzie used to feed me hot fudge sundaes to make me gain a little weight. She always said that it wasn't fair I could eat the stuff and not gain an ounce while she just looked at it and put on five." She slanted him a provocative grin. "But I know you're a sucker for lost causes. I'll order a hot fudge sundae for dessert and let you drool over it."

"I don't drool," Mark protested lightly. At least not over a hot fudge sundae, he added silently, wondering if she'd noticed the small slip she'd made, and if McKenzie was her real name. Investigations were like big puzzles, little random pieces often popping up here and there. Put together, they eventually gave him the whole picture. This one—his personal investigation into one beautiful and mysterious Jenny "Wilson"—was no different.

Leaning back in his chair, he decided that she hadn't noticed because she was too busy teasing him. His glance slid down her long slender throat, coming to rest on her breasts. "I don't think you're skinny," he murmured softly.

Jenny felt warmth rush through her. His glance was like a physical caress, and she could only wonder what it would be like to go out with him on a real date. Abruptly she raised her card a little higher and tried to ignore him by concentrating on the menu. But the feeling of warmth remained.

"Are you ready to order?"

Jenny nodded, but didn't lower the menu. It had just occurred to her that after everything he'd done for her it was only fair that she should pay the bill. Unfortunately, it wasn't a situation she'd ever been in before and she didn't know how to deal with it. She took a deep breath, angled her chin and said in her best teacher's voice, "There's something I want to say before I do.... This dinner's on me."

Mark's brows drew together in a straight line. Usually, he didn't have an ego problem with splitting the bill, though he balked at having a woman pay for his meal. This was the nineties, women were touchy about their independence and Mark had learned long ago that the meal was more enjoyable if he didn't argue the point. It had also never been important to him. But with Jenny it was. "I invited you, not the other way around," he pointed out firmly.

Jenny clasped her hands in her lap. "I know I should have mentioned it before."

"It wouldn't have made any difference. Look, one meal isn't going to bankrupt me."

An indignant look came into Jenny's eyes. "I should hope not. With the taxes I'm paying I would like to know where the money's going if not for salaries."

"Then consider it a tax refund," Mark said, tongue-in-cheek. "The next time we'll discuss it beforehand."

Jenny wasn't very comfortable with it. But without bringing up the touchy matter of gratitude again there was little she could do. "Is that how it's done?" she asked seriously. "You discuss it beforehand?"

Stunned, Mark looked at her, thinking of nuns and cloisters again. It had never occurred to him that she'd been so cut off from life even before her divorce. "That's how it's done normally," he said very calmly, allowing none of the rage burning inside him to show. It was a complete mystery to him how this unworldly woman had managed to remain unharmed for three years. "The next time, if you insist, we'll split the bill. But don't ever mention it to my brothers. They'd never let me live it down."

There wasn't going to be a next time, Jenny thought. But it would be useless to argue with him, so she switched the subject. "Tell me about your family."

It was a tall order, but it kept the conversation on neutral ground during their meal. Mark didn't mind her curiosity. He talked about his parents and his three brothers, who worked in the family construction firm. With every childhood prank he recalled, she became less nervous and laughed more. She was hardly aware that she finished all of the lobster bisque and two-thirds of the scallops that she'd ordered. Talking about his two sisters, Mary and Erin, he realized just how different their lives were from Jenny's. Mary was about Jenny's age, and married, with a baby daughter and a husband who adored her. Erin was in law school and shared an apartment with three other girls. They were happy, confident young women. And with four brothers to look out for them, they would remain that way. Jenny had no one to lean on, no one to laugh with, he thought as he finished his steak.

"So you're the oldest," Jenny said, looking at him with quiet satisfaction. The distraction had worked. He seemed more relaxed, softer somehow, and sometimes a smile even reached his eyes. Life had taught Jenny one vital lesson. Everything passed. Good times, bad times, even nightmares. It was the bright memories that made a person want to go on. "What I don't understand is why you moved out here in the first place. You seem to be a very closely knit family."

Mark shrugged. "I used to work for the NYPD. My ex-wife came from Suffolk County. I transferred out here after we got married."

Jenny gave him a startled look. "I assumed that she was from California."

Mark shook his head, bitterness seeping into his voice. "She's an electronics engineer and moved to Silicon Valley after the divorce."

"I'm sorry. I didn't mean to pry," Jenny said swiftly, reaching for her wine. The woman sounded utterly selfish. First she'd made Mark move out to Suffolk County so she could be closer to her parents. Then, after the divorce, she'd moved clear across the country to separate the father from his son. Long Island had a flourishing high tech industry and Jenny felt certain that his ex-wife could have found a job here. Some women, she thought grimly, didn't know just how well-off they were. If a man ever loved her enough to even contemplate switching jobs and moving away from his family, she might, just might, consider marrying again some day. Someday, when Jamie was an adult and all her troubles were over.

At the thought of her son, Jenny slanted a look at her watch. Almost three hours had passed since she'd left the house, she thought in consternation. Swiftly, she put down her glass and rose to her feet. "I'll just check on Jamie," she said and walked to the pay phone in the lobby.

A very pregnant young woman in a bright red dress was already using the phone. Leaning against the wall a few feet away, Jenny searched in her purse for a coin. The evening had been a precious gift and for a few hours she had allowed herself to lose sight of reality. But the pretense had gone on long enough, she told herself sternly, her fingers closing around the coin. She could never forget that she was a woman on the run.

The woman finally finished her conversation and hung up, turning to Jenny with an apologetic smile. "My son has the flu," she explained, placing a hand on her stomach. "I know I shouldn't have left him, but this may be my last evening out for some time."

Jenny felt a twinge of envy. "When is it due?"

"Tomorrow. And it's a she this time," the young woman said, walking past Jenny into the nearby rest room.

With a sigh, Jenny picked up the phone and punched in her number. She'd always wanted more children, but she had miscarried twice after Jamie's birth. In a way it had been a blessing. When the doctor had warned Burke it would be dangerous if she became pregnant again, he had lost all interest in her. For the last three years of their marriage they'd had separate bedrooms.

"*Lady*—cold, useless," a voice seemed to whisper in her ear. It felt so real that Jenny's head spun around. The pregnant woman passed her with a smile, the door of the rest room swinging back and forth behind her. With a deep breath, Jenny pushed back the past and concentrated on her call, frowning when she heard a busy signal. Hanging up, she retrieved the coin. There was no reason to worry, she told herself firmly. Lizzie was just talking to one of her friends. Still, her fingers were trembling slightly when she reinserted the coin.

"Busy?" Mark suddenly said from right behind her.

Jenny nodded. For such a large man he moved very silently. "Lizzie must be using it."

Noticing the fine tremor, Mark took the receiver from her hand. "Or you punched in the wrong number." After everything he'd learned tonight he was beginning to understand how she had managed to hide for so long. She didn't trust anyone. Even now she hesitated before telling him her number. It was a hell of a way to live, he thought, waiting for the call to go through. Lizzie answered the phone after the first ring and Mark handed the receiver back to Jenny.

"Is everything all right, Lizzie?" Jenny asked, trying to keep the urgency from her voice.

"Great. Jamie's asleep. He fell asleep about thirty minutes ago. And I'm watching a movie. Did you try to call before?"

"Yes, but the line was busy. Why?"

"Someone called just before you rang, and at first I thought it was you, but it must have been a wrong number," Lizzie said. "When I picked it up no one answered, and then whoever it was just hung up."

At the mention of the call, she'd automatically stiffened, but with a rueful grimace, Jenny forced herself to relax. The phone call had no other meaning beyond that of an ordinary wrong number. She was behaving like an idiot, seeing ghosts behind every corner, and it would have to stop. "I'll be home soon."

"Take your time. I want to see the end of the movie, anyway."

"What are you watching?"

"One of your videos. *Dirty Dancing.* I just lo-o-o-ve Patrick Swayze. Isn't he sexy?"

Jenny chuckled at the dramatic words and her eyes flew to Mark. He was leaning against the wall next to the phone, watching her with a softness in his eyes that made her catch her breath. Then Lizzie added cheekily, "Your date looks a little like him. So take your time and enjoy."

"Brat," Jenny said succinctly, blushing furiously. "I'll be home in half an hour." Swiftly, before Lizzie could add another outrageous suggestion, Jenny hung up. From the smug grin on Mark's face there was no doubt that he'd heard every word of Lizzie's comment. Perhaps she'd been around teenagers too long, Jenny thought, but she couldn't resist the sudden urge to taunt him. She placed her hands on her hips and looked him over with reckless provocation. "Very sexy," she pronounced, imitating Lizzie perfectly.

Mark felt his pulse quicken and desire rip through him. If the place hadn't been so crowded he would have reached for her then and kissed her breathless. Instead, he flicked a punishing finger over her nose. "I dare you to repeat that when we're alone. Are you ready to order that hot fudge sundae?"

Abruptly, Jenny shook her head. She didn't know why she felt suddenly cold, but she had survived on her instincts too long to ignore them. "I need to get home."

Lizzie was still glued to the screen when Jenny entered Jamie's bedroom twenty minutes later. "You're too early," she wailed. She was sitting on the floor with a bowl of popcorn in her lap and a can of soda in her hand. "Can I stay and watch the end of it?"

Jenny looked at her son, curled up on top of the bed with a blanket wrapped tightly around him, breathing evenly. Everything was fine, she thought, relief flooding through her. Cautiously, she climbed over Mush, lying right next to the bed, to place a soft kiss on her son's warm, flushed cheek.

"I'll walk you back home when you're ready," she agreed. It would have seemed churlish not to invite Mark in for a cup of coffee, but she wasn't at all certain that doing so had been a wise move. Lizzie's presence would act as a buffer, she decided. Straightening, she glanced at the screen, estimating that the movie would last about another twenty minutes.

Which meant she had another twenty minutes before she pushed Mark out of her life.

She would miss him, she thought. She had never known a man with such unstinting generosity in him, and the thought of what she had to do made her heart twist painfully. It was then that she realized that she had made an unforgivable mistake. She had carried the pretense too far. Somehow the evening had turned into a real date. Perhaps it had happened after their crazy kiss in the parking lot. Perhaps it had happened during their meal or when she'd tossed the challenge at him in the foyer.

"Come downstairs when the movie's finished," she said and walked out of the room, closing the door behind her. Her chin firmly set, she headed for the stairs, more determined than ever to end it here and now.

Mark was studying a lithograph of Montauk Point Lighthouse, when she came down the stairs. "Ever been out there?"

"Many times as a child. With Jamie only once," Jenny said lightly, then abruptly stopped on the bottom step. The words had slipped out easily, making her wonder how many other mistakes she'd made during their meal. Then she realized that she felt no twinge of panic at the possibility. He was slipping beneath her defenses, every one of them, she thought resentfully, walking over to where he stood.

"Jamie's sound asleep. Lizzie's watching the rest of the movie." She practically flung the words at him, daring him to comment. She was spoiling for a fight. She needed the anger to help her get through the next few minutes.

"I'll take her home," he offered with a flash of humor, taking the force out of her fury.

Jenny's eyes narrowed. He'd left his tie in the car and had opened the top buttons of his shirt on the way back from the restaurant. His jacket was flung over the arm of a love seat in the nearby living room. He looked comfortable, relaxed—and as indolent as a sleek, well-fed cat. Only his eyes were sharp and alert, those patient knowing eyes that saw too deep. Abruptly, she turned to the closet, took off her coat—which she hadn't taken the time to remove earlier, so intent had she been on checking on Jamie first—then hung it up. "I'll make the coffee."

Mark followed her into the kitchen, watching her fill up the coffee machine and measure coffee into the filter with swift practiced movements. For the moment he was content to watch her move from cabinets to counters, seeing her stretch to reach for items or replace them. But carefully banked desire was drumming inside him as he waited for her to run out of things to do.

She flicked a button on the machine, then turned around to face him, her nails biting into the palms of her hands. "It was a lovely evening. I enjoyed it." She'd known that it wouldn't be easy. Now, facing him, the words refused to come. She turned away and paced to the dinette table, her heels clicking on the tile floor. She gripped the back of a chair tightly. "And I owe you more than—"

"You owe me nothing," Mark cut her off firmly. Leaning against the counter, he knew where she was headed with this. She was trying to work her way through the mountain of debts she thought she owed him before she told him to get lost. "I enjoyed the evening as much as you did."

Jenny spun around. "I wish you weren't so damned patient or so—nice."

"I prefer sexy," he said dryly, his stern mouth softening. "I knew you'd chicken out."

A brief smile lit her face, then vanished abruptly. She wasn't going to pretend she didn't know what he was talking about. "I wish we were kids. If you'd asked me to go steady then, I would have said yes." She grimaced. "I don't think you would have asked me out, though. You must have been one of those Irish rogues who only had to flex their muscles and smile and the girls would faint at your feet."

"Not faint," Mark said, grinning. "I assume you weren't one of them?"

Jenny shook her head, her voice dry with self-mockery when she said, "I was what was generally referred to as a good girl and a geek. I was skinny, wore braces and had a mob of curls when straight hair was in. I consistently made high honors, was a member of the track team and the student council, practiced music at least an hour a day, and the rest of the time, if there was any left, my nose was stuck in a book. I rarely gave my parents trouble. They were my best friends." She grinned suddenly. "Even if you'd asked me out, my father might have scared you away. He was very protective of me.''

''I doubt he would have scared me away.'' Mark felt tenderness well up in him at the picture she sketched of her high school years. Oh, he would definitely have been tempted, he thought. ''I had quite a problem with authority for a while.''

''Did you?'' She glanced at him, trying to imagine what he'd looked like. His unruly hair would have been longer, his eyes not so patient, bristling with aggression instead. He would have worn tight jeans and T-shirts, cocky one moment, brooding the next. Jenny felt blood drum in her ears. She wouldn't have been able to resist the teenager anymore than she could resist the man now. Her skin burned, her body ached, and she wanted nothing more than to be touched by him.

She drew her eyes away from him, focused on a straw wreath hanging on the wall and said firmly, ''The bottom line is I'm not a kid. I've escaped from one hellish marriage, and I'm still trying to piece my life back together again. Jamie is my whole life. I don't have the time or the inclination to date.''

With a single succinct word, Mark crossed the space between them, pulled her into his arms and kissed her firmly, impatiently. Her surprise changed to instant longing and she opened up to him. It was what she had wanted from the moment she'd run into him in the parking lot. Her mistake had been not to run from him then. Now it was too late.

She'd deal with her mistakes later, later when she could think again. This wasn't the time to question why he was the one, the only man, who had cracked the ice. Right now she only wanted to taste the pleasure, feel the heat. Insanity.

That, too, she would deal with. Later.

Her arms slid around his strong neck. She had to stand on her toes to deepen the pressure of his mouth without putting too much strain on his ribs. Stretching, she arched against him, feeling his heart pulse lightly, quickly, matching the rapid beat of her own. Matching her hunger. She felt wanted, desired and suddenly the touch of his mouth wasn't enough. She wanted more. What would it be like to make love with him? What would it be like to touch his skin? It was madness to think along such lines, to imagine what it would be like to feel Mark's rough hands on her.

And then imagination turned into reality as his hands slipped beneath her sweater, sliding over her back to the edge of her bra, strong hands with callused skin, hands that protected and excited at the same time. Like his mouth. Like the man. He was her nemesis and she couldn't resist him, even when she felt his thumbs brush gently over her breasts.

Through the thunder roaring in his ears, Mark heard the creaking of floorboards above them. He tore his mouth from hers. His lips were no longer demanding but soothing as he gently skimmed over the pulse at her temple, her cheekbones and down her neck. "After I take Lizzie home I want to come back," he said, his eyes locked on hers. He saw desire there, matching his own clawing need, and his hands tightened around her waist.

Jenny drew a steadying breath. For the first time in her life, it would be easy to say yes, she suddenly realized. She wanted him. More than she'd ever wanted a man. And if it had been mere sexual attraction that drew her, she might have left her door open and taken the chance of disappointing him. But she was falling in love with him and that frightened her.

She heard a door close and Lizzie's footsteps as she came down the stairs. Reality slammed into her with the force of a hurricane. She took a step back, then another, before she managed to say in a low voice, "I'm not ready for this." Then she brushed past him and met Lizzie in the foyer. By the time she'd taken money from the billfold in her purse, which she'd left on the table in the hall, she had herself back under control. "Mr. Lawton offered to take you home," she said, avoiding another look at Mark.

Lizzie slanted her a puzzled look, but she didn't protest or make another of her outrageous comments. Mrs. Wilson was her favorite teacher, funny, understanding and easygoing, but only up to a point. She had seen that firm expression once before, when a jerk at school, Ricky Torres, had tried to crowd Mrs. Wilson. The class still wondered what she'd said to him after that day's session, but the kid was real careful these days not to get on her bad side again. "All right," she said. Shrugging into her coat, she batted her eyes at Mark. "Too bad I live next door."

"Brat," Jenny said, managing a small laugh. "You better behave yourself. He's a cop."

With a toss of her head, Lizzie opened the door. "I'll wait outside."

Jenny carefully placed her billfold on the table, and picked up the folded up cotton socks she'd forgotten to return earlier. "I'm sorry, Mark," she said, holding them out.

He wanted to shake her. Snatching them from her, he walked out the door without looking back. If he had, he would have done more than just shake her and his loss of control scared the hell out of him.

Only, after he'd shut the door, he realized that he didn't have any valid reason to come back. And pride wouldn't allow him to knock on her door without one. Oh hell, he thought, frustration and anger clawing at his gut. Perhaps it was better this way. He'd become too involved, too fast and too deep. He needed a few days to cool off. "Hop in," he said to Lizzie, opening the door of his car for her. Joining her in the car, he started to pull out of the driveway, in his anger not even noticing that a branch scraped the roof.

Lizzie slanted a thoughtful look at his hard face. "Mrs. Wilson is a real sweetheart," she started a little hesitantly. "I think she's scared to date again. That's what my mom said to my dad the other day. And she was real nervous before you came."

Mark didn't comment. Jenny was always nervous and frightened, he thought grimly, shifting into drive. He wanted to help her, but she refused to give him a reason to become involved. She considered him as much of a threat as that ex-husband of hers. Besides, he wasn't going to discuss her with one of her students! "Nervous?" he asked, his foot poised on the gas.

"Yeah, like fussing over the sweater she was wearing."

"Was she?" Mark asked, his mouth softening as his eyes, drawn to one last look at the house, watched the lights go out one by one on the first floor. Slowly he eased the car forward. Maybe tomorrow he'd drop by and judge for himself.

"Hmm. Real nervous," Lizzie added for good measure. Suddenly her expression turned to one of dismay. "Look, someone stole Mrs. Wilson's mailbox."

Mark slammed on the brakes, shifted into park and got out of the car. Parting the yews, he stared at the empty hole in the ground, then took a brief look around. "Does it happen often around here?" he asked, getting back into the car.

Lizzie shook her head. "Not on this street. There aren't too many kids living around here."

Mark took a calming breath. Most likely one of her students with an attitude had been responsible for the prank.

But then again, it might have been a ghost.

# Chapter 7

There was nothing terribly sinister about mailbox theft. Kids were the usual culprits. They did it because they were angry or, because they were bored, for sport. It was so common that the precinct handled the reports over the phone and, unless requested, didn't bother to send a car to the "scene of the crime." Mark himself had lost two and, like many an irate homeowner, had spent the next few nights in a chair hidden behind a fence trying to catch the vandals. Jenny's had needed replacing, anyway. There was no reason for his gut to twist itself into knots, he told himself as he pulled into her driveway to tell her about the theft.

But after having spent nearly a whole day with her, he found it difficult to remain objective. Her fear was rubbing off on him.

Frowning, he closed the door of his car and slanted a look at the dark house. The only light burning was in the upstairs center window, the one immediately above the front door. It had to be Jenny's room. She had probably chosen that particular room for its location, so that she could hear the noises if someone tried to force the door. Though what she would do, should that happen, was more difficult to predict. She wouldn't sic the dog on the man, of that he was fairly sure. She would try to protect that big old warrior the same as she tried to protect him, he thought grimly. He dragged a frustrated hand through his hair.

He wished he could be sure that she would at least grab Jamie and the dog, and run out the back door to call 9-1-1 from her neighbor's house.

Hands balled in pockets, Mark stared at the flower bed of bright yellow mums at the edge of the floodlights. The bed was free of leaves and was carefully prepared for the coming winter with a thick layer of mulch to protect the roots from frost. Ample space between the plants allowed them room to grow. She was slowly turning this place into a permanent home. Thoughtfully, he glanced from the flowers back to the window. Jenny might not be aware of it yet, but her running days were over.

And while she was defending her home, there was a good chance that she'd send the dog and her son to safety.

Lines of tension curved around Mark's mouth. He had learned a lot about her during the past twenty-four hours. Enough to know that the mailbox theft would jolt her, even if it was only a prank. Enough to know that she'd try to hide her apprehension with a grin, or a sassy word. And enough to fear that she would do something stupid in an act of desperation if the bastard came near her son again.

Slowly, Mark walked up the steps to the porch. The glimpses of terror he'd seen in her eyes were so strong they sliced through him like shards of glass every time he saw them, ripping him raw. Her fear was very real, but the cop in him didn't believe in ghosts, in danger that couldn't be seen. Was the bastard still searching for her? Or was she still so locked in her nightmare that she felt him breathing down her neck even if he wasn't?

The fact was, that for the last fifteen months at least, she hadn't seen or heard from the man and it was entirely possible that he had finally given up the search.

Restlessly, Mark turned his back to the door, crossed the porch and braced himself on the weathered wooden rail, trying to look at the problem objectively. The breeze had died down to a mere whisper, rustling in the few remaining leaves. The smell of humus and wet grass filled the air and the moon hung like a big jack-o'-lantern above the treetops.

He had lost his detachment where Jenny was concerned and he needed a few minutes to regain control. He didn't know when it had happened. Perhaps when she'd tried to sic the dog on him and had looked at him with her lopsided smile. Perhaps it had happened when she'd run into him in the parking lot, when he had caught a glimpse of the woman she could be, funny, a little shy, wanting to reach for life. So many events had been packed into this long, crazy day, that it was difficult to say when it had begun. And oddly enough, the one scene that stuck in his mind more than any other was Jenny's attempt to pay for the meal.

It had suddenly struck him just how innocent she was, how sheltered her life must have been before she'd married that bastard. Swearing, he gripped the railing tightly and his jaw set hard when he imagined the kind of prison her marriage must have been.

To hell with detachment, Mark thought and strode to the screen door, but found it locked. The noise alerted the dog, though. He came charging from somewhere in the house, barking furiously. "All right, old warrior," Mark said firmly, pitching his voice low enough to be soothing and loud enough to filter through the door. "We're going to have to come to some understanding. I'm not the bad guy. I'm trying to protect your mistress, just like you. So stop barking. You're waking Jamie up."

To Mark's amazement the barking stopped, changing to a low growl instead. He kept talking, wondering if Jenny was going to open the door, or if this time she was determined to keep him locked out. With a grimace he propped his shoulder against the wall. He couldn't blame her if she did.

He had rushed her and kept up an unrelenting pressure all day on more than one level, keeping her off-balance continuously. Perhaps it was better to back off and cool it, he thought, turning away. The dog began to whine as he walked toward the steps. Mark's mouth twisted wryly. At least he'd made some progress there.

"Oh, don't tell me that he's come back." Jenny's muffled voice suddenly drifted to the outside. Mark turned back, waiting. Seconds later the porch light came on.

Jenny unlocked the door, uncertain which would be worse—to realize the porch was deserted and that Mush had barked again at the family of squirrels that visited every night, or to find Mark outside her door. After he'd left, the house had suddenly seemed so silent and deserted that she'd gone upstairs and taken a hot shower to ease the tension, hoping it would help her sleep. She had told herself stoically that she was glad he had left without another word. But now, opening the door, she held her breath.

He stood with one foot on the steps, poised to leave, his body turned toward her, waiting. The taut look on his face made her stomach tighten and her hands fumble with the lock. "What happened? Did your car break down?"

Mark shook his head, slowly walking to the front door. He started to tell her about the mailbox. But one good look at her through the glass of the screen door and he changed his mind. Her face was bare of makeup and hair curled damply onto her forehead. She wore gray sweats with the logo Save the Whales on it and the top was at least two sizes too big. She looked vulnerable and tired. Maybe it was no more than a prank, but he wanted to be with her when she found out.

"My car's fine. Open the door, Jenny," he said quietly.

Up close his face looked grim. This was no social visit, she suddenly realized, wondering what could have happened now. Anxious, she opened the door, forgetting about the dog. Mush slipped past her, baring his teeth and growling at Mark.

"I thought we'd come to an understanding," Mark said, holding the door with one hand while the other slowly stretched out. Mush's weight shifted to his front paws as he leaned forward and sniffed in the scent cautiously. Then, with another stretch, he pushed his wet nose into the large steady hand and licked it, before retreating to Jenny's side.

"Just what understanding is that?" Jenny asked, slanting a slightly resentful glance at Mush. Little by little Mark was winning over the other members of her small family. It made her feel, suddenly, like an outsider and envious, too. Her heart ached with the need to accept the hand of friendship and the protection he was offering her.

"The one about us," Mark tossed at her, the fine lines around his eyes crinkling.

Jenny felt the ache spread to her throat. Before she could say anything childish, such as telling him to leave her dog alone, she walked down the hall. "The coffee's still hot. I'll bring the mugs into the living room," she said over her shoulder.

Without waiting for an answer, she walked into the kitchen, her stomach tied into knots, wincing as her bare feet hit the cold tile floor. She had turned down the heat only minutes ago, but the tiles already felt like ice. She looked over her shoulder, realizing that Mush hadn't followed her. "Traitor," she muttered darkly, getting mugs from a cabinet and putting them down on the counter with unnecessary force.

Pouring coffee, she hoped that Jamie had slept through the noise. He was used to the dog's bark and the events in the past two days had taken their toll. When she had covered him with a thick comforter and turned off the lights a few minutes ago, he hadn't stirred.

Mark was squatting in front of the fireplace when she entered, holding a long match to the log. Mush was lying a few feet away, his head on his big paw and his thick tail thumping against the floor. She placed one mug on the square wooden coffee table, then retreated to the end of the couch farthest from Mark, watching the flames begin to lick at the wood. Curling up with a pillow and cradling the cup for warmth, she asked, "Are you going to tell me what brought you back?"

Mark glanced over his shoulder, his gaze connecting with hers. "Nothing earth-shattering. You lost your mailbox."

"But I saw it when we got home!" Jenny felt her mouth go dry and there was a cold knot of pressure in her stomach. Taking a steadying breath, she hugged the pillow a little tighter and sipped her coffee, feeling its warmth run down her throat. Don't panic, she told herself sternly. It's just a prank. She managed to keep her voice steady when she said, "Mailboxes get stolen all the time. I've been meaning to replace that rusty old thing, anyway."

But she couldn't prevent her thoughts from straying to another time, when Burke had removed their mailbox so he could intercept her mail more easily. Especially the letters from Aunt Alys. A cold fist gripped her heart.

Mark saw the convulsive movement of her fingers and watched her struggle for control. Dropping the match in the fireplace, he twisted around, gently prying the cup from the tight clutch of her hands. Placing it on the table, he clasped her hands between his palms. "I'll put another one up for you tomorrow."

For a moment Jenny looked down at the hands encircling hers completely. Strong, warm, capable hands with blunt nails and fine black hairs curling around a steel watch. So unlike the smooth manicured hands of her nightmares. She'd never been more tempted to stop fighting and place her fate and that of her son into his scarred hands. Then she raised her head and looked at the lines etched around his eyes and the grooves bracketing his mouth. He had his own mistakes to deal with and she couldn't burden him with hers.

Slowly, she shook her head and withdrew her hands. On impulse she pushed back the unruly hair falling onto his forehead and said gently, "Your ribs are never going to heal if you don't give them a rest. I can do it."

"Do you know how?" Frustration made him surge to his feet. Rocking on his heels he looked down at her and watched her eyes narrow at the challenge.

"I've learned all kinds of useful things over the years, Mark. One of them is not letting macho guys rile me."

"I believe that," Mark said with a grimace. "You won't even let one come close enough to rile you."

Jenny flashed him a grin. "That's the idea." Then her smile faded abruptly and she turned toward the fireplace, watching the small flames leap and crackle. "I can remember cleaning the fireplace the second day after we moved into the house. I didn't want to wait for the chimney sweep. It was August, humid, in the nineties. There was no furniture in this room. We sat on pillows, with the windows wide open, and roasted marshmallows. The neighbors must have thought we were nuts."

"Jenny—" Mark began, his voice hoarse. A deep aching tenderness welled up in him. She stirred all kinds of turbulent feelings in him. Compassion, yes, but also admiration for her courage and her determination, her humor and her spunk.

She went on as if she hadn't heard him, her glance flying to the cornice moldings. It had taken her days to strip off a hundred years of paint. She had sanded the wood, stained and varnished it and almost lost a thumbnail putting the pieces up again. She glanced at the hardwood floor she had stripped on her hands and knees, afraid that machines would damage the old wood. And with each new room she had tackled, her confidence had grown.

At the thought of having to leave everything she'd built here, she suddenly felt excruciatingly tired. Resting her head on the back of the couch, she closed her eyes. "I don't know if this is a prank or if he's found me," she said quietly. "He once took the mailbox out for six months and had the mail sent to his office. I don't want to leave here. I don't know where to hide next."

Her voice was calm, but Mark found the unbearable weariness in her eyes even more disturbing. He jammed his fists into his pockets to keep from pulling her into his arms. "He wants you to keep running, to make mistakes. You're playing right into his hands," he said quietly.

Let Mark decide if he wants to become involved. The words crossed her mind again, more tempting than before. "Nothing's going to stop him. He'll never give up, until Jamie is an adult." At the thought of Jamie, strength flowed back into her voice, along with a quiet determination to protect her son. "If I gave you a name and an address could you guarantee Jamie's safety?"

He sat down beside her, and drew her head against his shoulder. She was so weary she didn't protest. "I want to help you, but I can't do it without a few facts."

Jenny tilted her head and looked at him. He was strong, reassuring, dependable. Gently, she raised her hand and stroked his jaw, feeling small bristles scrape against her skin. He had a strong beard, and would need to shave twice a day. Burke, she recalled, had never been able to grow a full beard. "You can't be here all the time, you know. He may show up tomorrow or it could happen a year from now. All I know is that he isn't going to give up."

Perhaps it was all in Jenny's imagination, Mark thought, but he wasn't willing to take the chance of her getting hurt again. "I won't let anything happen to you and Jamie. You can't go on alone like this, Jenny. You need help, so why not take the leap and trust me?"

She stared at him, wishing she could. It would be so easy, she thought. All she had to do was lean against him, allow his arms to close around her and shift the burden onto his broad shoulders.

Mark saw her indecision and said quietly, "Sometimes talking about the past helps to put it into perspective."

Jenny looked down at her hands, noticing that it was ten minutes to midnight. Midnight, when respectable ghosts returned to their closets, but her own demons never slept. "It's a lousy bedtime story," she muttered, wavering.

Grimly, Mark stared at her bent head. Her hair had parted, revealing the long, vulnerable nape of her neck. It would make a lousy bedtime story. He knew how ugly life could be, how cruel, how violent. It wouldn't shock him, though he doubted that he would find it easy to sleep afterward. But if he could convince her that her ghost was no longer haunting her, at least she would get some much needed rest. "I think I can handle it." Gently, he laid a hand on her shoulder.

She swayed forward and rested her forehead on his chest. "I don't know why I should trust you," she muttered into his shirt, still fighting. "I don't like cops."

"We'll tackle that problem some other time," Mark said mildly, gathering her close. Burying his hand in her soft silky waves, he tenderly pushed her head onto his shoulder and held her. "Right now I'm off-duty. All I am is a man who cares about Jamie and you."

"Don't tempt me," she muttered, her voice suddenly breaking as emotions swamped her. Tears shimmering in her eyes, she raised her head. "I don't want to fall apart. I'd hate myself afterward and I've traveled that road too many times before to risk it again."

Nervously, she twisted the soft cotton fabric of her pants, a new fear clogging her throat. His opinion of her was important, mattered more than it should, and she was suddenly very much afraid to see the shame she had lived with for so long reflected in his eyes. He laid his life on the line for strangers continuously. How could he possibly understand that she had failed to protect her own son? She moved away a little and looked at him, one corner of her mouth tilting up, saying hoarsely, "I think I'd prefer the cop right now." The cop wouldn't judge her, she thought soberly. He would listen with an air of detachment, objectively and without emotion.

It was the man who made her feel weak and defenseless. It was the man who was the greatest threat.

Abruptly, she pushed herself to her feet and walked to the fireplace. Crouching in front of it, she took a log from the big copper kettle to her left and placed it into the flames, watching sparks fly up. "He came into my life when my parents died," she said quickly, not wanting to give herself more time to change her mind about this. "Granny was fighting cancer, and after the plane crash she just slipped away. My only other close relative, my mother's sister, lived in South America at the time. She came for the memorial service, but she couldn't stay. He was a stranger and it was easier to be with him than with the friends I'd known all my life. I wanted to put the past behind me, I wanted to stop hurting and they reminded me of what I'd lost.

"He was respectable, well educated and ambitious. If he hadn't been, my parents' friends might have interfered. Granny liked him, too. She died content, believing I'd found someone to care for me."

She paused for a moment, folding her arms in front of her, bleakness overtaking her.

"It took me five years to find out what kind of man he was. Our marriage wasn't warm and happy like my parents'. There was no real closeness. He had affairs—that was my fault—but he was discreet and I closed my eyes to it, because I had burned all my bridges and had no place else to go.''

At least the bastard hadn't assaulted her sexually. Mark released a silent breath of relief at the thought. He slanted a grim glance at her averted profile. She was beautiful enough to turn men's heads, warm and passionate. If her ex had looked for excitement elsewhere it sure as hell hadn't been her fault.

''He wouldn't have let me go anyway, though I didn't realize it at the time. It took me five years to find out that he had married me for the airline settlement. He was away on business in Europe when I received a check for 1.8 million dollars. I didn't want it, didn't need it. My parents had left me financially secure and I was working as a substitute teacher. To me it was blood money and until that moment I'd believed he felt the same. So I put it into a trust fund for Jamie. When he found out what I'd done, he—he went over the edge.''

Wearily, Jenny brushed a hand across her face. ''I don't have to tell you what happened next. I'm sure you've heard it dozens of times before. He was sorry afterward, of course, apologized and tried to make up for it.''

Until the next time, Mark thought grimly, controlling the rage burning inside him.

''It went on for two years. I tried to leave several times. I tried to divorce him, even went to a lawyer.'' Bitterness crept into her flat voice when she added, ''Wife abuse is not permissible evidence in some states and had no bearing on a custody hearing, I was told. I wouldn't have gotten full custody of Jamie, so I stayed. Until my aunt returned from overseas. She convinced me to leave. We were at his parents' house at the time and he was always careful to hide his rages from them and I thought I would be safe. But he lost it that day. Jamie rushed to help me and he—Jamie's grandparents rushed in as he fell down the stairs, arriving too late.'' She hesitated, facing her demons once again. Not a day went by that she didn't blame herself for what had happened next.

"When he hurt Jamie, he broke the chains. I guess he'd always known that if he ever did, nothing would keep me from divorcing him. Jamie was in the hospital for six weeks and I got the divorce. Afterward, he told me that it wasn't the end. He was never going to give up his son.''

For a while after she'd finished, Mark said nothing, didn't trust his voice to be steady and calm. For a cop the sight of abuse was almost as common as mailbox theft. It was ugly, unforgivable, but he usually dealt with it objectively. Only this was personal. He was involved, had been involved from the moment a young boy had asked him if he was a good cop. He was hurting for her and for Jamie. And he was furious. But he would deal with his emotions later, in private.

Now he concentrated on her. Pity or anger wasn't what she wanted or needed. If he made a move toward her now, she would push him away. Looking at her across the small space between them, he said, his voice flat and quiet, "You're right, it's a lousy bedtime story. The stuff of nightmares.''

Her hand trembled as she ran it through her hair. If he'd judged her and found her wanting, he was hiding it well. The way she felt right now, she couldn't have taken it if he'd touched her, but his flat words steadied her. With his restraint he acknowledged that she was strong enough to deal with it without clinging to someone for support. He always seemed to know what she needed, she thought. Some demons did vanish at midnight.

But others did not.

"I know he hasn't stopped looking for me,'' she said with a quiet intensity.

Mark frowned, examining the motives. A son, money, a beautiful young woman who had managed to defy the bastard and had bested him. Murders had been committed for

far less. Still, it had been three years since her escape. Time
enough for the ex's rage to cool, to assess his losses and go
on with his life, possibly find another victim. "Jenny, when
he made those threats, he was furious," Mark pointed out
quietly. "Also, it takes a lot of money to keep up a search
indefinitely. And from what you've just told me, he lacked
sufficient funds."

Jenny stared at him for a long moment, while hope fractured inside her, splintered and died. Burke didn't have to
be rich, she thought grimly. He could afford to sit back and
wait. Wait for her to make more mistakes, like the one she'd
made tonight. "I know there's nothing you can do," she
said, her voice devoid of emotions. "So why don't we drop
the subject. It's getting late."

Mark got to his feet and rubbed the back of his neck,
where a headache was beginning to form. Twice today she
had looked to him for help. And twice he'd let her down.
Whether the threat was real or imagined, he wanted to help
her and Jamie. He needed to see them happy and safe. His
feelings for her had gone beyond the physical. He wanted
her, but not just for a few nights of passion. He could wait.
"The only thing that can be done at this point is to check
your ex-husband out, and for that I need his name and address," he said quietly. "I won't be able to run a complete
make on him because this is not official business and I can't
use all the obvious resources available to me. But I can call
in some favors."

"No. I don't want you to." The words burst out of her in
a rush of guilt and alarm. She had wanted him to believe in
her. But she didn't want him to become involved, because
she hadn't told him the complete truth. Deceptions. So
many deceptions, she thought. Would she ever be free of
them? "I appreciate the fact that you're willing to help," she
said huskily, backing away from him, from temptation.
"More than you'll ever know. But I don't want you calling
in any favors for me. I'm not worth it."

Mark saw panic darkening her big eyes, a mixture of dismay, regret and fear clouding them. Suddenly the last four words she'd spoken clicked with something she'd said earlier. *"He had affairs—that was my fault."* The words ripped through him, and the fury he'd so carefully controlled until now surfaced, and with it the desire he'd been holding back. "Don't ever compare me to him," he said harshly and hauled her against him, determined that this one ghost wasn't going to haunt her tonight. He tilted her head and took her mouth fiercely.

Heat sizzled. Thunder crackled and lightning flashed.

Jenny hadn't known that a kiss could hold so much heat. It seared her lips, burned her throat and set her body on fire. She didn't want it. She shouldn't want him. It was wrong.

And she should push him away. But her hands went around his neck, pulling his mouth closer, and her body sought his warmth.

The reasons, the deceptions, the lies. What did they matter? What mattered was this heat, this feeling of freedom. It was as if she'd waited a lifetime to feel and want. She moved urgently against him, needing him.

His hands went beneath her sweatshirt, seeking her soft smooth skin. She tasted of toothpaste and coffee. Her body was tautly stretched against him, eager, burning, hot. Her small breasts were firm and fit perfectly into his hands. At his touch they hardened, swelled, heated. A groan broke loose in his throat.

The sound was more beautiful to Jenny than any sound she'd heard before. She arched back as he touched her breasts, his hands gentle yet firm, his rough palms fanning the heat within her as the flames leaped higher. Mindlessly, she reached for him, brushing aside his collar, tugging at the buttons of his shirt, desperate to touch him as he touched her. Feverishly, her hands slid over his hair-roughened skin, her fingers touching the bandage.

It was as if a bucket of ice water had been emptied over her head. She froze, then snatched her hands away, pushing out of his arms, stumbling against the couch. Shaking, she braced herself against its sturdy back, blood still drumming in her ears, bitterly grateful that the heat was fading.

Mark fought for control, his body racked with need, his breathing ragged. Through narrowed eyes he watched her shake her head, saw her chin go up before she turned fully toward him. His lips compressed angrily. He'd had about as much rejection as he could take for one day. "Don't say a word," he warned her harshly. Snatching up his jacket, he stalked from the house.

Mark burned rubber backing out of Jenny's driveway and he did the same sliding into his. Walking into his kitchen, he tossed his jacket onto a chair, snatched a beer from the refrigerator and jerked off the tab, pouring the cold bitter brew down his throat.

Emotions were still churning inside him. Anger, desire, frustration. Leaning against the refrigerator, he closed his eyes. A mature man of thirty-seven didn't leave the house one morning and come home that same night burning for a woman he'd just met. That was his partner Jay's style, not his. He never rushed into relationships.

He had known Carolyn six months before he'd asked her to marry him. He'd always wanted a family of his own, but he'd hesitated to take the leap because cops made lousy boyfriends and husbands. Most of his partners had tried matrimony and failed. But his parents' marriage had survived the odds, and he'd figured that his own would, too, if he was willing to give it a chance.

They'd married six months later. A week after their honeymoon he'd caught a bullet and from then on their marriage had gone downhill. The transfer to Suffolk County had only been a temporary patch to their ailing relationship, delaying the inevitable for a few years. If it hadn't been for Tim they would have split up long before that.

Frowning, he turned off the lights and carried the beer with him down the hall to his bedroom. Since he hadn't bothered to turn on the heat, the place was cool. He remembered many a night when he'd stayed long past his regular hours at headquarters because he didn't like to come home to a cold silent house.

But a cold house and loneliness were lousy reasons to ever risk another mistake. He knew that a home could be just as cold and empty when shared by two people who couldn't stand the sight of each other.

He needed some distance. Just because he was twisted in knots now didn't mean that what he was feeling for Jenny was going to last. Unfortunately, until he knew if the threats were real or imagined, he couldn't walk away from her. Turning on the lamp on his nightstand, he suddenly realized that he still didn't have an address, still didn't have the bastard's name.

He shrugged out of his shirt, frowning uneasily.

Damn it, what was she hiding? She wasn't lying to him of that he was certain, but she wasn't telling him the whole truth, either. He rubbed the back of his neck, then slanted a look at his watch. It was past midnight and he was tired, but his mind was in overdrive. There was an urgency filling him, the same urgency he'd felt when he'd looked at the empty spot where the mailbox should have been. If Jenny refused to give him the answers, he was going to have to do some checking on his own.

He picked up the phone and dialed the night desk of the big *Long Island Daily,* hoping that Hank Gillis was on duty tonight. Hank's memory rivaled that of a computer; he could recall events, names and dates from way back. A few years ago Mark had helped him locate his daughter, who had run away from college with a rodeo clown. He and Hank still met occasionally for a drink. The phone rang on the other end, once, twice. "Come on, Hank, pick up the phone."

He answered on the fourth ring, his voice hoarse from too many cigarettes. "Hank. Mark Lawton, here ... No, I'm okay... Yeah, let's meet next Friday. Hank, I need some information. Do you recall a plane crash somewhere in Southern Europe about twelve years ago?"

Hank groaned. "My wife, Toby, walked out on me that year, that's all I remember. I came home one day and she'd cleared out, moved in with a guy from Sands Point with a million dollar house and a limo. She didn't only take my daughter, Stacy, with her, either, she took Sam, my Doberman pinscher, too. I walked around in a fog for months. But you know that story."

"Not about Sam," Mark said, kicking off his shoes and lying down on the bed, trying to hide his disappointment. But he knew how Hank had felt. He, too, had come home one night to an empty house. Unlike Hank, though, he'd known that Carolyn had planned to leave, but she hadn't told him when. He could still remember the shock when he'd walked into Tim's room and had found it bare, the bed stripped, the closet and toy chest empty. "Did you ever get him back?" he asked, picking up his drink.

"Yeah." Hank chuckled gleefully. "That was a stroke of luck. He must've jumped the fence one day. Toby hadn't bothered to change the tags yet and a girl called me at the office to let me know that she'd found him. I tell you, I drove over to Sands Point like a shot." He paused a moment, then added slowly, "I remember the girl to this day. She had the biggest, saddest brown eyes you've ever seen."

Mark blinked and his hand tightened around the receiver so hard that his knuckles showed white. There had to be millions of girls with big brown eyes, even big, sad brown eyes, who liked dogs and who lived in an upper class North Shore community, but he had to ask, "What else do you remember about her?"

"Not much. Only that she was very slender and that she had gorgeous thick, blond, wavy hair that reached all the way down to her waist. Why do you want to know? Is there a story in it for me?''

"This one's personal," Mark said firmly, but his eyes were gleaming. "You don't happen to remember a name, do you?"

There was a momentary silence, then Hank sighed with regret. "Sorry. I'd like to help you, but I wasn't kidding when I said that I don't remember much of those first few months."

## Chapter 8

"Is Mark coming today?" Jamie asked when he bounded down the stairs for breakfast the following morning, dressed for Sunday school in brown slacks and a tan blazer.

"I don't know." With a few deft tugs Jenny straightened the collar of his white shirt and the thin sweater he wore over it. She had asked herself that question at least a hundred times during the night. Inwardly she winced when she recalled last night's scene, wishing she could erase it from her memory, wishing she had never given in to the impulse of confiding in him.

In the clear morning light it seemed dangerous and reckless. Due to her need for warmth, she had endangered the both of them.

Pouring two glasses of orange juice she joined Jamie at the table. "Some kids took our mailbox last night. When you come back from Sunday school we'll have to buy a new one and put it up."

"But you said we would go to the movies today, because we didn't make it last night." Jamie put a pale blue napkin into his lap, then reached for the cereal box and filled his bowl.

He was more concerned about missing the movie than the theft. Jenny breathed a small sigh of relief. She wanted to keep his life as free of anxiety for as long as possible. "The mailbox comes first," she said firmly. "If there's time afterward, we can go."

"We'll never see it," Jamie muttered with his mouth full, giving her an angry look. For the first time he noticed that Jenny was dressed in jeans and a blue cotton shirt. "Aren't you going to church?"

Jenny shook her head. "I asked the Shermans to take you and they'll be here soon." Over the brim of her juice glass she watched him eat, words of caution hovering on her lips. She waited until she heard the honk of the Sherman's station wagon before saying, "I want you to stick close to Mike and not wander off by yourself."

Something in her tone must have alerted Jamie, because he froze with his hand on the storm door and looked at her over his shoulder, his eyes suddenly aging from young to old. Solemnly, he said, "Don't worry, Mom. I'll be careful."

Jenny sighed as she followed him outside. Leaning over the porch railing, she watched Jamie climb into the back of the car and waved at the Shermans, forcing a smile on her face. "Thanks. I appreciate it," she called out.

Dottie, a slender brunette with hazel eyes and a warm smile, stuck her arm out of her open window and waved back. "Any time."

Jenny watched the car drive down the road, then looked at the bright blue sky. It was barely ten, but the sun was warm on her skin and she was reluctant to return to the coolness of the house. Today promised to be one of those beautiful fall days the Island was famous for and this might be the last one until next spring. Would she still be here? she wondered. Would she see the daffodils and tulips she had planted with such hope bloom?

She sat down on the porch steps, leaned against the corner post and closing her eyes, raised her face into the sun.

When she heard his car drive up, she didn't stir, though tension immediately flowed through her. She purposely kept her eyes closed, afraid of what she would see in his face, listening instead to the opening and closing of the car door, listening to his smooth long steps on the walkway.

At the bottom of the steps, Mark stopped and watched the light shimmer in her hair and the sun warm her face. Faint mauve shadows were visible beneath the thick fan of her lashes. She had probably spent the night pacing, wearing a hole into her carpet, he thought. "I'm one problem that won't go away. So you may as well open your eyes," he said quietly, hooking his thumbs into the pockets of his black jeans.

Jenny finally looked up at him. He stood with his back to the sun, his face in the shadows, his thick hair tousled as if he'd run his hands through it recently. His casual light gray shirt was open at the neck and the sleeves were rolled up, revealing strong forearms. God, he looked good, she thought, her heart quickening at the lean powerful sight of him. She wanted to run her hands over his hair-roughened skin and move into his arms. "I wish you would go away," she said, her voice grave and her eyes serious. "I've made a lot of mistakes in the past, mistakes Jamie is still paying for. Letting you into my life would be another big one."

"That's just what a man wants to hear first thing in the morning," he said with a hint of humor in his voice. Sitting down on the step below hers, he leaned back on his elbows, stretching his long legs out in front of him. Her face was only inches away from his, her chin resting on her drawn up knees. He watched a small grin form small dimples at the corners of her mouth. In another ten years lines would deepen the dimples and, surprised at himself, he realized that he wanted very much to be around to see them. He forced his mind back to the present. "If you want to talk about mistakes, I made some last night, too."

Jenny shook her head, wishing he wasn't always so generous. She had no defense against that. "What you said was true. I know I can't keep running and I shouldn't uproot Jamie again. But it only makes me more cautious not to complicate my life."

Mark controlled the swift surge of impatience and looked around the garden. "Where is Jamie?"

"At Sunday school." At the distraction, Jenny slanted him an annoyed look. Her glance settled on the long powerful lines of his body, the flat stomach and the narrow jeans riding low on his hips. Her heart contracted, and her pulse began to throb with need. Firmly she turned her attention elsewhere, to the tip of her white sneakers. "And Mush is in the backyard," she added, so he wouldn't interrupt her again. She took a small breath and went on, determined to make him listen. "I know I encouraged you yesterday. I guess I was trying to pretend that I was just like other women. But I'm not. No one in my position should ask anyone into their life. And you're not just anyone. You—"

"That's nice to know," Mark murmured, giving her a hot look from beneath lowered lashes.

Jenny felt the impact and swiftly raised her eyes to the maple tree a few feet away. "This isn't a joke," she said fiercely. They were fugitive and cop, and there was nothing funny about the situation. Whatever he stirred in her, it could never mean anything. "I can't keep warning you off, Mark," she added with a touch of weariness.

Impatience glinted in his eyes, but his voice was still mild. "Who asked you to? I'm thirty-seven years old, old enough to make my own decisions."

"But you know nothing about me. I could be lying to you."

"Are you?" he asked her quietly, watching a fly settle on her hair.

Jenny thought of the fake IDs in her billfold and the secrets she was keeping from him and said evasively, "I told you the truth last night."

But not the whole truth.

Mark noted the evasion, wondering how long it would take her to trust him enough to reveal her real name. Patience. Raising his hand, he waved the insect off, running his fingers gently through her waves, marveling at the soft, silky thickness. Raising one thick strand, he watched it curl around his finger. "Did you always wear your hair short like this?"

"It used to go almost down to my waist." Exasperated, Jenny looked at him, trying to ignore the small shivers generated by his touch as he brushed the strand behind her ear. It had been her one claim to beauty, her ex-husband had always said. Her voice was expressionless when she added, "People always commented on it. So I cut if off."

Another puzzle piece fell into place. Possibly two. From her flat comment it was obvious that the bastard liked long blond hair. Jenny had been the girl Hank had described last night. "I like it this way," he said simply. "It won't get in the way when I make love to you." Feeling her stiffen, he dropped his hand with a crooked smile.

Jenny gave him a level look and gathered her courage. "You don't know me well enough to jump into a personal relationship."

He might have met her only a short while ago, but he knew more about her now than he'd known about Carolyn when he'd married her, he suddenly realized. "I know enough," he said firmly, calmly. "Two nights ago I met a woman who thought nothing of braving a storm. A real toughie—so tough in fact that she sicced a dog on me. But that toughie took one look at a battered, unshaven cop who should have scared the hell out of her and invited him in for a cup of coffee.

"And yesterday I saw a woman who laced into DiNigro, trying to shield a son from his father's anger. You've pushed me away repeatedly, because you're afraid that *I* would suffer if you asked me for help. You're neat to the point of obsession. If you could, you would save the world. I'm sure the World Wildlife Fund loves you dearly." Mark saw her eyes open wide and he almost grinned. And since that guess had paid off, he tried another one. "And you think that you have nothing to offer a man."

Agitated, Jenny ran her hand through her hair. "What I am, is frigid," she said in a low voice.

"Rot," Mark said succinctly, and clamping his hands around her waist, he lifted her as if she were a feather, settling her down on his thighs. "If you'd let me, I would've stayed last night."

Jenny braced herself on his shoulders, trying to squirm off his lap. But his hands were holding her in place and she didn't want to hurt him. "Out of pity, maybe, or out of your stupid sense of duty. You're always trying to remove threats," she said, tossing his phrase back at him.

Mark shot her a disbelieving look. "Is that why you think I kissed you?" As incredible as it seemed she believed exactly that. "Jenny," he said with aching tenderness. "You're a fool. I don't go around kissing women out of a sense of duty."

His eyes intently focused on her, he traced the shape of her mouth with the tip of his finger, until her lips began to tremble beneath his touch. They began to open as if to speak, but no words escaped her. With tantalizing softness, he moved on, skimming across her cheekbones, tracing the dainty shell of her ear.

Jenny's skin began to tingle and a lump formed in her throat. For a moment she was quite self-conscious about sitting on his lap right there on the porch steps and she shifted, trying to get to her feet.

"Relax," Mark said softly, "No one can see us. When the neighbors bring back Jamie, you'll hear the car before it turns into the driveway."

Jenny doubted she'd hear the roof fall in over the drumming in her ears. But she didn't want him to stop. There was such tenderness, such gentleness in his touch that she couldn't turn away from him. And it never changed, remaining achingly tender, tantalizingly soft as it slowly trailed down her neck. She could see her eyes darken with desire and need, and she realized suddenly that for the first time he was letting her see how he felt, leaving himself wide open for her rejection.

With the same slow care he drew her mouth to his and followed the path already sensitized by his touch. Lightly, his lips skimmed over her face, setting her skin on fire like the kiss of the sun. He used neither pressure nor demand. There was only his patient, gentle caress. Still barely touching her, he returned to her mouth and deepened the kiss. Shifting his hold, he slowly circled her waist and lightly moved his big, strong hands up her rib cage and down again, feeling the small tremors of her response.

He deepened the kiss ever so slightly, a lure for her to increase the pressure, waiting for her desire to flicker to life. Her lips parted, her tongue meeting his. Her shy response excited him, and heat began to spread to his loins. But he needed more. He wanted her to touch him, to need him. Gently his hands moved across her breasts, lightly cupping them, feeling the nipples harden, pushing against the soft fabric of her blouse. She moaned into his mouth, a soft, yearning sound, and her hands raised to his face, cupping it, drawing him closer.

Jenny felt him withdraw slightly, but she wasn't ready yet to stop. She wanted the beautiful feeling of being desired to last a little longer. It seemed as if she had waited a lifetime to feel like this. Her hands went to his shoulders, holding on to him, pressing against the hard length of his body, desperate to touch him as he touched her.

Slowly, her hands slid down the strong column of his neck, feeling the warmth of his skin, the strong corded muscles flexing and contracting beneath her fingertips. The beat of his pulse was becoming more rapid beneath her touch, telling her that he desired her, too. His response was all the encouragement she needed. Her hand slipped beneath the open collar of his shirt, stroking the firm flesh beneath it, lightly rubbing her palms over his hair-roughened skin.

Mark almost lost control then. He pulled her against his chest and pressed her head into his shoulder, absorbing her shudders, taking deep slow breaths, liking the sensation of her body sprawled on top of his. So much for his intention to keep their relationship light and friendly, he thought with a wry grimace. She went to his head. Gently, he stroked her hair. "Are you all right?"

Nodding, Jenny raised her head and sat down on the step next to him. "I should be asking that question," she said, her voice low and slightly embarrassed, though she felt like grinning. "How are your ribs?"

"What ribs?" Mark teased, raking his hair back. Then his face sobered and he asked quietly, "What's wrong?"

Jenny hugged her knees tightly, lowering her chin on them. "I just realized how much I've been missing. It's been so long since I've even thought of doing things like necking on front stoops."

"This went a little further than necking," Mark pointed out dryly.

Jenny bit her lip. "I know. And I don't know how to deal with it lightly."

Mark started to say that he wasn't exactly dealing lightly with it, either. He hadn't felt so much need and desire in years. He looked at her, serious. Whatever steps he'd taken in life had been his choices, his decisions and his mistakes. No one had forced, threatened or beaten him into them. He'd always had complete control over his life.

Jenny hadn't had those choices. Since the day her parents had died, control seemed to have been taken out of her hands. And she was only now beginning to realize how much she'd missed, how much had been taken from her.

Slowly, he stood up and pulled her to her feet. His voice was a little rough when he said, "The only thing you have to deal with at the moment is a mailbox. What type of box do you want? What kind of post? Do you want to put it in the same place? If you plan on a concrete foundation, you may have to choose a different spot or clear out some of the yews."

Bemused, Jenny shook her head. "I don't know. I haven't the faintest idea." But she knew a con job when she heard it. She was being railroaded into something, though she had no idea what it was.

Placing an arm around her waist he drew her with him down the driveway and pointed at the low-hanging branch of an oak tree. "That should come off, or I soon won't have any paint left on the roof of my car."

Jenny tilted her head back and looked at him. She suddenly realized that he was giving her a choice, letting her decide whether she wanted to see him after today. No more pushing and prodding, his steady gaze told her. We'll try it on your terms.

Jenny knew she was strong in many ways. Over the last few years, she had lived on the edge continuously, and often the going had been rough. But at the moment she didn't have the strength to pretend that she didn't want him in her life. "I don't have big clippers," she said gravely, "but we can get some when we go to the hardware store." She licked her suddenly dry lips and added in a rush, "And a concrete footing sounds good."

With a squeeze to her waist, Mark released her and walked to his Blazer. "I brought clippers just in case and a pole digger, too." Before she could change her mind, he clipped the branch. Watching it fall, he prayed that he was doing the right thing in luring her out of hiding and making her face life.

"I like the white garage," Jamie said an hour later in the hardware store, pointing at a white plastic mailbox with black shutters and a steep black roof.

"It matches the house," Jenny agreed, but her gaze was drawn to the brick-red barn standing next to it. "This one would, too." Opening the flap she took a peek inside, imagining what it would look like filled with Christmas cards from relatives and friends. Brick-red barns evoked visions of rolling green hills, golden fields ripe with corn and old farmhouses in the distance. Safety, peace, permanence. The things she wanted most out of life. Things the man watching them from a few feet away was trying to make her believe in.

She looked over her shoulder at Mark, leaning against the shelves behind her. "I'm sorry. This can't be very exciting for you."

Mark shook his head and smiled faintly at her. "Take your time," he said gently. He enjoyed watching Jenny and her son make the selections and discuss their choices. Especially now. There was a lightness about her that he hadn't seen before. Not once since they'd left the house had she mangled the strap of her purse or run nervous fingers through her hair.

"Which one do you like better, Mark?" Jamie asked, coming to his side. Taking his hand, he drew him to the display. "The white one isn't as big. But we only get newspapers and bills, so it doesn't matter."

Mark's gaze connected with Jenny's over the head of her son. Jamie might not see the significant difference between the two boxes, but Mark did. Jenny's expressive face showed hope and longing every time she glanced at the barn. But Mark also saw uncertainty and fear, as if she didn't dare believe in a bright future yet. Putting up the barn would be like waving a red cape in front of a bull. An act of defiance, rebellion and courage. If the bastard had been behind the theft of the old one, he would see the significance of the new one, too. Mark wanted her to have that badge of courage, though, wanted her to choose the barn. And more than that, he wanted her to trust him to keep them safe.

But he was also afraid of what it would do to her, if it, too, disappeared. Her hope and trust were too new, too fragile, and he didn't want to see them crushed. "Why don't we let your mother decide," he suggested firmly.

Jenny glanced at Jamie's hand, clasped firmly in Mark's big one and tears pricked her eyes. She wanted so badly to believe in the promise of a future that small gesture implied. Blinking, she turned back to the display. She trusted Mark enough to know that he would *try* to help them, *try* to protect them.

But seeing them standing there so close together, Jenny couldn't help but remember that he had chosen his job over his son, that he was so committed to it that he had settled for visitation rights only. Swiftly, she reached for the white garage. "This will look great," she said with forced brightness.

"I told you so," Jamie said, a pleased grin on his face.

Jenny didn't look at Mark, but she could sense his disappointment. "Now all we have to do is find a post and the cement," she said quickly, eager to have it all done with. "How about Chinese food afterward?"

It took them the better part of the afternoon to put up the box. Despite Mark's protests, Jenny dug the hole, using the pole digger, sinking it deeper and deeper into the sandy soil. They had chosen a new sight—right next to the driveway—

and soon the pile of dirt on the blacktop pavement grew. She wanted to anchor the post in so far that it couldn't be stolen again.

Occasionally Jenny stopped to observe Mark and Jamie assembling the mailbox a few feet away. Mush was sleeping in the sun. It was such a normal family scene, Jenny thought, watching Jamie put the red flag on the box with Mark's help. A can of beer stood next to a can of soda. Plastic bags and cartons littered the lawn and a slight breeze rustled in the treetops. Next door, the Shermans ran their mower, shredding and bagging leaves. Whenever they deposited yet another bag at the curb for tomorrow's garbage pickup, they waved. Of course, if things had been completely normal, Jenny would have invited them over for a drink after the chores were done, the way her parents, years ago, had invited their neighbors, Sheila and Randy. She sighed. Maybe next spring, she thought, sinking the digger back into the hole.

Mark watched her for a moment, then turned his attention back to Jamie. "Nice and easy," he said, guiding the boy's eager hand. "The screw has to go in straight. And don't tighten it until you've put in the others." He'd forgotten what it was like to spend a lazy Sunday afternoon doing little chores, teaching a young boy how to use a screwdriver and answering the dozens of questions leaping from his eager mind.

Jamie's nose was wrinkled in concentration as he gave the screw one last turn. "How's that?" he asked.

Mark tested Jamie's work for slack, raising the flag and lowering it again. "Looks good to me," he said, ruffling Jamie's hair. Stretching with lazy contentment, he looked at Jenny again.

Her face was flushed, her eyes bright and there was a streak of dirt on her nose. He imagined her face heated with passion as he made love to her, and fantasized about what it would feel like to have her hands slide over him. He could almost taste the flavor of her skin. He would peel the clothes off her while she was watching him, her big brown eyes filled with longing, trust and need. Just thinking about it made his pulse race.

Restlessly, he got to his feet. "Ready to let me do the rest?"

Jenny dropped a load of sand on the growing pile and sent him a teasing grin. "I hate to bruise that macho ego of yours, but I'm done." She saw his eyes narrow, and felt a tingle run down her back.

"Jenny," Mark warned blandly, cupping her chin. "Don't think you're safe because Jamie's watching."

"You wouldn't dare!" Her eyes challenged him and she tried to turn her head away, but his hold merely tightened. With a mixture of alarm and excitement she watched him lower his head.

"That was a mistake," he muttered, his breath fanning her skin. Gently, his thumb stroked over her lips. "Macho guys don't back down from dares."

"I take it back. You're a wimp." Twisting free, she leaped across the pile of dirt, raced up the driveway and past his car. Behind her she could hear his sneakers pounding on the blacktop, coming closer. Excitement welled up and laughter, too. Mush started to bark. Eager to join the fun, he raced toward her, almost tripping her.

Mark caught her by the shoulder before she lost her balance, spinning her around. Falling against him, Jenny braced herself against his shoulders, laughter bubbling in her throat. Just as Mark's head came down to kiss her, Mush leaped up, licking her face. And then Jamie cried from behind them, "I knew you'd catch her." The mixture of frustration, humor and disbelief crossing Mark's face was priceless. Jenny tilted her head back and chuckled out loud, laughter rippling from her throat in helpless abandon.

Hearing it, a sharp urgent need shook Mark. He had to have her. He was desperate for the hope and promise of her.

Instinctively he knew that he would be cold and empty for the rest of his life without her.

It was at that precise moment that he lost his hold on sanity and tumbled head over heels in love with her.

If Jamie hadn't been standing but a few feet away, he would have carried her into the house and made passionate love to her. With an enormous effort, he banked the desire racing through him. Still, for a fleeting few seconds, he pulled her hips tightly against him.

Jenny felt the pressure of his hardness and, startled, her eyes focused on him. Awareness ripped through her and her smile changed, becoming sharper, edged with need. Then Mark dropped his hands and she stepped back, belatedly wiping Mush's exuberance from her face with her sleeve. "I can't remember the last time I laughed so hard."

Jamie gave her a puzzled look. "What was so funny?"

Jenny sent Mark a mischievous grin. The dangerous glint in his eyes made her retreat hastily to the pole digger, but she tossed over her shoulder, "Why don't you ask Mark!"

"Mush licked your mother's face," Mark said as he followed with Jamie at a slower pace. Desire shot through him at the thought of having her naked beneath him, of tasting every part of her soft, white skin.

"I still don't see the joke. She doesn't like it when Mush licks."

Mark saw Jenny's lips twitch in amusement, she was obviously enjoying his predicament. He glowered back at her. "Your mother must have thought it was funny. Why don't you collect the tools. We're ready to put the mailbox in."

At his words Jenny felt apprehension ripple down her spine and her smile vanished abruptly. Playing time was over in more ways than one, she suddenly realized. How long would it be before he began demanding answers?

With a sigh she carried the pole digger to his car. She guessed she would have to take the chance and tell him the whole truth. She cared too much for him to deceive him much longer.

It didn't take long to pour the sacks of premixed concrete into the hole and place the pole with the attached mailbox into it. Gathering all the cartons and tools together, Jamie said, "Mom, there's a bracket in here to put a name on the mailbox. What d'you want me to do with it?"

Her arms filled with empty bags, Jenny's eyes locked with Mark's. The air between them suddenly crackled with a silent question.

*When are you going to tell me?*

"Mom? Did you hear me?"

Jenny licked her suddenly dry lips. "Yes, I heard you," she said, but it was Mark she was talking to.

The phone rang faintly in the distance. Jenny tossed the empty bags aside and ran toward the house, grateful for the reprieve. She didn't want him to disappear from her life, but if she wanted him to stay, she would need to tell him the truth. Her conscience demanded that. Tonight, after supper, when Jamie took his bath.

"I'll be back in a minute," she tossed over her shoulder as she leaped up the steps. Running into the kitchen, she grabbed the phone. "Hello?" she asked, breathing hard.

Silence answered her.

Jenny felt a chill feather down her heated skin. She caught her breath, expelled it slowly, then asked again, "Hello? Is anyone there? Answer me."

The silence deepened, shifted, becoming more menacing. Jenny's hand flew to her throat. *It's just a wrong number,* she told herself sternly. *Hang up.*

But her arm wouldn't obey her. She stood there, frozen, unable to speak, unable to move. How long the silence lasted she didn't know. But as the seconds ticked by the certainty grew.

*Burke had found them.*

# Chapter 9

"Mom, Mike's here. Can I go over to his house to play?"

The sound of Jamie's voice reached Jenny through the buzzing in her ears, galvanizing her into action as nothing else could have done. She slammed down the receiver. Dimly she could hear the boys' high voices mingling with Mark's deeper one and Mush barking for attention. Everything was normal, she told herself. It was just another wrong number. Slowly, she expelled the breath she'd been holding and walked to the foyer, trying to steady her shaky knees.

"—I put the flag on the mailbox all by myself," Jamie was telling his friend as she approached. He looked up at the giant next to him, who was scratching the dog between the ears. "Didn't I, Mark?"

"You sure did," Mark said lightly, but his eyes were on Jenny, searching for an answer to the subtle shift in her mood.

"That's kid stuff," said Mike. "I helped my dad repair the mower this morning." Mike, a slender, dark-haired boy with horn-rim glasses and a cowlick, was a year older than Jamie and topped him by at least an inch.

"It's not! We poured concrete into the hole, too."

Jenny decided to interrupt before they escalated into an argument. "Everything cleaned up outside?" she asked Jamie.

"Yeah. I put the brackets with the tools."

"Thanks." Jenny felt Mark's eyes on her, but she avoided looking at him. She carefully picked a twig out of Mike's dark hair. "Did you finish bagging the leaves?"

Mike nodded. "Only in the front, though. Dad said it's getting too late to start on the back. Mom wants to know if it's all right for Jamie to eat over at our house. We're making hamburgers and hot dogs on the barbecue."

Jenny looked at Jamie's eager face. If Burke had made that call, he could be anywhere, in a store two miles away, in Denver, or in Dark Water. He could even be in Europe, playing a game of cat and mouse with her. She didn't want to let Jamie out of her sight. Yet the cruel game, she knew from bitter experience, could go on for weeks or months.

"That's fine," she agreed, determined to keep things normal until she knew for certain that it was Burke. For now, Jamie should be safe at the Shermans'. Besides, she needed to talk to Mark alone, without Jamie around, although the decision she had to make, made her stomach churn. If she encouraged him to stay around, she would have to tell him the truth. Her conscience demanded that of her. Checking her watch, she was surprised to see it was already past four. "I'll pick you up at seven."

"So early?"

"Tomorrow's school. And I still have to check your homework," Jenny said firmly.

"Oh, all right. Come on, Mike." He didn't say goodbye to Mark.

He assumes Mark will still be here when he comes back, Jenny thought, following the two boys out on the porch. She wished she could be as certain as her son. Intensely aware of Mark standing in the doorway behind her, she watched the boys cut through the bushes separating the two properties, waiting for their voices to fade. What was she going to do? she wondered. Leaning against the railing, she kept her back to Mark, hoping that he hadn't noticed her agitation.

Her glance swept over the green grass, past the bushes and trees to the mailbox, barely visible from the house. Had Burke driven by here this afternoon? Had he watched them laugh and play? she wondered. Sudden anger rushed through her at the thought. Her hands curled around the railing and her mouth compressed into a determined line. She refused to allow him to spoil this one perfect day for her.

*And there could be other perfect ones.*

"It's so peaceful here. So quiet. It's hard to believe that New York is only an hour's ride away. Do you ever miss the city?"

Mark gave her a narrow look, wondering if it was the phone call that had shaken her, or if the name bracket was the cause of her agitation. Until the moment she'd teased and taunted him, he'd been content to go along with the pretense that everything was normal, that they were just a man and a woman who enjoyed each other's company.

But pretense wasn't enough anymore. What he felt for her was too real, too strong.

With a small sigh he stepped out onto the porch and joined her at the railing. Like Jenny, he wanted to prolong the inevitable confrontation for a few minutes more. "When we first moved out here, the silence grated on my nerves," he answered. But it had been the silence *inside* their house that had really gotten to him. Until they had moved out here, he hadn't realized how little he and Carolyn had in common. "Then Tim came along. Kids have a lot more freedom out here."

Drawn by the wistful sound in his voice, Jenny looked closely at him. "Why did you settle for visiting rights only?" she asked, her eyes searching his hard profile.

Mark shrugged. "I felt it was best for Tim. When Carolyn and I first separated, she moved back into her parents' home, and Tim was enrolled in the Patchogue school district. Carolyn's mother took care of him when he came home. He was better off with them than with a baby-sitter at my house. Besides, he was already hurting. I didn't want him drawn into a custody battle. And I assumed that Carolyn would stay here on the Island and that I would still be able to take him to soccer practice and basketball games. I never thought she'd move to California. I would have fought her otherwise."

She had done him an injustice, Jenny thought with a quick flash of remorse. "Is Carolyn going to spend Christmas with her parents? Maybe she's planning to move back."

Mark shook his head. "She's met someone else. They're going away together over the holidays."

His voice was carefully flat. Jenny wondered if he still cared about his ex-wife, or if he just didn't like the thought of another man raising his son. "Have you ever thought of going back to court?"

Mark dragged a hand through his hair. "It's too late. Carolyn doesn't want to come back to Long Island. Besides, Tim's happy out there, and he likes the guy she's dating. It wouldn't be fair to disrupt his life again. He's never forgiven me for abandoning him."

Jenny shook her head fiercely. "But you didn't abandon him! If you made any mistake at all, it was in believing that your ex-wife would place Tim's happiness above her own bitterness. She sounds like a very selfish—" Appalled at her words, she bit her lip. "I'm sorry. I shouldn't have said that."

Mark's eyes gleamed at her heated defense of him. "No. I liked it." It was an odd sensation, this feeling of wanting

Jenny's support. He had rarely bothered to explain himself to anyone, about anything, during the last few years. He'd certainly never felt a desire to explain his actions to a woman. But Jenny was different. He had never known anyone like her. She was fiercely loyal and very protective of those she cared for. Unfortunately this fierce protective streak of hers was also keeping her from confiding in him.

Their eyes locked and once again tension crackled between them. Jenny was the first to lower her eyes. "How much longer will it take for the concrete to set?" she asked with sudden urgency, glancing at the mailbox.

Mark grimaced. "Twenty-four hours." Frowning, he studied her profile, wondering if the phone call was the reason for her agitation. "What's the matter?" he asked quietly.

"Nothing," Jenny said evasively, looking down at his large, long-fingered hands, still coated with dust from handling the bags of concrete. "You'll want to wash. Let's go inside."

Mark followed her into the kitchen, turning on the faucet to wash his hands. He wondered if she'd ever trust him enough to confide in him. Frustration curled in his stomach, but he managed to keep his voice calm. "If whatever is bothering you isn't important, then you won't mind telling me about it."

"Oh, for heaven's sake! Don't you ever give up?" Jenny snapped. Mark's mouth compressed angrily as he rinsed off the soap. With a sigh, Jenny relented. "I'm sorry. I didn't mean to snap at you. It was nothing, really. Just a wrong number." The caller could have been one of Jamie's school friends. Kids were shy when they called a friend but got a parent on the phone instead, and often didn't identify themselves. It had happened before, and more than once a day.

But for years she had trusted her instincts, lived by them, survived by them. And now her instincts were warning her that Burke *had* found them.

Frowning, Mark dried off his hands on a paper towel. Jenny had mentioned the call Lizzie had told her about yesterday, but two wrong numbers in two days, and a stolen mailbox were hardly anything to get steamed up about. But Jenny was more than angry. She was scared. "Tell me why you're so upset."

Jenny snatched a can of soda and a beer from the refrigerator, hesitating. She knew Mark doubted that Burke was behind the incidents and she could hardly blame him. A cop had to work from hard facts, not shadows. "When Burke was away on business, he used to check up on me," she explained in a low voice. Placing the two cans in the center of the table, she sat down. "He'd call two or three times in the middle of the night. He never threatened. He never identified himself. He didn't even talk. But I knew it was him."

Slowly, carefully, Mark dried his hands on a paper towel, trying to keep his emotions separate. But the image of Jenny sitting in the darkness listening to threatening silence with no one to turn to made him furious. This ghost was becoming a real menace! He tossed the paper towel into the trash can and joined her at the round table, choosing the chair opposite hers. Pushing the cans aside, he took her cold hands between his warm ones, chafing them. "There are ways to find out if it is him, but I'll need your help."

"To tap my phone?" Her lips twisted bitterly. "He's too smart to be caught that easily. He'd never stay on the line long enough to trace the call."

Mark's eyes hardened, anger flickering in their depths. "Catching him is beginning to seem like the easy part. Contrary to popular myths, it only takes a few seconds these days to trace a call. The tough part is getting you to trust me. I want to help you, but I need your cooperation."

"It wouldn't do any good! He's not threatening me with anything tangible," she said roughly. "I'll dissolve the damn trust. He can have the damn money."

"And then what?" Mark asked her calmly. "Do you honestly believe that he would be content then?"

"Why not? It's all he ever wanted! He never cared for Jamie, or for me." Abruptly, Jenny withdrew her hands and pressed them to her burning eyes. "I wish it were true. Actually, in his twisted way, he does care for Jamie." She felt the old ugly demon of worthlessness creep up in her again. "Sometimes I remember the good times. There were good times. In the very beginning. That's what makes this all the more frightening."

But she'd never felt the contentment and warmth she'd shared with Mark today. Burke had rarely taken time off to play with Jamie. And she'd never felt completely at ease with him. She realized that now. There had always been the constant feeling of being judged, of coming up short of his expectations. There had always been subtle, emotional threats.

"I keep telling myself that I should have recognized his potential for violence. But then I wonder if it was me who drove him to it. After Jamie, I had two miscarriages. Now I thank God for them. But at the time it made me feel—useless. We were both only children, and we had planned to have a big family. I think he began to hate me because I made him feel like a failure. I know I failed him, both as a wife and as a partner."

The way she would fail Mark if she didn't send him away. No, she added soberly. She would more than fail him. She would ruin him.

Mark almost lost his cool then. He clamped down on the white-hot rage surging through him, but his voice was harsh when he said, "Stop blaming yourself. You had just lost your parents. It takes time to recover from a shock like that. You didn't fail him. Damn it, he's a calculating bastard who saw a chance to get rich quick, and jumped at it. He intimidated and manipulated you from the beginning, and when that failed, he resorted to violence."

She looked into his hard face. He wasn't telling her anything that she hadn't told herself a hundred times before. Wearily, she said, "Maybe so. But when it comes right down to it, it was *my* mistake, *my* failure. I should have recognized him for the man he was."

"At twenty?"

"And how old were you when you got your badge?" Jenny asked pointedly. Placing her hands on the table, she pushed back her chair, got up, and paced to the sink and back again. "He's out there," she said, "playing a cat-and-mouse game with me. I know you have doubts, but—"

"Even if I didn't, what could I do?" Mark interrupted angrily, surging to his feet. He rounded the table and stepped into her path. The need to shake her was so strong he jammed his hands into his pockets. "Just once, forget that I'm a cop."

"I can't," Jenny said, her voice distant and sad at the same time. She felt cold. Unconsciously, she rubbed her hands over her arms, trying to warm herself.

Mark swore softly, wondering if she would ever get past the hurdle of his job, or if, like his ex-wife, she would always resent it. "I once made the mistake of falling for a woman who couldn't deal with my job," he said, his face as grim as his voice. "I want you Jenny, enough to risk getting hurt again, but you've got to meet me halfway."

Jenny looked at him, torn between her need for him, and her fear of the demons of her past. "I want you, too."

Mark's mouth twisted bitterly. "You want the man, maybe. But that's only a part of me. You don't want me enough to look beyond the badge. Hell, you don't even trust me enough to tell me your real name. I'd like to know who I'm planning to make love to."

Jenny turned away from him, looking out the patio door, watching a blue jay settle on the red bird feeder. "I never really believed I could be safe before. I want to stop running. I'm not just talking about staying in this house, but about trusting another person again.... I care for you more than I care for anyone save Jamie. But it isn't enough."

Turning back to him, she raised her hands to his face and studied his strong features. She wanted desperately to believe that she was woman enough to make him happy. She needed to believe that he cared enough for her and Jamie to put his job on the line for them. "For myself, I'd be willing to take that risk." She dropped her hands and stepped back. "But I can't afford to trust blindly, not with my son's life."

She took a deep breath. Her need for this man was so great, she was going to take a gamble. "I'll make you a deal," she said hoarsely, not looking at him. "I'll tell you what you want to know if you'll help me defend myself. Help me buy a gun and teach me how to use it."

Stunned, Mark stared at her profile. Whatever he had expected, it wasn't this. He couldn't imagine her with a gun in her hand, no matter how desperate she was. He gave her a quick shake. "Jenny, I'm not sure what you have in mind, but taking the law into your own hands won't solve anything."

She stared at him with bitter eyes. "Just what are people supposed to do when that very same law is failing to protect them?"

Mark struggled against anger. "You're asking for a hell of a lot more than trust. You're asking me to put my job on the line."

*That's exactly what I would be asking of you if I told you the truth, if I allowed you into my life.* Silently, Jenny stared at him, holding her breath, waiting for his decision.

Mark stared at her with hard eyes. And suddenly the missing pieces of the puzzle fell into place. The truth hit him with stunning force. She wasn't talking about the gun itself. Like his badge, the gun was only a symbol of his job. Now he realized why she was so damn secretive about names, why she kept pushing him away. And why she wanted a commitment before she placed her trust in him.

*Jenny had kidnapped her son.*

*Jenny was a fugitive from the law.*

Emotions raged inside him: bitterness, pain and a sense of betrayal. Damn it, she had lied to him. Well, maybe not lied; but she had set him up. Grimly he said, "This cop may be burning out, but he has too much respect for the system to abuse it. If you want the bastard dead, hire a hit man." With grim satisfaction he saw her flinch, and her eyes widen with shock. Her skin turned very white and for a moment her mouth moved soundlessly.

How much had he guessed? she wondered, staring into his hard, angry eyes. She drew a deep shuddering breath. Releasing it, she said very quietly, "If I'd wanted him dead, I'd have hired a . . . professional long ago, someone without integrity or scruples. I would never use you." But she had, she suddenly realized. She had tried to do just that. Maybe she hadn't set out consciously to use him, and never to kill Burke. But she had encouraged him to spend time with her by not trying harder to get rid of him. Knowing how he felt about his job, knowing that she would hurt him, would fail him, she had still put her own needs above his.

"What I wanted you to do was kill the demons inside me," she said, her voice quiet and defeated. "Only, no one can do it for me. I realize that now." No one could give her back her self-respect but herself. She might be on the run from the law and hiding from Burke, but mostly she was running from herself, from the shame and the guilt and the helplessness. And until she was strong enough to come to terms with her past, she would never have the normal, happy life she wanted and she would never be Jenny McKenzie again.

Very quietly she said, "Please leave. Forget that you ever saw Jamie and me."

Mark tried. He drove to Mulligan's, a favorite hangout of his where cops wound down after a shift before returning to their homes, or, more often than not, stayed for hours, because they had nowhere else to go. No woman, he told himself grimly, was worth risking his badge for, was worth losing his integrity, his honor. And if DiNigro ever got wind of this, he *would* lose his badge. Nothing came between him and The Job; and he wasn't the only one who felt that way.

Most of the boys at Mulligan's did, too.

Walking into the dimly lit restaurant, he stopped, letting his eyes adjust to the darkness. The place reeked of stale beer and smoke. The ceiling fan swirled the blue smoke into the air, burning his eyes. He'd kicked the habit eight years ago, but for a moment, he wanted a cigarette so badly he was tempted to put money into the machine and get himself a pack. Country music blared from the jukebox; George Strait was singing about how hard second chances were to come by.

He shut out the sounds and smells and looked around.

"Hey, Lawton. Over here." Jay, his partner, had spotted him, and was waving from the bar. Slowly, Mark picked his way past crowded tables, stopping for a few words with friends on the way. Roper, from vice, slipped from the stool next to Jay's, muttering something about getting home before his wife sent out a search party. He was one of the lucky ones, Mark thought. Taking the vacated seat, he ordered a Scotch.

Jay's reddish brows drew together over sharp blue eyes. The last time he'd seen Mark touch the hard stuff had been the night his wife moved out. "For a man who's been on vacation for ten days, you look like hell," he teased. "I called you earlier. Where were you?"

"Some vacation!" Mark reached for his drink, which the bartender had quietly placed in front of him, wondering what Jay would say if he told him that he'd been out shopping with a fugitive. Jay was three years younger and four inches shorter, with the lean build of a runner, a thatch of red hair and cool blue eyes. They had been partners for five years and there was little they didn't know about each other. Mark even knew that Jay still kept Marcy's picture in the drawer of his nightstand three years after his divorce. Jay had a sentimental streak. But even he would draw the line at risking his badge.

Frowning, Jay tossed back his beer. "If you're still worried about Houligan, they released the kid today. I dropped by the hospital on the way over here."

Mark smiled faintly. "Thanks. I talked to the nurse early this morning." He took a second swallow of his whiskey, welcoming its bite. Knowing that Pete Houligan was going to be all right had eased his conscience, but that had only been a part of his problems. He'd made an error in judgment that night. And he'd made an even bigger one becoming involved with Jenny. Grimly he stared into the glass. Maybe he was losing it, he thought. She had given him enough clues, she had even warned him repeatedly that he didn't know what he was getting into. But like a fool he had ignored her words.

He tossed back the rest of his drink, wanting to erase her from his mind. Trying desperately to pretend that he wasn't involved already, and all the way up to his neck, with a woman who probably had a warrant out for her arrest. Trying and failing miserably. He still wanted that bastard ex-husband of hers dead.

And he still wanted Jenny.

Scowling, he pushed the glass across the counter and ordered another.

Jay studied Mark's grim profile. "If you really plan on getting drunk, let's go to my place, or yours. I won't remind you that you're on duty tomorrow. I'll even make your excuses to the captain. He'll understand. He's been worried about you, too. You've been bottling things up since Tim left, and it's about time you let loose. But I would prefer not to have to lug your two-hundred-pound carcass in and out of cars."

"Two hundred and five," Mark muttered with a hint of humor in his voice. "I never realized it before, but midgets seem to have one thing in common. They're always trying to scale people down to their size."

Jay released a small sigh of relief. At six feet, he wasn't a midget by anyone's standard, but the joke showed Mark wasn't terminal. "Want to talk about midgets?"

"No." Mark took another deep swallow from the refill he'd just gotten, then set the glass down with a thud. Jay was right. Getting drunk never solved anything. At best, it was a temporary escape. And he hated hangovers. Besides, when he woke up he'd still see her big brown eyes and her lopsided smile. He'd still hear the clear sound of her laughter as he'd heard it this afternoon. And he'd still have to deal with the fact that he had fallen in love with a fugitive.

And he'd still have to decide what he was going to do about it.

But first he needed some distance, so he could look at the situation objectively. Damn it, he had only known her two days! How long could it take to get control of this hunger that was still churning inside him every time he thought of her? With a hard set to his jaw he turned to Jay. "Fill me in on some of our cases."

Jay gave him a disgusted look, but said obligingly, "They caught Brandon in Florida two days ago. He denies being anywhere near his ex-wife's apartment the night she got killed, and he's given us the names of enough witnesses to keep us busy for a week."

"Damn!" Mark swore beneath his breath as he recalled the crime scene in question . . . and the victim's shoulder-length blond hair. What if Jenny's ex had homicidal tendencies? And then another grim thought occurred to him. What would happen if DiNigro began making inquiries about Jenny? She might have fake IDs, but he doubted that her cover would hold up under careful scrutiny. She could be taken away in handcuffs, and Jamie returned to a father who had nearly killed him. Reaching in his pocket, he tossed money on the counter, then turned to Jay. "I've changed my mind." When Jay slid from the stool, he shook his head. "This is something I've got to work out on my own."

Getting back into his car, he drove home at a slow pace. Mulligan's hadn't calmed him. Trying to explain his problems to Jay wouldn't have helped either. When it came right down to it, he wasn't sure what would. But he had the feeling he wasn't going to give up the woman he wanted.

Traffic on the expressway was light tonight and he stayed in the slow lane. He wasn't in a hurry, anyway. He had no real place to go. His house might be fully furnished, but it lacked the warmth of Jenny's place. He sighed. Both Jenny and Jamie had made him feel like a hero, a blue knight on a white charger riding to the rescue. He'd needed someone to believe in him and both Jenny and Jamie had accepted him, despite his scars, despite his failures. He'd fallen for a warm, perceptive, traumatized angel who was frightened of the past. Now her words came back to haunt him. *"You don't want this. You know nothing about me."*

Mark slowed down at the exit sign and turned on his blinker. She *had* warned him, more than once. But he'd ignored her warnings, because he had wanted the angel. Rescuing damsels in distress had appealed to him, as a man, and as a cop. That was why he'd ignored all the half truths she'd tossed his way, as well as all the warnings.

He hadn't realized that he'd done anything wrong until she'd knocked him over the head with talk of a gun.

After everything she'd told him, he still hadn't believed that her ghost was real. He'd failed her, just like the lawyers she'd gone to for help. Like the judge who, for some reason, had decided to give her ex-husband custody of their son. His mouth twisted grimly. She had driven the point home with a vengeance. For what it was worth, he did believe her now. Now, after he had pushed her away.

On his way home he drove past her house. The lights were on but her car wasn't in the driveway, he noticed. With a sigh, he headed for his own home. In the empty rooms, he finally faced the fact that he had a decision to make.

It wasn't a matter of Jenny's guilt or innocence, he realized. He had a fair idea of what could have happened to give her ex partial custody of Jamie. Like Chris, Jamie had probably been too scared to testify against his father. With the law having failed her, Jenny had had no option but to take her son and run.

Mark stopped at Tim's room, his glance sliding over the bare walls, over his empty bed. If anyone ever harmed Tim, he would feel absolutely murderous. He would probably beat the guy to within an inch of his life. But in the end he would let the system take care of him. And his gut told him that a social studies teacher couldn't live outside the system any more than a cop could, or Jenny would have hired someone to "take care" of her ex-husband long ago.

All right. Fine. So he understood her motives. Where did that get either of them? Jenny needed more than understanding. She needed help. A good lawyer could straighten out the legal mess, but that would take time, and his gut was telling him that time was running out.

Walking into the kitchen to make himself a cup of coffee, Mark filled the machine with water. If the ex had filed charges against Jenny, he was using official law enforcement channels to hunt her down. The bastard didn't need to spend a penny of his own money on the search. He could afford to sit back in his chair and wait for her to make a mistake, which would draw the attention of a cop. Which it had.

With slow controlled movements, Mark counted four scoops of grounds into the filter, covered the can and returned it to the cupboard, flicking the switch to turn on the machine. The good news was that he didn't have to use official channels to hunt down the ex-husband. There wasn't a decent officer in the country who wouldn't be happy to help him. He knew that he would have all the cooperation he needed to find that bastard and put him behind bars. And he was going to stick to the rules because he didn't want to give the ex a chance of getting off on some technicality.

The bad news was that he still needed a name and address. Without those, his hands were tied as surely as if he were wearing his own handcuffs. He needed facts that only Jenny could provide, and she didn't trust him enough to even reveal her real name. Until she stopped running, until she trusted him, there wasn't a damn thing he could do except keep an eye on them. And show her that he believed in her.

It was past ten when Jenny walked down the driveway to check on her mailbox. With nightfall the air had turned chilly and her breath came out in small white clouds. Mush raced ahead of her and scurried into the bushes alongside the road. "Don't go far," Jenny called after him as she ran a critical but approving eye over the little garage. Gently she pushed against the post. When it refused to budge, she pushed a little harder. It still wouldn't give. Satisfied, she stepped on the sand she'd filled in earlier, then stomped on it, trying to pack the dirt firmly, keeping her ears and eyes tuned for dangers in the night.

She wondered if she would ever feel safe again, as safe as she had earlier today. Not once while Mark had been here had she looked over her shoulder, she realized suddenly. Not in the store, and not out in the garden later on. Perhaps that was why the crank call had shaken her so badly, she'd let her defenses down.

With a final, angry kick at the dirt, she stepped into the road. Mark had been furious, she thought, and disappointed, too. It was difficult for a man who believed so strongly in the system to understand what she had gone through, the sense of abandonment, of betrayal, of total disbelief. Her mouth tightened grimly. She hoped he would never learn what it meant to be an outcast, to live a constant lie, to have no one to turn to for help except your family.

And to know that every time you asked them for help you would hurt them.

For a moment she looked at the spot where Jamie and Mark had assembled the mailbox. Over the past few hours she had nursed a temper, and whether it was justified or not had nothing to do with it. She was angry with Mark for pushing the issue, for not trusting her not to use him, for making her face her demons all over again.

If she was honest with herself, she had to admit that he had no real reason to trust her. Maybe she hadn't lied to him, but she hadn't told him the full truth, either. Still, he had hurt her with his doubts and scorn. She'd hoped that they had come far enough in their relationship for him to accept her for who and what she said she was.

With a sigh, she picked up a pebble and threw it across the street into the vacant, heavily wooded lot. She had wanted too much. The trouble was she wanted his trust without being completely honest with him. She wanted his support without having to reveal the reasons for her secrecy.

She wanted his love and commitment without taking the risk of commitment herself.

If she was angry with Mark, she was disgusted with herself.

After Mark had left she'd driven to the shopping center and called her aunt to ask for the lawyer's address and phone number. She would call for an appointment tomorrow, she thought. She would talk to Ms. Stein and then decide if she was willing to take the risk. She had Mark to thank for that, too, she thought with a bitter smile. And in return she had hurt him. Like she hurt everyone else she loved.

Mush suddenly emerged from the bushes across the road. Instead of running toward her, he stopped in the middle of the street, poised, his ears pointed, listening. Apprehension feathered down her spine and she called to him sharply. "Mush, let's go back inside." He ignored her. Moments later Jenny heard the sound of a car engine and she rushed into the road. Her fingers curling around the dog's choke collar, she started to pull him toward the curb.

He refused to budge. Seconds later, she saw twin circles of lights leap over tree trunks and bushes. She tugged at the chain with all her might, dragging eighty pounds of unwilling dog across the road. Headlights trapped her as the car came around the curve. With her heart beating high in her throat, she watched the lights come closer and closer, and slanted a frantic look at the house.

Five feet away from her, the car came to a full stop.

# *Chapter 10*

Suddenly Mush started to bark and strain at the chain. Recognizing the Blazer, Jenny expelled the breath she'd been holding. For a moment she'd feared that the car belonged to Burke. Would she ever stop running from him? she asked herself wearily.

With a sigh, she released Mush. Like a flash he raced to the car, leaping up at Mark in frenzied welcome. Jenny stood watching him, her heart in her eyes, hope surging.

"Still siccing dogs on me, I see," Mark said lightly, looking at her over the top of the car door while stroking the dog's head. Mush groaned with pleasure, and his tail thumped rhythmically on the pavement.

A small grin tugged at Jenny's lips. "I couldn't hold him. He must have recognized the sound of your car." Squinting, she tried to see past the blinding whiteness of the vehicle's headlights. Why had he come back? she wondered, her heart beating erratically. Damn it, she'd told him to stay out of her life. Sending him away had been the best thing she could have done for him. "What are you doing here?"

"Same as you, I guess. Checking up on the mailbox. I see you filled in the hole." And she had packed the dirt tight, he noticed, relief flooding through him. At least she didn't plan to run anytime soon.

"I did it right after you left," Jenny said quietly. *Please get back into your car and leave,* she pleaded silently. She didn't have the strength to keep pushing him away.

Instead, he closed the car door. Reaching into his shirt pocket, he crossed the space between them in two long strides. "I wrote down phone numbers where you can reach me, if you need help."

For long moments Jenny stared at the slip of paper, swallowing hard. He did believe that the threats were real, and he was willing to help her. Reaching for the note, she tucked it into the pocket of her shirt. "Thank you," she said, a catch in her voice.

With an impatient grimace, Mark shoved his hands into his pockets. "I'm getting tired of telling you not to thank me. It isn't gratitude I want from you," he growled. Taking a hand out of his pocket, he raked it through his hair. "I blew it this afternoon, Jenny. I admit that at first I had doubts the threats were real, but for what it's worth, you convinced me." His lips twisted wryly. "Shocked me into it."

Jenny stared at him uncertainly. "You were willing to help me anyway," she pointed out quietly. "But I had no right to involve you so deeply. I see that now." There was such hunger on his face, such need in his eyes that she wanted to reach out to him. She knew he was asking her for a second chance and she was so very tempted to give it to him. But a second chance for what? she asked herself bitterly. So that she could hurt him even more? She slid her hands into her pockets, curling them into fists. "What I told you to-day... it's all I can give you," she said somberly.

She looked over her shoulder, at the place where she'd watched him with Jamie. Then she looked back at him, her chin angled determinedly. "It was a lovely weekend, Mark. The best I've had in a long time." She smiled faintly. "But I'm just not ready yet to meet you halfway."

Mark looked straight into her eyes and said quietly, "We've only known each other for two days, Jenny. We'll deal with your ghost first. Once he's gone from your life, we'll talk again."

Jenny kicked a small pebble with her sneaker. She knew exactly what her feelings were for Mark. She wanted him. She wanted him in her life, in her bed and as the father of her son. She wanted to be there for him; she wanted to be the one he could turn to when the chips were down. She wanted to see desire and need darken his eyes for her, Jenny. She wanted to be a woman again for him.

But she carried a burden around with her from the past, and she wasn't young and naive enough to believe that love conquered all. She had come a long way in the last three years. She'd like to think that she had earned respect as both a mother and a teacher.

But the woman in her was still riddled with self-doubts, guilt and fear. And as long as she was hiding behind the name of Jennifer Wilson, she didn't have the right to draw him into her world of lies. She would only destroy him. And that wasn't caring.

She raised her head and said quietly but firmly, "I'm the wrong woman for you, Mark. I can only hurt you, and I couldn't deal with that. I've hurt too many people in the past already. You were right. A lover or a mate has the right to know who he's making love to. And he also has the right to find his mate waiting for him when he gets home. I can't promise you that I won't run again. I could tell you my real name, but it wouldn't mean anything, because I'm not that person."

Yet.

He could feel her slipping away from him. He suddenly realized that the deeper her feelings went for him, the more afraid she was to fail again. "All right. I'll leave for now, but I'm not giving up on you." When Jenny started to protest, he placed his thumb over her lips, and added, "I could tell you that you're stronger than you think you are, but I guess that's something you have to find out for yourself."

At his words, her resolve weakened and she covered his hand, pressing it against her cheek. "You're not making this easy for me, Mark," she protested hoarsely.

One corner of his mouth kicked up and his thumb stroked her bottom lip. "Did you expect me to? I happen to think that you're worth fighting for." He could feel her lip quiver beneath his touch and saw her swallow. With infinite gentleness he tilted her face up and lowered his head, kissing her with tantalizing tenderness.

Jenny stiffened at his caress, tears pricking her eyes. She knew she should run back into the house and lock the door against temptation. Perhaps if he'd been angry she might have found the strength to resist him, but his belief in her and his gentleness were her undoing. With a muffled sob, her hands lifted to close around his head, burying her fingers in his thick hair, seeking the strength of his body and the moist heat of his mouth, wanting him so much her throat was raw with pain.

With her last ounce of strength she eased out of his embrace and stared at him with troubled eyes. "This wouldn't solve anything," she said wearily. "Please don't make it more difficult for me."

Mark's face tightened and his hands curled with frustration. "If you change your mind, or if you need help you know where to find me," he said gravely. Looking past her, he added, "I'll keep an eye on the mailbox. Good night."

"Good night." Jenny watched him walk back to his car and slide into it, sudden tears shimmering in her eyes. "Damn you, Mark," she swore softly. It had taken all of her strength to push him away tonight, how could she keep doing it day after day? She wanted to be strong enough not to pull him into her problems, but she wasn't strong enough to fight her feelings for him, too. The sooner she made an appointment with the lawyer, the better, she thought.

"Are you sure you don't have an earlier opening?" Jenny asked the following afternoon. The moment she'd returned from school, she had sent Jamie upstairs to change while she called the lawyer's office. Now she was being told the next available appointment was in three weeks. She didn't want to wait three weeks for an appointment! "I need to talk to Ms. Stein as soon as possible. This is a rather urgent case."

"All of Ms. Stein's cases are," came the patient reply. "Her associates handle the less complicated ones. But with the Thanksgiving weekend coming up, her schedule is more crowded than usual. If you would prefer to talk to one of the other counselors, I could give you an appointment the Wednesday before the holiday."

Frustrated, Jenny ran a hand through her hair, tapping the tile floor with the tip of her black shoe. "I prefer to see Ms. Stein," she insisted. From what Aunt Alys had told her, Ms. Stein had once been in a similar situation years ago, and would understand what she was up against. Jenny needed the best lawyer; she couldn't afford to settle for less, because this time there was no room for mistakes.

If she lost the case—

Dear God, what was she going to do if she lost Jamie? Panic rushed through her and she almost hung up. But she wasn't committing herself to anything more than a consultation. "I'll see you the Monday after Thanksgiving, then."

"Fine. Ms. Wilson—" the secretary's voice hesitated briefly, then said quickly, "We have an emergency number you can call if your situation becomes desperate in the meantime."

Jenny's hand clenched around the receiver, realizing that the secretary was offering her the number of a shelter where she could take refuge if she needed it. The fact that there were now shelters showed just how many women were afraid of the men in their lives. No one, Jenny suddenly thought with fierce anger, should have to live with constant fear. "I hope I won't need it," she said soberly, but added the number to the list Mark had given her last night. Hanging up, she pinned the emergency list on the wall above the phone.

"What are those numbers?" Jamie asked, walking into the kitchen just then, gym tote slung over his shoulder.

With a sigh, Jenny held her hand out to him. Wrapping an arm tightly around his shoulders, she explained, "You know that Mark went back to work today. He won't have a lot of time from now on. So he gave me some telephone numbers, in case we need to get in touch with him."

"You mean, in case Mr. DiNigro starts yelling at you again?"

"Good example," Jenny said swiftly, wondering how much longer she could keep things normal for him. "And speaking of phone calls. We've had a few anonymous calls in the past two days. I don't want you to answer the phone anymore. Let the machine take messages instead."

Jamie stiffened and turned his head, looking at her with anxious eyes. "What kind of calls? Like the ones you used to get?"

Softly, Jenny caught her breath and her hand tightened on his shoulder. "Do you remember them?"

Nodding, Jamie said slowly, "You used to turn on the music box so I wouldn't hear the phone ring. Burke didn't like me playing with the carousel; he always called it a baby toy. Once, I remember you yelling at him that if he ever broke the carousel, we'd leave. I threw it out the window the next day. Burke got real mad with you that night. I could hear you crying for a long time and I felt real bad." With a sob he turned into Jenny, hugging her tightly, his body shaking. "The next day we went to visit grandma. And then Aunt Alys and Uncle Ralph came and later—"

"Shhh, it's all right, sweetheart," Jenny whispered into his hair, her voice rough with tears. She could remember the morning she'd found the broken pieces of the carousel as clearly as if it had been yesterday. She'd known then that she would have to leave. The music box had always reminded her of the one her father had brought back from one of his trips to Germany. It had been her link to the past, a memory of happier times. "Everything will be fine, Jamie. I promise you. We're going to stay here, in this house, and no one will ever hurt you again."

With a slightly embarrassed expression, Jamie stepped back and wiped his eyes with the back of his hand. "Did you tell Mark about Burke? Is he going to lock him up?"

With a shake of her head, Jenny poured him a glass of milk and handed him two chocolate chip cookies to tide him over until supper. "He knows the story, but I didn't mention any names. We have to keep our secret a little longer."

"But why?" Sitting down at the table, Jamie gave her a puzzled look. "How can he start looking for Burke if he doesn't know his name?"

"It's a little complicated," Jenny said evasively, pouring herself a glass of orange juice. Until now she had hidden from him the fact that she'd kidnapped him. As far as Jamie was concerned they were hiding from Burke, not the law. But she couldn't shield him much longer, not if she went ahead with her plans.

Perhaps it was time to give him a simple lesson in how the legal system worked. Pulling out a chair, she sat next to him, cradling the glass in her hand. "Mark can only arrest a man, he can't keep him locked up indefinitely. Only a judge can do that."

Jamie bit into his cookie. Chewing, he looked at her with old, knowing eyes. "The judge in Dark Water was a friend of grandma and grandpa's. Is that why he didn't lock Burke up?"

Jenny shook her head. "That may have influenced him, but he tried to be fair. A judge cannot make a decision based on his feelings, just as I cannot give a bad student an *A* because I like him as a person. What do you remember about the last few days at the hospital, just before we left?"

Jamie stuffed the other half of the cookie into his mouth, frowning. "Grandma said that she was taking me home with her, and she got mad when I started crying. I tried to tell her that it wasn't because of her, but that I was scared of Burke. She said his temper was all your fault, because you made Burke angry."

Wincing, Jenny chose her words carefully. She wanted him to keep some of his illusions. "Your grandmother loves Burke very much. And she lied to protect him."

Jamie looked at her soberly. "The way you lie for me?"

Jenny hugged him fiercely. "No! You didn't do anything wrong. Never, never feel guilty about the lies, do you hear? We have to keep Burke from finding us. On the other hand, if you cut your classes, I won't protect you."

Jamie's bottom lip quivered. "But she didn't like me. Was it because I locked Biddie into the shed? She said that it was my fault that she died."

There had always been something strange about Biddie's death, Jenny thought. Jamie had played with her ex-mother-in-law's poodle in the shed that fateful day, but he'd been as inseparable from the little dog as he was from Mush. Biddie's being locked in there was a total mystery. "Biddie's death was an accident," she repeated firmly. With a gentle smile Jenny brushed back his hair, wishing that she didn't have to recall the nightmares again. But sooner or later they would both have to talk about the events, because it had been Jamie's testimony that had tipped the scales of justice the wrong way. "I'd like to believe that your grandma also lied because she didn't want to lose you. You see, she was afraid that if Burke went to jail, I would never allow you to visit them again. She was wrong. Your grandma and I didn't get along too well, but I would never have done that to her."

"It doesn't matter, Mom. I don't ever want to see them again." Jamie reached for the glass of milk, took a big gulp, then pushed back his chair. "Can we go to karate now?"

It was past eight when Mark drove by Jenny's house that night. All day long, while he'd worked his way through the paperwork that had accumulated during his absence and had caught up with the ongoing investigations, she had been at the back of his mind.

He glanced at the mailbox. By now the concrete had set hard enough to make it tough for a man to pull the post out with his hands. Everything appeared to be normal, he thought, looking at Jenny's house. Smoke curled from the chimney and the lights in the living room were on. Faintly, he could hear the dog bark as he slowed down at the curb. For a moment, Mark stood with the motor idling, willing for her to open the door and at least wave at him.

She didn't. And the door remained closed.

Mark felt a sudden urgent need to park the car and knock on her door. He was willing to back off and give her time to sort her feelings out, because he realized that he'd pushed hard all weekend long. But he'd only done so because he had been afraid she would start running again and that he would drive by her house one evening to find it shrouded in darkness, finding nothing but cold ashes in the fireplace.

He wanted a place by her fire. He wanted the warmth, laughter and contentment he had shared with them. He wanted to unlock the passion Jenny was capable of.

But how much did he want it? And how much was he willing to sacrifice for it? Jenny and Jamie needed a sense of security and safety he couldn't provide. Even if all the threats were removed she would still want someone she could count on to come home to her every night.

He grimaced. For the first time in his life, he was getting a taste of what cops' wives went through every day. They could never be certain that their husbands would return to them at night. Every morning they faced the risk that they would be left with only cold ashes.

How would he feel if he drove by Jenny's house one night to find her gone?

He would feel like hell, he admitted. Shifting into drive, he pulled away from the curb. But he would never have to face that scenario, because she was determined to keep him out of her life.

From the upstairs window, Jenny watched him pull up at the curb and held her breath. Behind her she heard water running through the pipes, and Jamie singing off-key in the bathtub. She hadn't told him yet that she had sent Mark away, perhaps because she was so very tempted to run outside. She had even had a valid excuse ready. Chris hadn't been at the dojo today and she was worried about the boy. But before she could break down her resistance, Mark pulled away from the curb. With her arms wrapped around herself, Jenny watched until the lights had disappeared, feeling more lonely than she had in years.

She watched him drive by on Tuesday night.

On Wednesday he came a little earlier, as she was folding the laundry. Chris had missed another class today. It wasn't the first time he'd skipped several classes in a row, but she hadn't known the reasons for his absences then. When she heard Mush bark, she stopped and raced outside, but Mark had already turned around and left. As Jenny watched his taillights disappear, she felt an inner emptiness growing within her. She hadn't realized before just how empty her life would be without him.

It was late by the time he arrived at the house on Thursday night, and Jenny was already in bed. He was wearing her down, she thought, listening to the sound of the engine. If a man cared for her enough to drive by her home every night to make certain that she and her son were safe, then he was already so involved that even her being wanted by the law wouldn't make him leave.

When Jenny didn't hear him drive by on Friday, she barely slept a wink. More than once that night, she reached for the phone to call him. But just as she thought she'd gathered enough courage, her own phone rang. The silent threat on her answering machine made up her mind.

"Can we drive by Mark's house on the way to brunch?" Jamie asked as they were leaving the house Saturday morning. "I haven't seen him all week."

With her hand on the doorknob, Jenny hesitated. Until now Jamie hadn't commented about Mark's absence and she'd been glad that he had accepted her explanation that cops didn't work regular hours. But she knew she couldn't avoid the issue forever. Sometime this weekend she would have to tell him the truth. "We'll do it on our way home," she said, closing the door firmly. She didn't want to upset him before class.

He swung the tote over his shoulder with a show of unconcern. Running down the steps of the porch, he tossed back over his shoulder, "Maybe he's going to drop by the dojo later on."

Jenny followed him at a slower pace, a troubled look on her face. "Cops work weekends, too," she warned, unlocking his side of the car.

Without another word, he flung his tote into the back, climbed into his seat and slammed the door. "Cops don't work all the time."

Sliding into the car, Jenny watched him jerk on the seat belt and fasten it with a snap. With a sigh of resignation she started the engine. "That's true," she said, shifting into reverse. "But Mark also has a large family. And he does have other friends."

"Maybe he's sick again," Jamie muttered as Jenny backed out of the driveway.

"I don't think so," Jenny said firmly, but the possibility had worried her, too. With a glance at her mailbox, she shifted into drive and shot down the road. In the darkness of her bedroom she'd also met a new demon, one she hadn't faced before. *Jealousy.* The mere thought of Mark spending the evening—and possibly the night—with someone else, had been a painful lesson, she admitted grimly. One she could have done without. It was also the real reason why she didn't want to drive past his house.

They didn't enjoy their meal. Jamie sulked. For once Jenny didn't try to coax him out of his mood. She was thinking of ways to draw Mark back into her life. Maybe she could invite him for dinner.... But the reason she'd sent him away still existed.

The phone still rang every day, the caller still silent. She was sure it was Burke.

It was drizzling when Jenny pulled into the parking lot at the dojo. Getting out of the car, she shivered in the damp cold. She would have to get warmer clothes for the winter, she thought as the breeze bit through her tweed jacket.

"Behave yourself," she warned Jamie on their way into the building.

Unfortunately the first person they met was the one she had hoped to avoid. DiNigro stood just inside the door, clad in jeans and a red windbreaker. At her entrance he turned and shot her a sardonic look. "I see you came without your bodyguard today," he sneered.

Jenny's mouth tightened angrily. Out of the corner of her eyes she saw Jamie stiffen and she swiftly placed a warning hand on his shoulder. "Go into the locker room and change," she said firmly, giving him a little shove. She watched him walk toward the back of the building, her glance sliding past the curious faces of the other parents before returning to DiNigro. "You don't frighten me," she said, her voice filled with contempt. "I deal with bullies every day. So why don't you keep your nasty little comments to yourself."

Angry, she started to brush past him, when she heard Jamie yell, "You're a liar, Chris. Mark doesn't beat up kids. He isn't like—" His voice broke on a sob.

"My dad's going to put him in prison. He said so," Chris yelled back. Thuds followed.

With a furious look at DiNigro, Jenny ran toward the locker room. But other parents were already converging on the small hall, blocking her way. She pushed and shoved her way through the crowd, a sob in her own throat. By the time she reached the hallway, Luke had already separated the two boys and was dragging them into his office. Grimly, Jenny followed him and led Jamie to the black vinyl couch at the end of the room. He was trembling and his skin was as white as the color of his *gi*. She gently pushed his head between his knees. "Take a few deep breaths."

Luke ushered DiNigro into his office and slammed the door. Angrily, he glanced from the pale Chris to the red-faced father. "This isn't going to work. I warned you last week that I wouldn't tolerate any more brawling. Your son is disrupting my school." He cast an apologetic look at Jenny, then turned back to the lawyer. "I'm probably playing right into your hands. I've a feeling you wanted your son to create another disturbance, so I would kick him out. Unfortunately I have a responsibility to my other students." His grim face softened when he looked at Chris. "If you need someone to talk to, call me." Then he opened the door, indicating that he wanted both son and father to leave now.

Troubled, Jenny watched DiNigro clasp his beefy hand on Chris's shoulder and shake him, propelling the boy out of the office. "I warned you to stay away from that kid," he growled, his voice vibrating with fury. "Get your gear. I'll wait for you outside."

Jenny flinched at the threat of violence in his voice. "Luke," she said urgently, turning to the black belt, "I'm worried. DiNigro's furious enough to hurt Chris."

With a sigh, Luke closed the door, his hands curling around his black belt in frustration. "Look, there's nothing any of us can do."

He looked past her at Jamie, who was watching them with dark, anxious eyes. "You okay?" When Jamie nodded, he suggested, "Why don't you change for class?"

Jamie made a slow, negative movement with his head. "I want to go home," he said, his voice flat, as if all hope had drained out of him. "Mom, can we go home?"

Jenny swallowed hard. "If that's what you want," she said gently.

Jamie got to his feet, stuffing his hands into the pockets of his jeans. "Can we drive by Mark's house?"

"Sure," she said, wondering if Chris's remark had been an idle threat, or if DiNigro had already started some legal action against Mark. She'd warned Mark not to become involved, she thought as she walked out of the dojo with quick anxious steps, one hand carrying the tote, the other firmly clasped around Jamie's wrist. Rain blew into her face and she lowered her head into the wind as she crossed the parking lot. She had warned him that she would bring him nothing but trouble, but he hadn't listened.

"What did Chris say to you?" she started to ask Jamie, when she suddenly heard DiNigro's voice snarling from behind the truck.

"I'll teach you not to repeat what you hear at home to other people. You stupid imbecile! Get into the car."

"I don't want to," Chris cried. A sob followed. A thud. And then a muffled cry.

Grimly, Jenny yanked Jamie back, wanting to spare him the sight. "Run back to the dojo and get Sensei Luke," she ordered.

For a moment Jamie stood frozen. "I'm not going to leave you alone."

Another cry came from behind the truck. Jenny brushed past Jamie. "Get Sensei Luke and stay at the dojo."

When she rounded the truck the scene that met her eyes was the one in her nightmares. Jamie crouching on the floor and Burke kicking him over and over again. Even the words were the same: "I'll teach you—"

Blindly, she lunged at the man, knocking him off-balance. He raised his fist. Jenny blocked the downward swing in the same way she had seen Jamie practice it countless times, then grabbed the strong arm with both hands. "Run, Chris," she gasped.

But the boy didn't move. He lay curled into a ball on the wet pavement.

DiNigro twisted free of Jenny's hold. He grabbed a fistful of Chris's hair, trying to drag him in the car, which stood with the door open only a few feet away. "Get in, you sniveling coward."

Jenny lunged at him again, nightmare and reality merging into one. She kicked DiNigro in the shin so hard he staggered back, releasing Chris.

And then Luke was there, hitting DiNigro's arm with the side of his hand, sending him crashing into the side of the truck. Holding him pinned there with nothing more than a hand at the base of his throat, he growled, "I'd love to beat the hell out of you, but that would be too damn easy on you. I'll let the cops have you instead."

Jenny knelt beside the crying Chris, helping him into a sitting position, pressing his face into her shoulder. At Luke's words, a cry of protest rose in her. Cops meant statements, hearings, maybe even publicity. All the things she'd tried so hard to avoid. Then she looked down at Chris sobbing in her arms, trembling.

And she knew she couldn't leave.

If she did, she would never be able to look at herself in the mirror again.

She would never be able to face Jamie without feeling that she had failed him yet a second time.

She would never be able to stand in front of a class again. How could she teach her kids about convictions and courage when she had none herself?

And she would lose the one man she wanted with all her heart.

*Second chances.*

The thought scared her to death.

When Mark and Jay arrived at the dojo forty minutes later, an ambulance was leaving the parking lot. A car from the Port Jefferson Police Department stood in front of the place. Inside parents crowded the small waiting room, hovering near the hall leading to the office and the locker rooms.

Mark slanted a look through the window into the dojo, where a class was in progress. A young black belt with oriental features was supervising the group. For a moment Mark stopped, searching for Jamie's blond head among the kids. Not finding him, he turned toward the office, Jay following silently behind him.

Jamie was hovering in the half open door to the locker room. "I knew you would come," he cried, launching himself at Mark. "The officer at the switchboard said they'd leave a message."

At Jamie's welcome a feeling of warmth stole over Mark. He squeezed the boy's shoulders, searching his face for signs of distress. "Why aren't you in class?"

"It's almost over now. Besides, I had to watch out for Mom. She looked kind of sick. They sent me out of the office, so I was waiting for you."

Jay, who'd been watching the entire scene, now stepped forward. He always felt a little awkward around kids. But ten was half adult; he figured he could handle it. "I saw a pizza place a few stores down. Want to come with me?"

Jamie looked from Mark to Jay. "I don't go with strangers."

A small grin tugged at Jay's mouth. "I'm a police officer, like Mark."

Jamie looked at him searchingly. "Can I see your badge?"

Jay reached into the pocket of his suede leather jacket. Looking at Mark, he was startled. There was a curiously proud expression on his face. Maybe his partner knew what he was doing after all, he thought, holding the tin out to the boy.

Jamie studied it with the same thoroughness he'd once given Mark's. Then he turned back to Mark and asked quietly, "Is he a good cop, too?"

"Jay's my partner."

Slowly, Jamie nodded. "I have to get my coat. Can I have a slice of pepperoni pizza and a cherry coke?"

When Jenny saw Mark enter the office, she shuddered with relief. He gave her a sharp, searching look, making sure she was all right first, then joined Luke. Through a haze, she watched the gray-haired, uniformed officer sitting behind the desk almost snap to attention as he asked, "Lawton, what are you doing here? This is village business."

He looked lean, powerful and fit, Jenny thought. The brown cord jacket stretched over his broad shoulders. His collar was open and he had loosened his tie. He stood with his legs slightly spread, his hands on his hips as he asked questions.

The whole last hour had taken on a surreal cast for Jenny. Chris had been taken away by ambulance. DiNigro had been led away in handcuffs. The two young officers had taken an almost fiendish delight in slapping them on. That, she thought, had been the one satisfying moment. But the worst part was still to come.

Luke was giving the officer seated behind his desk all the necessary information to file a report. Nervously, her fingers held the cup of sweetened coffee Lainie had brought her.

Her turn would come next.

All her lies were catching up with her, she thought. Which name should she use? Which date of birth? Was she widowed or divorced?

Definitely the latter, Jenny thought. The divorce was one of the few decisions she was proud of.

Should she stick with the rest of her lies and hope that no one would check?

Or should she tell the truth? That, too, would cause problems, Jenny thought. She didn't own a single ID with her rightful name on it.

Carefully, she sipped her coffee, feeling its heat burn her throat.

Making a stand had seemed the right thing to do out in the parking lot, when she had held a sobbing, injured child in her arms. But now, with the haze slowly clearing, she saw a tidal wave crashing onto the shore, washing away her carefully fabricated lies and leaving nothing but the stark truth.

Over the rim of her cup, she saw Mark turn and stride toward her, until he filled her vision, until she saw only him.

"Still a little shaken?" Mark asked. Her eyes were dark and slightly unfocused. Her lips had no color at all. There were bloodstains on her jacket and her white shirt matched the shade of her skin. Her jeans showed dark patches on the knees, where she must have knelt on the rain-soaked pavement. She hadn't shed a single tear. Mark figured she was about a finger's snap from breaking down, but she still managed to give him her lopsided smile.

"No, I'm fine. Did you see Jamie outside?"

"Jay, my partner, took him out for pizza and cherry coke."

"And he went with him, just like that?" Jenny asked, surprise in her voice. He had been very upset earlier and she had been prepared for a setback.

"Not before demanding to see Jay's shield and asking me to vouch for him."

Jenny wrinkled her nose. "I didn't know he'd called you, not until afterward. Thank you for coming."

Mark didn't comment. "Drink your coffee. Then I'll take you outside for a breath of fresh air."

Jenny raised the cup to her lips. "Thank you, but I want to get this over with and go home."

Mark scowled. "Why didn't you run inside and get Luke? Damn it, you might have been hurt."

The concern in Mark's eyes warmed her. Soberly, she said, "I wasn't thinking rationally at the time. But even if I had, I couldn't have turned away. What will happen to Chris now?"

"He'll probably stay with his mother's parents until the hearing. DiNigro will be forced to go to counseling. The rest depends on Chris and his mother. And on you." His eyes narrowed. "You realize that you'll have to testify at the hearing."

"I know." Taking a deep breath, she stood up and walked to the officer, who had signaled he was ready for her.

Telling the truth wasn't so difficult after all. Perhaps it was because she had stopped running. Or perhaps it had something to do with Mark, who leaned against the wall behind the desk; she spoke directly to him rather than the uniformed officer. She gave her true date and place of birth and told him she was divorced. As to her name, for Jamie's sake, she compromised. But the man watching her patiently would know who he would be making love to. That is if he still wanted her after she had told him the whole truth.

"My name is Jennifer Teresa McKenzie Wilson."

## Chapter 11

It was almost four o'clock by the time Mark followed Jenny and Jamie home. The drizzle had turned into a steady downpour, and upon arrival, they all dashed into the house. In the foyer Mush raced from one person to the next in greeting, his tail whipping back and forth. When he paused, and nudged Mark's hand in welcome, a small smile curved Jenny's lips. Feelings, deeply buried and closely guarded, flared to life, longings and needs so hot they seared the ice surrounding her heart. Mark had become an integral part of their lives, she realized.

It was too soon, though, she cautioned herself, her hands curling at her sides. Much too soon. She still had to tell Mark all the truth, and Burke was still out there, waiting. She couldn't afford new vulnerabilities, new weaknesses. She didn't want to love, ever again. Shivering, she clamped down on her feelings and made for the living room.

Drained, she sank into the soft cushions of the couch.

From the dark shadowy room, she watched Mark talk briefly to Jamie before sending him upstairs, then he turned on the lights. "Can I make you a cup of coffee?" she asked when he came toward her, anxiously searching his features for some kind of reaction.

She'd noted that her statement at the dojo had startled him, had seen it shake him out of the detachment with which he'd been listening to her. For a long moment his eyes had darkened with hidden emotions, then his control had snapped back into place. Now, new questions hung between them. More questions that she had to answer, she reminded herself. Her fingers curled into the damp fabric of her jeans. She had to tell him, she told herself. Yet still she delayed, torn in two, wanting to get it over with, but fearing his reaction.

Mark shook his head, studying her face. She looked pale and exhausted, and he hated to leave her like this. But Jay was waiting outside in the car for him. And they both had witnesses from the Brandon case waiting for them at headquarters. If they didn't shake one of their testimonies soon, Brandon would be released. They'd spent most of last night going over the evidence with a fine-tooth comb, but had found nothing. "I have to get back to work. Is there anyone who could stay with you?"

Jenny shook her head, inwardly sighing with relief at the unexpected reprieve. "I'm fine. I really had no idea that Jamie called you. I'm sorry we took you away from your job."

Until now he'd barely managed to control his rage and the need to hold her, but then, he hadn't wanted her to break in front of witnesses. Now he felt his control slipping again, and his eyes narrowed. "I wish you had called me instead."

Jenny, her fingers clutching the damp fabric of her jeans, hesitated briefly. Then she smoothed out the wrinkles and tossed caution to the wind. "I would have. But Jamie beat me to it," she said softly, her eyes holding his.

Mark sucked in his breath sharply. He hadn't known what to make of her statement earlier. A part of him had hoped that she'd changed her mind, that she wanted him in her life. Then he'd told himself that it didn't mean anything, that she had merely wanted to protect herself, in case someone discovered her real identity by accident. But now her hands rested on her knees without mangling the fabric of her jeans and there was a steady look in her big brown eyes. Slowly, he expelled his pent-up breath and started to reach for her— just as Jamie came leaping down the stairs.

Frustrated, Mark watched the boy drag his comforter behind him while Mush tried to catch the trailing end. He turned back to Jenny with a small, taut smile. "Damn," he swore softly, "the timing around here stinks."

The frustrated look on his face made her want to giggle with relief. Jenny felt warmth tingling in her cold fingers, heat spreading rapidly. She flashed him a small grin. "Jay's waiting, too. I'll see you later." Sensing his reluctance, she added gently, "Don't worry about us. We're fine, aren't we, Jamie?" she asked her son, who was trying to wrap the comforter around her legs.

Nodding, Jamie looked at Mark seriously. "I was supposed to sleep over at Mike's house tonight, but I just canceled it. I'll take care of Mom."

Jenny pulled the thick down comforter across her knees and gave Jamie a fierce hug. "Thank you, sweetheart."

Mark watched the two blond heads so close together, then cut an impatient look through the jungle of plants at the headlights of the waiting car, visible through the living room window. "Try to get some rest," he said, striding into the foyer. "I should be back in about two hours."

He was back two minutes later.

Outside the temperature had dropped, and with the wet cold seeping into him, dispelling the recent warmth, he made straight for the driver's side of the car. He waited for Jay to roll down the window, then said, "I'm staying. Roper can take over for me." Mark had just been given a second chance, and this time he was determined not to blow it. "Have someone drop off the car for me later on."

Jay nodded. "Will do. I'll keep an eye on Roper. Since you're off tomorrow, I'll see you Monday." With a glance at the house, he added soberly, "I don't blame you. This beats Mulligan's any day."

When Mark walked back into the house, Jenny and Jamie were huddled beneath the comforter, Mush lying on the trailing end at their feet. The dog noticed him first, but didn't stir. For a moment Mark stopped in the foyer, listening to Jamie's voice. "I like Jay. I told him about Chris and what he said about Mark and that I didn't believe him. Mark isn't like Burke or Mr. DiNigro."

Jenny hugged Jamie tightly. Over his head she slanted a look at the door, wishing Mark hadn't had to leave. When she spotted him, her eyes widened with surprise. "No, he isn't," she said, meeting Mark's gaze over the head of her son, wondering about his decision to come back.

She knew he had done it for her and for Jamie; but she hoped that he had done it for himself as well.

Mark had a strong protective instinct, but she didn't want him to stay out of a sense of duty and obligation, to stay only because they needed his help. Today she had proven to herself that she was strong, stronger than she'd ever thought possible. Strong enough, she hoped, to face Burke in court. She would like to have Mark's advice and support, but with or without his help, she was determined to give the system one more chance. "Did you forget something?" she asked softly.

For a moment Mark hesitated, searching for the right words, words that would show the full meaning of what he felt for them, then he said seriously, "I thought we'd roast marshmallows in the fireplace."

Jenny caught her breath, her eyes suddenly shimmering with tears.

With an eager grin, Jamie slipped out from beneath the comforter. "I'll get the marshmallows, if you start the fire," he told Mark. He started to run toward the kitchen, then stopped as another thought occurred to him. "Are you staying here tonight?"

"Jamie!" Jenny blushed furiously at her son's words.

"Well, if Mark stays here, I can sleep over at Mike's house." Jamie looked at Mark. "You can use my bed. We only have two, and mine's bigger than Mom's."

Jenny's blush deepened. "That's enough, Jamie," she said sternly. "And I don't think it would be a good idea for you to stay with Mike after what happened today."

"Why not?" He glared at her mutinously. "I won't have a nightmare, if that's what you're afraid of. It's different at the Shermans."

Jenny bit her lip. She understood exactly what he meant. The Shermans were a happy, normal family and to him that meant security, the kind of security he craved, that she couldn't give him. Unless she married again. But marriage was one thing she wasn't ready to even contemplate. "Okay. Go ahead and call Mike," she said quietly.

"All right!" Jamie rushed into the kitchen.

Jenny pushed back the blanket and got to her feet, giving Mark an embarrassed but apologetic look. "I'm sorry," she said, pacing to the fireplace, then turning to him. "He's frightened—"

Mark placed his hands on her shoulders. "There's no need to apologize," he said quietly. "I wouldn't have left tonight, anyway."

Jenny stiffened, panicking. She wasn't ready yet for a commitment of any kind. She needed more time.

Mark cupped her chin, stopping her words with the pressure of his thumb. "I'm in love with you, Jenny," he said deeply, his eyes steady on hers. "With every part of you. I want to be with you, make love to you. But that's *my* problem. I won't pressure you. I'll sleep on the floor, in Jamie's bed, or outside in my car. But I'm not leaving you here alone tonight."

Dear God, Jenny thought, shaking her head in mute rejection. *Love.* She didn't want the additional pressure and responsibility. Not until after she had dealt with Burke. "But you can't be. I don't want you to be."

Mark felt a stab of sharp pain, swiftly controlled. "I'm aware of that," he said with a wry twist of his mouth. "But it doesn't change anything."

"You don't understand," she said, fear roughening her voice. She had left the explanations too late, she thought despairingly. "I kidnapped Jamie. There's a warrant out for my arrest." The moment the words were out she wanted to call them back. Wide-eyed, she stared at Mark, steeling herself for his anger and derision. None came. What she read in his eyes instead was acknowledgment. Slowly, she expelled the breath she'd been holding. Leaning her forehead against his chest she asked, "How long have you known?"

Mark closed his arms around her, holding her tightly, tension flowing out of him. "Since you asked me to help you buy a gun."

Jenny closed her eyes briefly, feeling the strong, steady beat of his heart beneath her cheek. He'd known the truth for almost a week, she thought, tears pricking her eyes. If he had wanted to change his mind, he'd had plenty of time. "Why didn't you tell me you knew?"

"I didn't want you to start running again," he said quietly, burying his fingers in her soft silky waves. "And I wanted you to trust me enough to tell me openly."

For a moment the strength of his feelings for her caused a huge lump in her throat. A lifetime had passed since she had opened herself up to anyone. But then, he had come to mean more to her than she had ever intended to allow again.

"I trust you," she said simply. "The person I don't trust completely yet is myself. I'm still not Jenny McKenzie," she warned somberly. "I may never be. I've contacted a lawyer to clean up the legal mess. I'm trying to straighten out my life," she said, raising her head. "But I think we should keep our relationship platonic until after I've talked to Ms. Stein. I have an appointment for the Monday after Thanksgiving."

Frowning, Mark looked at her. He could see the shadows still lurking in her eyes and he doubted that she'd fear intimacy less tomorrow, or even the next day. "That's two weeks from now," he protested, silencing her objections with a kiss. She closed her mouth against his invasion, resisting him, and her hands started to push against his chest. Frustrated, he raised his head. "What if it takes months to straighten out this mess?"

Jenny stared at him in indecision. He had shown her passion; he had shown her that he wanted her. Deep down she'd known, from the time she'd gone out to dinner with him, that he would ask her to make love with him and that he wouldn't wait long. Mark was too hungry and too lonely. He loved her. The knowledge still staggered her. And she was scared that she would disappoint him, hurt him. She tried one more time. "Mark, I don't want you to risk your job for me. I was wrong to ask it of you before."

Mark slowly shook his head. "You asked me to believe in you. There's a difference," he pointed out quietly. He drew her to the couch and gently pushed her down. Joining her, he said, "I have a fair idea of what happened. So why don't you fill me in on the rest."

With her head on his shoulder and his strong arm wrapped around her, Jenny told him about the custody hearing, how Burke's parents had lied, and how worried she was that Jamie might still fear Burke too much to face him in court.

Mark shook his head firmly, the grim slant of his mouth softening when he said, "I think you're wrong. It wouldn't surprise me one bit if he went up to him and punched him in the stomach."

Jenny's mouth curved briefly, then straightened again. "Burke's a dangerous man. His threats have been subtle so far. He still calls. I let the machine answer the phone on the first ring and I've been able to shield Jamie somewhat. But I'm afraid that the moment he finds out I've hired another lawyer his tactics are going to change. Damn, I wish I knew what game he's playing."

"We'll find out," Mark said grimly. "This time he's not going to walk away free." Tilting her head up, he kissed her softly, then added lightly, "But I warn you, if you start running again with some idiotic idea of protecting me, I'll hand in my badge and come after you."

Stunned, Jenny stared at him, emotions churning inside her.

She wanted to yell at him that she wasn't worth the sacrifice. Yet she wanted to cry, too, because no one had believed in her like this since her parents had died. "The day you turn in that badge, you're not welcome here anymore. You could sleep in my driveway from now until doomsday and I wouldn't change my mind," she said hoarsely, tears pricking her eyes.

Mark watched a tear escape and slide down her cheek. He had never seen her cry before, he thought, gently catching the drop with the tip of his finger. His voice wasn't quite steady when he said, "Does that mean that as long as I have my badge I'm welcome in your bed?"

Jenny's eyes narrowed and she looked at him accusingly. "That's not playing fair. You said no pressure."

Mark stared at the wet tip of his finger, then back at her. The corners of his mouth kicked up. "Tough. Take it or leave it."

Inwardly she panicked, terrified that she would disappoint them both. "I'll let you know later," she said airily; but they both knew what her answer would be.

Mark felt a moment of panic himself after he'd taken Jamie over to the Shermans's place after dinner. Until now, he'd never worried over the physical aspect of a relationship. But then again, none had ever been this important to him. Hands in pockets, he strolled down the road, wondering if he had it in him to be patient, gentle and thorough enough when desire was flicking inside him like hot little flames.

When he entered the house, he smelled a subtle floral scent. The fire was burning brightly in the grate and the lights had been turned low. On the table stood an open bottle of wine, two glasses and some snacks. Candlelight and soft music.

Mark stopped at the doors, stunned. Jenny had set the stage for seduction, he thought looking at her. She was standing near the fire, dressed in a flowing hostess gown of white velour, the soft folds hinting at the slender curves beneath. It might take her days, weeks or even months to come to a decision, but when she finally did make up her mind, she did it wholeheartedly. Then he noticed that her hands were worrying the fabric; her eyes were huge and wary, and her lopsided smile was back in place.

Tenderness washed through him, softening the sharp edge of his desire. He'd been seduced before, but never by such innocence, he thought. With a gleam in his eyes, he leaned against the door frame. "Nice."

Jenny gave him an uncertain look. It had taken all of her courage to get to this point and she had expected something a little better than a bland 'nice.' "Aren't you coming in?"

"You want me to?"

Jenny's eyes narrowed with exasperation. He wasn't going to make this easy for her. Actually she couldn't blame him, she thought. She had rejected him often enough. "Suit yourself."

Mark flashed a mocking grin. "Candles. Soft music. A fire. You forgot the fur rug in front of the fireplace, but I'll let you seduce me without it."

Jenny's temper flared. She had agonized over the setting, had worried over failing. And he was poking fun at her! She flung up her hand and said, "Oh, forget it. Don't you dare laugh."

Mark shook his head, looking very serious. "I'll let you use my body without teasing you."

Jenny scowled at him. "Do you have to be so—so unromantic about it?" She tried to hang onto her anger, but a smile tugged at her lips. "You're impossible."

Mark's eyes began to shine. "I thought you didn't want romance and feelings. I didn't want to frighten you," he said softly. "You set the scene, Jenny. You follow it through. I'm still waiting for an invitation," he pointed out patiently.

Jenny's mouth went dry. The thought of love frightened her and she wasn't ready yet to deal with it. Maybe some day, when she believed in safety, she would find the courage to face this last ghost. "I'm supposed to seduce you?" she asked. She licked her lips. She'd expected him to take matters in his own hands. Setting the scene had been easy compared to what he was asking of her, but she had come too far to draw back now. Besides, the idea, once planted,

seemed appealing, she decided, a gleam coming into her own
eyes. She could break it off at any time if she was the one in
control, couldn't she? "I don't know how," she said a little
uncertainly.

Mark looked at her and asked quietly, "Don't you want
me, Jenny?"

"Yes." She took a swift breath and added softly, "So
much that it frightens me."

Mark smiled tautly. "That makes two of us." When she
gave him a startled look, he added huskily, "You're not the
only one affected by your past. I want it to be good for you,
but I'm scared I'll say a wrong word or make a wrong move.
So tonight you're going to have to tell me what you like and
what you want me to do."

Jenny's throat was suddenly clogged with an aching tenderness. She didn't know what she'd done to deserve this
generous man. She wanted to tell him how much it meant to
her that he cared, cared for her despite her past, despite her
flaws, but the words wouldn't come. She walked up to him
and showed him. Standing on her toes, she flung her arms
around his neck and pulled his head down to her. "Just kiss
me," she whispered against his lips.

Slowly, his mouth brushed over hers, teasing, then
tempting.

Jenny tightened her hold. "Deeper," she muttered against
his mouth. "And hold me."

Mark circled her waist with his hands, pressing her against
him, increasing the pressure little by little, tempting her
more with each stroke of his tongue.

She met his heat with equal passion, deepening the kiss,
leaning into his chest. An ache was spreading through her,
need rising. Raising her hands to the rough silk of his hair,
she drew him closer. She heard her name whispered against
her lips, but her mouth was taken again before she could
reply.

The kiss was different this time. A possession that drank her response, filled her, seduced her with the slow movements of his tongue. Muscles tightened deep within Jenny as a strange shiver raced through her, heat spreading, burning her and burning him.

She wanted, needed, to feel more of him. Restlessly, her hands slipped beneath his jacket, spreading over his broad chest, marveling at the hard contours. She felt the granite wall of his chest begin to soften, muscles shifting, quivering beneath her fingertips. A man's body seemed to respond in the same way as a woman's, she thought, excitement welling up at the discovery. "Slide your hands up to my breasts," she whispered against his lips.

Mark slowly raised his hands, feeling her fire spreading beneath the sensuous softness of her gown. Cupping her small firm breasts, he gently slid his thumbs over her nipples until they hardened. He saw her breath quicken, heard her low quiet moan and felt her eagerness and excitement grow.

Mark studied her face with a slow smile. There was a radiance to her skin, and her lips were soft and full. The glow of the fire made her hair shimmer like spun gold and her eyes were dark and mysterious, shimmering with newly awakened power. "You're enjoying this," Mark said softly.

Jenny smiled tautly. "I've never felt like this before," she said, reaching for him again. "I never knew that a man's body responded the same as a woman's," she whispered against his mouth.

"Not quite the same," Mark murmured, cupping the back of her neck with his hand.

Jenny pressed her mouth to his. "Make love to me, Mark. Now, right now."

With his mouth still on hers, he pulled down the zipper at her back, then lowered her to the couch. He touched her gently, exploring her shape through the softness of her gown. The material slithered sensuously over her skin, a breath of velvet and a whisper of heat. He took his time peeling away the layers and baring her skin. She moved with him, pliant as he was undressing her, unafraid, unbuttoning his shirt, sliding it off his shoulders.

For a moment, when her gown whispered down her legs, Jenny felt a hint of panic. She felt so vulnerable, dressed in only a few scraps of white lace. Slowly, she raised her hands to Mark's sculpted chest, lightly running the tips of her fingers over the dark curls. His skin was warm beneath her exploring touch, heat reaching out to her. She discovered a small round scar just below his left shoulder. A bullet wound, she thought. And the skin, stretching tautly over his ribs, was still discolored. Lightly, she traced the injury.

Mark held his breath. "It's not a pretty sight," he said quietly.

Fiercely, Jenny shook her head. He, too, was vulnerable, she thought. Bending, she trailed her lips over his injury.

With a groan Mark reached for her again. "Your skin is so soft, like silk," he murmured. Hunger ripped through him as he peeled away the last barriers and slid his hands over her slender form. She was beautiful. Her body was subtle, with narrow hips and strong, long legs. She was worth every bit of patience he could find, worth every bit of torment and pleasure she gave him while she explored him.

Jenny's hands trembled slightly as she reached for the buckle of his belt and helped him remove this last barrier.

Gently, Mark lowered her to the soft rug in front of the fireplace and laid down beside her. With his mouth hovering over hers, he suddenly stopped, drew back and groaned. "Damn! I should have made a trip to the drugstore after I dropped Jamie off."

For a moment Jenny looked puzzled, then comprehension dawned. Smiling, her arms curled around his neck. "Don't worry about it. I've been taking the pill for months for a medical reason," she whispered, drawing his head down.

In the glow of the flickering flames they discovered each other by touch and taste. Passion flared with the touch of their bodies.

Her small, firm breasts fitted perfectly into the palm of his hand and her skin tasted like wild honey. He lingered there, feeling her body shudder with each touch, each taste, and her hips began arching against him in small little thrusts.

In a single smooth movement Mark turned on his back and lifted her on top of him. Startled, Jenny braced herself on his shoulders, feeling uncomfortable in a position she'd never found herself in before. "The floor's too hard," Mark said, his voice gritty with desire and control. "I'm going to crush you with my weight."

Dazed, Jenny slid her hands over his chest. Hesitantly at first, her lips followed the path her fingers had sensitized, but with each kiss, with each touch, her hunger burned fiercer. Mark shuddered beneath the light scrape of her nails and the moist heat of her mouth. With each tremor her confidence grew, power swelling inside her, urging her on.

"Jenny." With the last shreds of control Mark reached for her, drew her mouth back to his, trying to slow down the pace.

But she didn't want to slow down. The fire burning inside her was urging her on. She lowered herself to him, gasping as she felt her softness suddenly stretched to its limits. He was big, but she wanted him and she was determined to have all of him. She moved slowly at first, then faster and faster, her hips moving like lightning. Pleasure ripped through Mark, tearing at the shreds of control he was holding on to. She placed her hands on his damp chest, feeling the thud of his heart beneath her palm. Then he went taut beneath her, shouting hoarsely, his hands biting into her hips as he urged her on to higher peaks.

Jenny felt a wild release rip through her, snapping the chains inside her. She felt the flames of freedom burning fiercer with each new peak, each new release. Higher and higher she soared to the sound of a magic flute, arching against the stunning pleasure rushing through her, before collapsing onto Mark's damp, heaving chest. He closed his arms tightly around her, holding her as if he never wanted to let her go.

They didn't talk for a long time. They were too exhausted, too fulfilled. The nearby fire crackled and hissed as they lingered, keeping their bodies warm.

Lazily, Mark's hand moved up and down her back in long firm strokes, soothing the shudders still running through her. Her head was cradled in the crook of his neck, soft puffs of air flowing over his heated skin. "Cold?" he asked gently.

Jenny shook her head. So much had happened today, she thought. She couldn't quite grasp it all. She had stopped running and hiding. She had stood up to DiNigro. And tonight she had discovered her sensuality. She smiled slowly, secretly. He didn't have to tell her that she'd been woman enough for him. She'd felt him shudder beneath her. She had heard him groan. She had seen the effect she'd had on him. God, it felt good.

Mark felt her small movement and turned to look at her. "What are you smiling about?"

Jenny raised her head and looked at him. "I've never been on top before."

His lips curved. "Like it?"

She slanted him a slow wicked grin. "No wonder men prefer the position. It gives them a sense of power and control." Slowly, she trailed a finger over his mouth and chin, trying to find words that would express the feelings churning inside her. Too much emotion, she thought, and said cautiously, "You have the most amazing effect on me."

Mark caught her finger between his teeth and nipped it sharply. It amazed him to feel strength flow back into him. Perhaps it was the way she looked at him—still a little dazed and quite pleased with herself. "So do you," he muttered, his hands cupping her buttocks and pressing her against him.

At the movement her eyes widened. Then she shook her head. "Will you listen to what I have to say? I'm not finished."

With a sigh of resignation Mark folded his hands behind his neck, bracing himself for another thank you. "Go ahead."

"I've never felt like this before," Jenny said softly, "beautiful and wanted."

Slowly, tenderly, Mark cupped her face and brought her mouth to his. "You are beautiful and wanted," he said. And loved. But those words he didn't say, because he knew she wasn't ready to hear them.

Early morning sunlight was flooding the living room when Jenny opened her eyes. Blinking, she followed the light dancing over empty wineglasses, and over the remains of the midnight snack she'd shared with Mark. For a moment her fingers itched to clean up the mess, the soiled plates and used paper napkins. Then, instead, she snuggled deeper into the pile of blankets. The arm around her waist tightened reflexively, pulling her closer against Mark's big warm body.

They had made love three more times, and each time had been different and beautiful. The last time, just before dawn, had been slow, languid and very tender. Then they had fallen asleep.

Cautiously, so she wouldn't wake him, Jenny turned her head to study Mark. With his tousled hair and the blue-black bristles covering his jaw, he looked like a pirate. She'd never realized before just how long and thick his lashes were. The scar on his forehead was healing nicely, she decided, her finger itching to trace it.

In one incredibly beautiful night Mark had shown her an intimacy between man and woman that was all about giving as well as taking, with a sharing of weakness and strength, of comfort and tenderness. She felt a closeness to him that was unlike anything she had known before.

For the first time in years, she had slept deeply and dreamlessly. For the first time since her parents had died, she was at peace. And she wanted to wake up next to him every morning, and face the day without fear. She wanted to believe in a future for them.

But as long as Burke was out there she didn't dare to believe.

Although she made absolutely no sound, his eyelashes suddenly lifted and he looked at her with clear, light gray eyes. Jenny realized with a start that he'd been awake for some time.

"I refuse to tackle ghosts so early in the morning," he growled, his voice still rough with sleep. Rolling onto his side he raised himself on one elbow, tangling his fingers in her hair. Her eyes were large and dreamy and the hint of anxiety disappeared at his words. The smile she gave him was enough to tempt him all over again. With a groan, he lowered his head and kissed her slowly, softly, seducing her. He could feel her soften, open, her hands reaching for him.

"The only problem I'll consider discussing now is a bed," he said lightly, but inside he was tense. Buying a bed would mean a commitment on her part, an acceptance that this hadn't been a one-night stand. He grimaced. He'd always thought of himself as a patient man, but she was teaching him otherwise. He hadn't known that he would need to hear her say that she loved him. Yet he did. More than anything he wanted her to say the words.

For a moment Jenny stilled beneath him, her hands gripping him hard, hesitating whether to pull him close or to push him away. She could tell herself a thousand times that needing and wanting him so much was selfish and unfair, but he had shown her a glimpse of heaven and she simply wasn't strong enough to send him away. Her arms tightened around his neck and she kissed him fiercely. "We'll need to buy a mattress, but I already have a frame, as well as enough furniture to fill this house."

At his puzzled look she grinned. "I even have a fur rug, if I remember correctly, and if the moths haven't gotten into it by now. When I sold the house, I couldn't bear to part with all my parents' belongings. Everything's been in storage since then."

Mark stared at her quietly, too moved to speak. He had wanted some kind of sign that she did care for him, that she wanted him in her life, but he hadn't been prepared for this. She trusted him enough to get her treasures out of storage. Maybe they weren't the words he wanted to hear, but it was more than he'd expected. "The moment I get back from headquarters, we'll drive over there."

Jenny saw the gleam in his eyes and she started to grin— then one corner of her mouth slipped. She rolled to her side and slipped from the covers. Reaching for the robe neatly folded over the end of the couch, she pulled it on. "We need to talk," she said.

"All right." He didn't move, but his eyes narrowed warily on her lopsided smile.

Jenny folded her hands in her lap to keep them from twisting. "I don't want you to read too much into this," she warned quietly. "It seems silly to buy a bed, when I have a storage room full of stuff."

His eyes never left her face. "I understand."

"I've lost people before," she said, looking down at her hands. "When Granny died, I could accept it, because she had been sick for a long time. It hurt, but I'd had months to prepare myself for the pain and loss. It's the other kind, the unexpected, needless kind of loss that hurts and keeps hurting.... When my parents died, I lost everything. It's taken me twelve years to find the courage to want to look at those memories. For the first time since their deaths I'm starting to believe in a second chance. You make me want to believe in a future, that I can have safety, and love. But I'm scared, Mark. Scared that I'll never be rid of Burke. Scared to love and lose again."

"Jenny—" Mark started. He wanted to pull her into his arms and make love to her, make her forget every hurt she'd suffered, every bit of pain.

Jenny shook her head. "No, please hear me out. I would never ask you to give up your job. It's not only that it's what you do for a living, it's what you are. I don't want to change you." She paused and a brief grin flashed across her face. "Except, maybe, take you down a notch or two occasionally."

She sighed. "What I really want to say is, I'm not ready to make a commitment. Maybe I'll never have the courage to risk that kind of pain again. All I know is that I couldn't bear it if anything happened to you. I wouldn't be able to bear losing you."

Mark had heard enough. He uncoiled in one smooth movement and lifted her, carrying her back to the pile of blankets, almost tearing the robe as he pulled it over her head. Then he lowered her on her back. Until now he'd treated her with gentleness and tenderness, letting her set the pace, pushing back his own needs, lest he frighten her. He'd wanted her to become confident in her own power first, before he showed her what she meant to him. Now time was running out and he might never have another chance.

He bent his head and blazed a trail of kisses on her face and down her neck, caressing her breasts with a fierce tenderness that made her groan and arch beneath him. He stroked her smooth, white skin from neck to toes and back up again, slowly stoking the flame that was beginning to glow in her eyes.

Jenny moved beneath him, slowly at first, hesitating, uncertain. This was different from their lovemaking last night. There was still gentleness and tenderness, but there was also a fierceness he hadn't shown before. For a moment the strength of his feelings made her want to draw back. Not because they frightened her, but because she was afraid that she would never be able to love him as he deserved to be loved. Only he wouldn't allow her to retreat, seducing her with the firm touch of his hands, arousing her with the heat of his mouth, torturing her with the pressure of his hard body until her arms closed tightly around him and her lips searched wildly for his.

Her feelings broke free, a strong, wild need to match his generosity, his belief in her. There was no room for nagging doubts. There was no room for fears. The fire burning inside her was so strong it melted the ice and consumed her fears.

He entered her slowly, with his eyes on hers. He filled her vision and filled her body until she saw only him, felt only him. Life began to pulse inside her. She rose to meet him, strength flowing into her with each thrust, urging him deeper, holding on to him as if she never wanted to let him go.

This, then, was love, she thought, as she came apart in his arms. A fire so strong it consumed mistakes and failures, cleansing her of the past. A fire so strong it glowed like a bright beacon of hope in the darkness, showing her the way to a bright future. *Home*. He had become home to her, she thought, clasping him tightly. He had become her roots. Her anchor. Her strength.

And her vulnerability.

Two hours later Mark sat at one of the computer terminals in the squad room, watching the screen come to life. Around him, men came and went, none of them paying attention to him. The detectives in his squad were used to seeing him come here on his days off. No one commented on his arrival, especially with the Brandon case still bogged down. Jay had raised an eyebrow when he'd strolled in fifteen minutes ago, and still occasionally sent him a puzzled frown, but he hadn't said anything.

Ignoring him, Mark typed in Jennifer Teresa McKenzie, then pressed the search command. Waiting as the computer flicked through the files, he let his eyes run over the office with its small, narrow windows and crowded desks. He could feel the hum of excitement as Roper suddenly looked up from the statement in front of him and shot to his feet, whistling. "Hey, Grayson, I think I've found something here. Now Simms and Rawlings were with Brandon..."

Mark grinned at the eagerness on Roper's lean young face. Searching for the truth, putting together a solid case that would hold up in court, was often tedious work. Sometimes it took years to find enough evidence to nail a suspect, but, when they finally broke a case, the satisfaction was great. It was no replacement for a boy's warm welcome, though, or seeing Jenny's eyes light up at the sight of him. He needed that, too. He wanted it all, job and family. But if it came to a choice, he decided, his eyes returning to the screen, he would choose the warmth.

There was no warrant for any Jennifer McKenzie.

Puzzled, he punched in Jennifer Williams next. Jenny had sounded so certain that her ex had filed charges against her, that he hadn't asked if it was just her suspicion, or fact. Minutes later his frown deepened. He tried one last time and punched in Wilson. Again a blank. "Ghosts," he muttered, frustrated. He was getting tired of them. Ghosts didn't make annoying calls. Ghosts didn't steal mailboxes.

Just what game was Burke Williams playing?

Then Mark played a hunch, and began to search another list, vacated warrants. And there it was. Jennifer Williams, wanted for violation of child custody order. Curious. Why had the warrant been canceled?

Mark logged off the terminal and walked back to his desk. Part of him was relieved that there were no outstanding warrants, because it would ease the pressure on Jenny and on their relationship. But another part of him felt uneasy. Reaching for the phone, he asked the switchboard to connect him with the Sheriff's department in Dark Water, Oklahoma.

If there was one place where he could get the information he needed, it was the place where the warrant had been issued. As the phone rang, he wished that Sheriff Reed would answer it. He wasn't nearly as forgiving or understanding as Jenny. But the young deputy who answered suited his needs even better. He was young, impressionable and eager to help. "I always wanted to work in a big city department," he said. "Maybe join a vice squad. Nothing exciting ever happens here," he complained. "I'm sorry I can't help you," he added, regret in his voice. "You can tell the cousin who's looking for her that we tried to locate Ms. McKenzie and her son for years. Mr. Williams really misses the kid and he's worried sick about him. From what I've heard, his ex was always a little strange."

"Strange?" Mark interrupted, his face hard.

"Well, you know. Frightened and seeing things. Mr. Williams finally decided to drop the charges against her two months ago, because he was concerned that she might harm her son and herself. If you do locate her, he'd appreciate it if you'd notify us.''

Over my dead body, Mark thought grimly. "Sure, I'll let you know," he said. He put down the receiver with studied care. For a moment he sat quietly, staring at the phone with hard, cold eyes. He was only now realizing what Jenny had been up against. Then another chilling thought occurred to him. There was only one reason why Burke Williams could have dropped all charges. He had found her and didn't need, or want, help from the law anymore. He didn't want a recent connection, on record, to his ex-wife. So that if she disappeared, no suspicion would fall on him.

What Burke Williams was planning was cold-blooded murder.

With sudden urgency, he dialed Jenny's number. The phone rang once, before the answering machine kicked on. He waited impatiently, hoping she would pick up the phone, knowing she wouldn't. Then he left her a terse message. "Jenny, I'm leaving headquarters now. Don't leave the house before I get there.''

# Chapter 12

When Jenny returned home after taking Mike and Jamie to Sunday school, the light on her message unit was blinking again. Fear leaped into her throat at the sight of it, shattering the happiness and peace that had been with her since Mark had left. Not even the thought of the warrant had been able to dim her mood, she thought, raking a hand through her hair. She was so tired of running and hiding that she'd felt more relieved than frightened that the truth was finally out. She wanted control of her life, and she wanted to live without fear.

She wanted to spend the next fifty or sixty years in this house with Mark, surrounded by their children and grandchildren. Surrounded by laughter, and contentment. And love.

But the red blinking light made her wonder if she would ever be free of Burke.

Perhaps one never stopped paying for past mistakes, she thought, her sneakers dragging on the kitchen floor as she made for the coffeepot. Her stomach churning, she only half filled the coffee mug, topping it with milk. On the other hand, if she married Mark, perhaps Burke would finally accept that both she and Jamie were beyond his reach.

In a sudden burst of anger, she erased the message without listening to it.

She wanted to marry Mark for only one reason, because she couldn't live without him. Loving like that was the greatest miracle she had ever known. And the greatest danger, too, she thought soberly. Because there would be no real safety for her if she married Mark. Every day she would have to face the fact that one night he might not come home. The fifty and sixty years she wanted might come to an end after only a few months. She didn't know if she could live with the uncertainty.

Worse yet, if she wasn't strong enough to see him off with a smile and a kiss every morning, if she failed him, she would destroy both their lives.

But Mark had already gotten so close to her that she didn't know if she could pull back. She didn't even know if she wanted to pull back, or, for that matter, if pulling back still made any sense. And the time was fast approaching when she must make a decision, for her own sake as well as his.

But how could she make a decision until she'd met with Ms. Stein? She needed to know that Burke was confined to her old life before she could even contemplate starting a new one. Uneasily, she sipped her coffee. Mark seemed so confident that this time she would win the custody battle, and he seemed to have no doubts that Jamie was strong enough to face his father in court. His confidence was rubbing off on her. She wanted to believe that this time the system wouldn't let her down. She wanted to believe that Jamie wouldn't buckle under the pressure and refuse to testify. She wanted to believe so badly that she was staking everything on it. The gamble frightened her.

Restlessly, she reached into a drawer for the telephone book. The system seemed to be working for Chris, she pointed out sternly, searching for the number of the hospital he was in. The boy had suffered multiple cuts and bruises, but the only reason he'd stayed at the hospital overnight was because the police had been unable to contact his grandparents yesterday. This morning he was supposed to be released into their custody. Physically he would heal soon enough; it was the emotional scars Jenny worried about.

Having temporarily memorized the number, she was walking to the phone when Mush started to growl. Jenny's stomach suddenly lurched, apprehension welling up. Mark had come back early, she thought, anxiously. It couldn't have been easy for him to find her name on the wanted list. Slowly, carefully, she put the mug on the counter and walked into the foyer. "Hush, Mush," she said to him. The dog, who stood on his hind legs, his front paws on the glass of the storm door, was looking outside. "I thought you recognized the sound of his car by—"

A boom suddenly rent the air.

The shock wave rumbled through the house, ringing the windows like crystal bells, shaking the floor violently. Dazed, Jenny threw out her hand to steady herself on the table in the foyer, watching bemusedly as the pottery crock with Jamie's paper flowers suddenly began a rapid slide on the polished surface. Lunging for it, to stop it before it reached the edge, Jenny was dismayed to see it shatter on the floor before she could reach it.

At that precise moment, Mush flung himself at the storm door in a frenzy, his big paws clawing at the glass. The simple latch wouldn't hold much longer under the onslaught of eighty pounds of fury, Jenny realized and raced to the door.

Fumbling, she tried to bolt it with one hand, while seeking a firm grip on Mush's collar with the other. Her hand was trembling so badly, she couldn't engage the bolt and the lock suddenly gave way. As the door burst open, Jenny gripped the choke collar tightly. Mush dragged her outside, pulling her across the porch.

Acrid smoke immediately filled her nostrils, and obscured her vision. Mush tried to charge down the steps, but Jenny grabbed the railing with her free hand, jerking him back. "Calm down," she ordered hoarsely, "I don't want you to get hurt. What if Burke's out there, waiting." For a moment she seemed to succeed. Mush was still straining against her hold, still barking, but he didn't jerk nearly as hard. Bit by bit, he seemed to relax.

Expelling a breath of relief, Jenny chanced a glance at the place where her mailbox should have been. It was gone, she realized as the smoke began to lift. All that was left were pieces of newspaper fluttering in the air. Burke had struck again, she thought, swallowing the lump in her throat. And in broad daylight this time. Perhaps because he hadn't been able to pull out the post last night. With an anxious look around, she started to drag Mush back inside, but he refused to budge.

Suddenly an engine roared to life nearby and tires screeched. Seconds later a silver sports car shot past Jenny's house. Mush flung himself down the steps in a sudden strong leap, almost pulling Jenny's arm out of its socket, causing her to lose her grip on the collar. He was off like a shot, streaking across the lawn, chasing after the silver Porsche. "Mush," Jenny screamed, "Mush, come back." But the German shepherd didn't stop. Moments later he had disappeared from her sight.

With a sob, Jenny leaped down the steps, fear lending her speed. She raced across the lawn, dodging rhododendrons, brushing past a spruce, cutting diagonally across her property. A sudden vision of Biddie's small, lifeless body flashed before her eyes. The dog had always hated Burke, she thought, as she sprinted down the road. Blood drummed in her ears and her breath started to come out in gasps as she raced down the road, making for the curve. With luck Burke would be long gone and Mush would have given up the chase.

The scene that met her eyes when she rounded the bend chilled her blood.

The Porsche had not driven off, but had slowed down to a crawl halfway down the hill. Mush was rapidly closing the distance, his powerful body stretched low to the ground.

''Mush,'' Jenny tried to yell, but her voice came out in a gasp. She dragged more air into her lungs and raced down the hill after the dog. Perspiration started to drip into her eyes and a stitch in her side sliced through her with each breath.

Ahead, the car screeched to a sudden stop, skidding on the dirt shoulder and spinning around. For a second it stood motionless, a menacing monster, engine revving, its dark windshield gleaming in the morning sun. Then it leaped forward, charging back up the hill, making straight for the German shepherd less than thirty feet away.

A high-pitched warning ripped from Jenny's throat. Mush slowed at the sound and made for the shoulder, trying to fling himself out of the way of the oncoming car. He almost made it to safety, but at the last moment the driver turned the wheels sharply, hitting the dog, flinging his big, lean body into the air. A sob wrenched from Jenny's throat as she watched the animal fall, hitting the ground, barely missing a big oak tree at the side of the road. Jenny didn't think, didn't stop. She kept running toward the place where the big dog lay so silent and still.

The car changed course again, leaped forward, now making straight for Jenny.

With her last ounce of strength, Jenny jumped for the shoulder of the road, wrenching her ankle as her feet hit uneven ground. The car shot past her, so close that she felt the snap of its cold draft and its hot, fuming exhaust. The monster, squealing in frustration and fury, slowed down once again, spinning around. With a roar it charged her.

Jenny felt pain shooting up her leg. Sobbing and calling Mush's name, she went on. If she could reach him in time and pull him behind the oak tree he would be safe. Her breath came in gasps as she skipped, hobbled and stumbled. Four more feet to go. She didn't dare look back, and kept her eyes fixed on the dog. When she saw his body twitch, saw him raise his head and try to get to his feet, a weak growl forming in his throat, she wanted to shout in relief. Swiftly, she grabbed him by his front legs and dragged him behind the oak just as the wheels crunched on the dirt a few feet behind her.

The car skidded to a stop.

Jenny crouched behind the tree, hovering over Mush's bloodied body protectively, wildly searching the ground for something to defend them with. Her eyes settled on a fist-size rock, and her fingers closed around it. Swinging around, she watched the car door slowly open. Her fingers tightened around the rock. Mush raised his head, snarling. He tried to struggle to his feet, then sank down again with a whimper.

Her heart beat high in her throat as she slanted another glance at the partly opened door of the Porsche. Why was Burke hesitating? Frantically, she looked up and down the road—and spotted a movement farther down the hill. Drawing a sharp breath, Jenny prayed that the car wasn't making for one of the properties at the bottom of the hill.

But Burke, having heard something, apparently wasn't taking any chances. He slammed the door and floored the gas. The Porsche shot forward and roared away down the hill, its gray metallic color soon blending with that of the road.

Jenny watched him pass the oncoming car. Relief flooded through her as she recognized Mark's black Blazer. Painfully getting to her feet, she hobbled into the road, waving, just as the Porsche disappeared around a distant curve.

Recognizing Jenny, Mark increased the car's speed, the Blazer surging forward. He should have sent a squad car to warn her, he thought grimly, coming to a skidding stop a few feet away from her. Shifting into park, he flung himself out of the car, crossing the gap between them with two long strides. Then he was checking her over, his mouth tightening when he spotted blood on her blue jeans. "Are you hurt?"

"No. I'm fine." Jenny flung herself into his open arms and clung to him for one long moment, absorbing some of his strength. Then she stepped back and hobbled back to the tree. "It's Mush," she said hoarsely, kneeling down at the German shepherd's side. "Burke tried to run him down with his car. He blew up the mailbox and Mush chased after him. That Porsche you just passed was him. I didn't see him, but I don't have any other enemies."

Mark swore silently. He'd been so damn close. "Do you remember the license plate number?"

Frowning, Jenny shook her head. "I don't recall any numbers at all. It was a late model silver-gray Porsche 944, with dark glazed glass. He had no plate in the front, that much I'm sure of. I don't know about the rear."

Mark surged to his feet. He strode to his car and picked up the receiver to his CB, giving the dispatcher what little information he had. Then he turned back to Jenny and said quietly, "I need a physical description of Williams."

This time Jenny didn't hesitate. Until now she hadn't known just how unbalanced Burke had become. He would have run her down, just like the dog. If Mark hadn't ar-

rived he would have killed her, she realized with chilling
certainty. "He's 39 years old, slender, six feet tall, silver-
green eyes, light brown hair. Speaks with a southern ac-
cent." Then she pushed back her terror and gently ran her
hands over Mush's blood-soaked fur, trying to determine
the extent of his injuries. There was a big gash on his left
hip, where the car had hit him. Blood welled from it slug-
gishly. The bone itself seemed to be broken or out of place,
and his breathing was very shallow. "We need to get him to
the hospital before he goes into shock," Jenny said as Mark
signed off the CB. "Do you have a blanket or a towel in
your car?" When he shook his head, she gave him swift in-
structions of where to find everything back at the house,
including her purse and keys.

Five minutes later Mark cautiously lifted the old warrior
and carried him to his car, gently laying him down on the
blanket in the back seat. "How's your ankle?" he asked
with concern as Jenny limped to the car behind him.

"It's nothing. I'm fine," she insisted. Climbing into the
back seat, she cradled Mush's head in her lap, gently pressing a towel against the gash while wrapping the blanket
around his shivering body.

Mark waited until she was settled and then he cupped her
face and wiped the tear stains with his thumb. Gently he
kissed her, before closing the door.

"What did you find in the computer?" Jenny asked after Mark had slid behind the wheel.

Shifting into drive, Mark hesitated briefly. She'd had
enough shocks for one day. Then he realized grimly that after this little incident the news wouldn't be much of a shock
to her anymore. "Williams dropped the charges two months
ago."

The waiting room at the Animal Emergency Hospital was
deserted. The smell of antiseptic hung in the air and, from

somewhere in the back, patients occasionally barked or meowed. Jenny shifted anxiously in the gray molded plastic chair.

The receptionist had vanished into the surgery room at the end of the hall to assist the vet. Ten minutes ago Mark had left to pick up Jamie from Sunday school. The Shermans had offered their help, but after this morning's attack, Jenny couldn't risk letting Jamie out of her sight.

With a sigh, she leaned forward and lifted the ice pack on the ankle she was keeping elevated, probing the tender flesh. She was relieved to find the swelling was going down. She certainly didn't need a sprained ankle on top of all her other problems, she thought, replacing the pack.

She reached for the cup of coffee Mark had bought at the convenience store next door before he'd left. Her hands were still trembling slightly as she raised it cautiously to her lips. She grimaced at the sweet taste of it.

In the last ten days her quiet, secluded life had turned into her worst nightmare, and it was suddenly all too much to absorb. Having her mailbox blown up in bright daylight. Watching Mush being run down and barely escaping death herself. The knowledge that Burke must have known for months where they lived was frightening because by now he probably knew every part of her daily routine. The mere thought that he had watched them for weeks made her skin crawl. And the cold-blooded way in which he was stalking her was terrifying. It made her realize all the more forcefully that she wasn't dealing with a rational man any longer.

Sometime during the last three years he had slipped over the edge of sanity.

Burke had never been able to deal with failures. He had always blamed someone else, mostly her, Jenny thought, cradling the cup, savoring its warmth. She guessed that she had eluded him for too long. And now he had decided on the ultimate punishment: death.

Suddenly the door at the back of the hall opened. Jenny sat up a little straighter and braced her shoulders, searching the round, freckled face of the red-haired receptionist anxiously. "Is Mush all right?"

Jane Peters sat down at her desk and smiled at Jenny over the counter reassuringly. "He will be, given time and care. Apart from the gash, he has two broken ribs and his left hip is dislocated. Dr. Whitman will be out directly to discuss the treatment with you. In the meantime, I need some information," she said, flicking on the computer screen. "Your name?"

"Jennifer McKenzie," Jenny said just as the door opened. Jamie burst into the room, followed by Mark.

Her son must have caught her words, because he stopped abruptly and looked at her with round, anxious eyes. "Mom?"

With a small smile Jenny held out her hand, her arms closing around him tightly as she repeated her name. She wasn't a fugitive anymore, she thought, her gaze connecting with Mark's. Burke didn't realize the mistake he had made. By dropping the charges against her, he had set her free. The system was no longer her enemy. This time the police would protect her and her son.

But who would protect Mark? she thought with sudden fear. Burke's fury would now be directed at him, as well.

It was then that she realized that the threats hadn't started until the night she'd gone out to dinner with Mark. That had been the night her mailbox was stolen, and when she'd received her first anonymous call. During the week she hadn't seen Mark the calls had continued, but her mailbox had remained in place.

Until last night.

Last night Mark's car had been parked outside her house. The sight of it must have pushed Burke over the edge. Jenny swallowed the bile in her throat. She hadn't realized just how closely Burke had been watching her. She couldn't live like this for the rest of her life.

"I don't want to be James Williams," Jamie shouted, tears swimming in his eyes. He stood in the kitchen, his body shaking, his hands balled into fists. "I don't want Burke to be my father again. He's a monster." Sobbing, he spun around and raced from the room, running up the stairs. Seconds later the door to his room slammed so hard that the lamp in the kitchen vibrated.

Jenny closed her eyes wearily and leaned her head against the back of the chair, wishing for just a few moments of peace. They had arrived home less than ten minutes ago, Jamie hadn't wanted to leave the dog behind and it had taken a great deal of patience to convince him that Mush would be better off at the hospital. Then Jamie had taken one look at the charred remains of his mailbox and had burst into tears.

Opening her eyes, Jenny looked at Mark, who was sitting next to her. "I never thought of that before. And it should have occurred to me, because I felt the same. The moment I got the divorce, I went back to my maiden name." Bracing her hands on the table she started to push herself to her feet. Her ankle was still tender, but it wasn't throbbing anymore.

Mark gently pushed her back into the chair. "Give him a few minutes to calm down," he said quietly, his hand resting on her shoulder. "He's been upset since I told him about Mush. He kept saying that he didn't want him to die like Biddie. Who's Biddie?"

Jenny swallowed, then tilted her head sideways, pressing her cold cheek against his warm hand. "Biddie was Jamie's grandmother's white toy poodle. He died the day Jamie fell down the steps. Someone had locked Biddie into the metal shed and he died of heatstroke. I always suspected that

Burke did it. Biddie always went for his legs. I guess Jamie finally made the connections between the mailboxes, the phone calls, Biddie and Mush. The worst of it is, legally, I can't change his name without Burke's consent."

Mark's eyes hardened and there was a grim slant to his mouth when he said, "Williams has gone over the edge. He's not rational anymore. He made a mistake today, though, and he's going to make more."

"I realize that. Still, when I think that he must have been watching us for months, it makes me sick." Jenny reached for Mark's hand, holding on to it. "What scares me is that he's not just some stranger stalking me, but someone who knows how I think and feel. I know he's planning to kill me, but I also know that first he's going to punish me by destroying the things I value most. And it's easy for him, because he knows my weaknesses."

"Do you have any?"

Jenny smiled briefly, as he'd expected her to, but she wouldn't allow him to sidetrack her. "He destroyed the mailbox because he knew it was important to me. He tried to run down Mush. And he knows that you're important to me." Her hand gripped his so hard, that her nails were biting into his skin; Mark ignored the pain. "Until he's caught, I don't want you to come around anymore."

Mark squeezed her shoulder reassuringly. "He's not going to hurt any of us. Now before you go talk to Jamie, I want you to give me information about Burke's place of business, his address, anything you can think of. Oh, and tell Jamie to change into jeans. We have another mailbox to put up."

Jenny's eyes narrowed angrily. "You're not listening to me."

But he was, and what he heard made him want to push just a little more. Right now she was very close to admitting just how she felt about him. He knew that if he took her in his arms and kissed her, he would get the words out of her. But then again, he had always known that the deeper she felt for him the greater her fear for him would be. However, he decided not to force the issue—she didn't need any more stress at the moment. Cupping her chin, he kissed the protest from her lips. "For now you're official police business, and I'm staying. Once he's caught, you can tell me to get lost."

"Maybe I will," Jenny threatened, then capitulated, "Burke works for Global Airlines..."

When Jenny went into Jamie's room a few minutes later, he had already changed into a pair of black jeans and a red sweatshirt. He was calmer, but anger and fear still lurked in his eyes. For a moment Jenny stopped in the doorway, looking at the jacket tossed across the desk. The rest of his clothes were scattered over the floor and the bed. "Feel better now?" she asked, watching him sit down on the bed to pull on his high tops.

Jamie tightened the laces, tied them loosely, then looked up at her. "Can I keep the name Wilson?" he asked.

Jenny's heart wrenched at the flat sound of his voice. Sitting down on the bed beside him, she put an arm around his shoulders. "A name's not really so important," she said gently. "Did you feel different every time we changed names?"

Jamie shook his head. "But Grandma always said that I looked like Burke when he was little. I don't want to be like him!"

Jenny felt a twinge of guilt at his words and her voice was fierce when she said, "You're not anything like him! I've always thought that you looked just like Grandpa Mc-Kenzie."

Hope flared in Jamie's eyes and his mouth tilted slightly at her words. "You think so?"

"I know so!" Jenny said firmly, squeezing his shoulder reassuringly.

Then his mouth drooped again and he shook his head. "You're just saying that to make me feel better. Grandma showed me pictures and I did look like Burke—a little," he modified after a brief hesitation.

Jenny breathed a small sigh of relief. Slowly, carefully, she said, "I'm not saying that you didn't inherit any looks from Burke. But looks alone aren't important, Jamie. Burke is a very sick man, sweetheart. You're good inside. You could never hurt anyone."

Jamie bit his trembling lip. "I hurt Chris," he said, his voice thin.

Dear God, Jenny thought, her heart aching for her son. "There's a difference," she said gently but firmly. "You had a fight, but you didn't enjoy hurting Chris. Burke does. He likes to hurt people, people that are smaller than him. It makes him feel big and strong. It's a sickness." She hugged him tightly. "You are *nothing* like him. And you do look like my father."

Jamie frowned. "I wish you had a picture of him."

It was a fifty-minute drive to the storage facility and by five it would be almost dark. Jenny hesitated, slanting a quick look at her watch. It was almost noon already and they still had to buy and put up a mailbox. Also, the storage facility lay in an industrial complex and the area was deserted on Sundays. What if Burke followed them there? she wondered uneasily. Still, if they didn't do it today, she would have to wait until the following weekend and Jamie needed what was there now. "I have pictures," she said, "loads of them. Would you like to take a ride and get them?"

Jamie's face brightened eagerly at the thought. "Could we? And can we get your music box, too? The one Grandpa McKenzie gave to you?"

Jenny expelled a small sigh of relief. "If we can find it," she cautioned. "There are a lot of boxes to go through."

Before Jenny went downstairs, she swiftly changed into a clean pair of jeans and a bulky blue cotton sweater. Evenings were getting chilly, she thought as she went downstairs. Mark was sitting at the dinette table, talking on the phone, the cord stretched tightly across the room. For a moment their eyes met in silent communication. Jamie was fine, she signaled.

Making sandwiches that they could eat on the way, Jenny half listened to Mark's conversation. Apparently, he was talking to his partner, Jay, giving him the information he'd written down earlier, discussing contacting the Denver PD. "Checking with Global Airlines headquarters will have to wait until tomorrow, but see if you can get the passenger lists from today's flights...."

Cutting thick slices of sourdough bread, Jenny grimaced. Police dramas on TV always neglected to show the tedious side of investigations, the long hours spent checking and sorting through information. She heaped ham, roast beef and salami on the slices, adding lettuce, tomatoes and cheese.

Wrapping the sandwiches in plastic, she looked again at Mark. For a moment she watched him lean forward, watched the denim shirt stretch over his broad shoulders. Need welled, a desire so strong, it almost propelled her across the space separating them. If she'd felt more confident, she would have gone over, wrapped her arms around him and nuzzled his neck, the way the young Jenny might have done before she'd married Burke.

Instead, her fingers curled around the edge of the counter. She was older now and much more cautious. Perhaps too cautious, she thought, returning the meat to the refrigerator and the bread to the basket on top of it. But when she finally told Mark that she loved him, she wanted to be free of the past and she wanted to say the words without doubts. He deserved that much from her.

Listening to his voice, a feeling of security stole over her. For so long she'd had no one to lean on. She was beginning to depend on him, she realized, but the thought held no threat. She knew that she was strong enough to stand on her own two feet and face storms alone. Yet it felt good to know that he was just across the room, and that he cared. And the closeness they'd shared last night had been beautiful.

But was it worth the risk of opening herself up to pain again? With a sigh, she slid the sandwiches into a bag. She would find out soon enough, she thought, suddenly dreading the trip, dreading the pain when she opened the door to the past.

They made two stops before they were ready to go. First Mark made a brief stop at his house. Waiting in the car for him, Jenny looked around curiously. The leaves had been raked and a pine tree recently braced, she noticed. Still, the house looked deserted. When Mark returned to the car a few minutes later, he wore a gray sweatshirt, and his black leather jacket.

And a gun.

Jenny caught a glimpse of it as he slid behind the wheel. For a moment their eyes met and she whispered, "Maybe we should postpone the trip until it's safer."

Mark looked over his shoulder, watching Jamie buckle himself in.

The boy raised his head, reached for the bag of cookies Jenny had packed for him and grinned. "I'm ready," he announced.

Glancing back at Jenny, Mark shook his head. Jamie needed this now. Mark started the engine.

Their second stop was the hardware store.

"The post is a bit charred on top, but doesn't need replacing," Mark said as they walked inside. "Jamie and I can put it up when we get back. It won't take long."

This time there was no agonizing over the choices. Mark went straight for the red barn. Jenny wanted to protest. Not because she didn't want it; she did. What she didn't want was the fierce disappointment she knew she'd experience if this bold red barn was destroyed, too.

"It's only a piece of plastic," Mark said gently, holding the box out to her once he'd paid for it. "If it disappears, we'll just buy another one."

It was more than a piece of plastic and they both knew it. It was a badge of courage and a token of his love. Jenny clutched the box tightly, her eyes filling with tears. "It's a deal."

# Chapter 13

On the long drive toward the city Jenny kept the box at her feet. She wanted it there to elevate her ankle should it start to swell again, she told Mark and Jamie. Jamie believed her fib, but one look into Mark's gray eyes and Jenny realized that she hadn't deceived him. He knew that she was dreading the pain almost as much as she feared Burke.

They didn't talk much on the trip. Mark kept the police channel open. Jamie was fascinated and asked question after question, which Mark answered patiently. Jenny was content to listen, watching the rearview mirror for any sign of the Porsche. Mark did the same, and for the first time, Jenny realized that the thought of the gun in his belt was reassuring.

Halfway there, Jenny opened the bag of sandwiches, handing them out to Jamie and Mark. She was beginning to relax a little. So far, there had been no sign of the Porsche. Maybe, just maybe, after this morning's incident, Burke had decided to hole up somewhere.

To distract herself, she glanced at the landscape flying by. Because eastern Long Island depended on groundwater for its drinking supply, there were no high-rise apartment buildings, and the single homes were spaced far apart and surrounded by trees.

When they reached the exit to her former hometown, Jenny sat up straight and her hand curled around her purse. Anxiously, she watched the rearview mirror, expelling the breath she'd been holding. No car had followed them. Then she looked out the window, a sudden curiosity about how much things had changed in her old neighborhood rising within her.

With a small reassuring smile, Mark reached across and covered her twisting fingers. "You've never been back." It was a statement not a question.

Jenny shrugged. "It was too painful. And I didn't want to take a chance of running into old friends."

The two-lane road was dense with traffic and lined with shops. A few miles north, she spotted the beauty shop where she'd always gotten her hair trimmed. It was under new ownership, and so was the boutique where her mother had bought her clothes. "There's the store where your grandpa always bought his fishing gear," she said to Jamie, excitement welling up. "And over there is the pet store where grandpa bought Terry, my first and only dog, a black Scottish terrier." A grin suddenly tugged at her lips. "He was a little devil. He chewed up your grandfather's deck shoes, a fishing pole and one of my feather pillows. God, what a mess that was," she recalled with a grin.

In the back seat, Jamie scooted to her side of the car and pressed his nose to the window. "What happened to him?"

"Your grandmother was allergic to pets and we had to give him to friends. I had an aquarium for the longest time after that." She turned to Mark and found him watching her with a softness that made her heart skip a beat. On impulse, she covered his hand on the steering wheel and squeezed it. "Thank you. I'm going to be all right."

Ten minutes later Mark pulled up at the storage facility. The area was surrounded by a tall fence and guarded by security. As they pulled up at the gate, a young blond guard, with his cap set at a jaunty angle, stepped from the booth. Jenny handed him a small plastic laminated ID, the only one she owned with her real name on it.

He glanced at the small photo in the right-hand corner, then went into the booth to return moments later with a computer key card in his hand. "You haven't been here for awhile," he said. "The unit is straight down this lane. Last one on the right."

"Thanks." Jenny's hand curled around the key, and she perched on the edge of her seat as Mark drove past the long white building.

Five doors down, a young couple was loading up a U-Haul truck, lugging boxes, a tricycle and a baby bed. They stopped and waved at them. Jenny waved back.

The moment Mark parked in front of the tall white garage door, Jenny jumped from the car. "I had the lock changed three years ago," she explained when Mark and Jamie joined her.

For a moment she looked at the door, the card key grasped tightly in her hand. She felt the pain, dulled now by time, but still there. It would never leave completely, but she could live with it, she realized. She felt a sudden eagerness to handle all the familiar things, and to share her childhood memories with Jamie and Mark.

Slowly, she put the card into the slot and turned the handle.

"Here, let me do that," Mark said, covering her hand. Together they pulled the door open and pushed it up.

A wave of musty odor drifted toward them. A thick layer of dust covered everything. On the left, boxes were neatly stacked from floor to ceiling, three rows thick. The rest of the space was filled with furniture, tables, chairs, headboards and tall cabinets, all draped with sheets. The top of a grand piano was covered with odd-shaped cases. Her mother's musical instruments. For a moment Jenny just stood there, staring at everything, recalling the day she'd watched the movers stack the boxes. She'd felt so lost then, so alone. Now the two people she loved best in the world stood next to her. Slowly the last twelve years, and their pain, faded away.

She was startled out of her reverie when Jamie said from right beside her, "Yuck, what a mess." He took a step inside and cautiously raised the sheet closest to him. "A bike," he cried, his voice high with excitement. Before Jenny could stop him, he tore off the sheet, sending a cloud of dust into their faces.

Gasping, Jenny took a hasty step back, bumping into Mark. Sneezing himself, Mark steadied her and drew her with him into the bright afternoon sun. For a moment they stood there coughing and sneezing and trying to wipe the dirt from their faces. Then they looked at each other and grinned. Grins turned to laughter while the dust settled around them.

"Jamie, you—" Jenny gasped, sneezing again. But her son was too busy dragging the bike out of storage to pay any attention to what she'd been about to say.

"Hey, this is neat," he cried, running his dirty hands over the streamlined shape of the yellow ten-speed. "There's even a pump to blow the tires up with. Can I ride it?"

They spent the next few minutes brushing dust off the bike and blowing up the tires, then watched Jamie try it out. "He's always wanted one," Jenny said, rubbing her itchy nose. "But I was afraid he'd stray too far from the house. He's been riding Mike's occasionally."

Mark watched Jamie pedal to the end of the lane and turn around. "Want to take it home with you?"

For a moment Jenny hesitated, tempted, then shook her head. "I'll have it shipped to the house with the rest of the stuff," she said, wiping a smudge off Mark's chin. "You didn't know what you were letting yourself in for," she said lightly.

"Beats Mulligan's," he said, kissing her before drawing her into the storage room.

"Mulligan's?" Jenny asked, frowning.

"That's where cops' wives send all search parties."

Jenny wrinkled her nose. "A bar. I should have known. Is that where you spend your evenings?"

Mark looked at her sharply, then asked slowly, "You have a better suggestion?"

"We'll talk about it tonight," she promised him, squeezing past a chest and a table. A small confident grin spread over her face. She doubted she would ever have to send out a search party for him.

For the next half hour, they shifted furniture and opened boxes, unearthing all manner of objects and memories. Paintings, china and crystal. Christmas decorations. At one point, Jenny held up a foil star she had made in school when she'd been about Jamie's age. Gently, she replaced it, closed the large box it had been in and handed it to Mark. "Did you see a metal trunk?" she asked, watching him restack the box.

"At the back behind the furniture."

Jenny grimaced. "Figures. That's the one with the albums in it."

The trunk was heavy and unwieldy, and it took them a few minutes to drag it outside. Wiping her hands on her scruffy jeans, Jenny watched Jamie ride around the U-Haul truck again. "Stay in sight," she warned him. Turning back to Mark, she said, "All I need to find now is one particular box with a *J* on it."

Mark groaned. "Do you have any idea how many boxes have a *J* on them?"

Jenny chuckled. "I had a lot of stuff. I never threw anything out."

It took them another twenty minutes to locate it. By that time the sun was beginning to set. As Mark carried it outside, the U-Haul truck five doors down started to pull away, its rough engine sounding like a rumble of thunder. Waving briefly, Jenny checked on Jamie, who was riding toward the end of the lane. Then she sat down on the metal trunk, drew the box closer and pulled off the tape.

Cautiously, she took out tissue-wrapped bundles, but didn't open them. It was getting dark and she wanted to be gone before nightfall. Searching quickly, she finally, way at the bottom, found what she'd been looking for—the small music box—its odd shape easily distinguishable.

Slowly she unwrapped it. The tent-like, fluted roof appeared first, its red paint cracked with age and chipped in two places. Four delicately carved black horses with red saddles and bridles became visible next. Gently, she ran a finger over the cream posts decorated with green garlands and tiny flowers, remembering the night her father had given it to her. "Dad brought it back from one of his trips to Germany," she said softly to Mark, who was kneeling beside her. "It was one of my most precious possessions. Jamie used to have a similar one. When it broke, I promised him that some day I would give him mine," she explained, winding it up.

Listening to the tinkling sound of Brahms' Lullaby, she could almost hear her father's booming laugh and her mother's softer voice, their love reaching out to her across the space of time, happy memories easing the pain of loss. Meeting Mark's eyes, she saw the same steady, warm love reflected there, and the last of her doubts vanished. Tenderly she wiped a smudge off his chin and whispered a little unsteadily, "I love you, Mark."

For one long moment Mark forgot to breathe. For one long moment he lost himself in the softness of her big brown eyes. He read acceptance in their depths, acceptance for what he was and what the future might bring. Slowly he let out his breath. "I love you, too," he said hoarsely. Framing her face, he kissed her sweetly, lingering for long seconds while the gloom around them deepened. Then he drew her to her feet and said impatiently, "Let's pack up and go back home."

*Home.* The word had such a happy ring to it. "I found the music box, Jamie," she called out, eager to see his face when she handed it to him.

No one answered her.

Mark turned, his voice sharp and loud when he called out himself. The lane was deserted. There was no sign of the boy. In two large strides he vaulted into the car, Jenny racing to the other side. Clutching the music box in one hand, she scrambled into the seat and closed the door just as the Blazer shot forward.

They raced past the slow moving truck to the guardhouse. One look at the unlit cubicle and the closed gate and Mark turned in the opposite direction, toward the other rows of storage spaces. In the swiftly falling dusk each lane looked gloomier than the last one. All were deserted.

"He must have gone through the gate," Jenny said hoarsely, fear roughening her voice. She sat perched on the edge of her seat, her free hand braced on the dashboard.

The truck had pulled up right next to the booth. As they doubled back and pulled up behind it, the young woman hopped out of the vehicle and called out a message. "The guard's making his rounds," she said. "Lock the gate behind you when you leave."

Jenny couldn't wait for the truck to move past the gate. She jumped out of the car and squeezed between the truck and the booth. When she spotted Jamie about 150 yards down the road, she expelled a breath of relief.

Seeing her, he came racing toward her. "Look, Mom, see how fast I can go."

Jenny bit her lip to hold back her angry words, afraid to startle him and make him fall. The truck began to pull through the gate. The moment it had passed her, she waved at Mark and said, "Jamie's fine. He's out on the road."

Suddenly, a low-slung car shot out of the gloom, barely visible in the fading light. It raced past the truck, cutting Jamie off, then braking so hard it fishtailed on the gravel of the parking lot.

Recognizing the Porsche, Jenny felt fear grip her throat, strangling her. She opened her mouth to shout a warning, but no sound escaped. Through the rising cloud of dust she watched Jamie try to avoid running into the car blocking his way. He skidded sideways, then fell, disappearing from her sight.

*Jamie.* She had to reach Jamie before Burke could pull him into his car. A sob wrenched from her throat as she broke into a run. Suddenly the car leaped forward, charging toward her. Abruptly Jenny stopped, spun around and raced back to the gate, trying to reach Mark and the Blazer, hidden from her view by the booth.

As she reached the white wooden structure, she stepped onto a pebble and felt her ankle give. Pain shot through her and a cry tore from her throat. Stumbling, she fell against the building. A frantic glance over her shoulder showed that the Porsche was less than ten feet away. Facing it, she braced herself against the impact, an anguished cry ripping from her throat.

"Ma-a-rk!"

Mark whirled around. He'd backed the car out of the driveway, parking it behind the booth. Reaching for his gun, he raced toward the gate. As he passed the booth, he heard the roaring sound of a high-powered engine, then the crashing sound of splintering wood. The sturdy structure shook and groaned under the impact.

"Jenny!" Fear shot through him and his hand tightened around his gun. The silence following the crash was eerie. There were no screams, no groans, nothing but the sound of the engine roaring and tires spinning. "Jenny, are you all right?" he shouted, his voice hoarse with dread. "Damn it, answer me." When she didn't respond, he swore viciously.

Reaching the corner of the building he forced himself to slow down, controlling the mind-numbing fear. With his back flattened against the wall, he cautiously glanced around the corner, afraid of what he would see.

At that moment the Porsche backed up, spewing a cloud of dust into Mark's face. Momentarily blinded, he drew back, cursing and wiping the grit from his eyes with his free hand. Then he chanced another look.

A bullet whizzed past his head. Ducking, he swore. "Damn!" His finger tightened on the trigger, hesitating. He didn't dare open fire until he knew where Jenny and Jamie were. Again he looked around the corner, expelling a breath of relief when he spotted Jamie scrambling to his feet at the end of the parking lot and Jenny running toward him, limping badly. But his relief was short-lived. The Porsche was backing up at high speed and heading toward them.

Mark didn't dare hesitate any longer. He had to stop Williams before the bastard could reach Jenny. He fired twice, aiming for the tires barely visible beneath the low broken fiberglass bumper to avoid any chance of hitting the two people he loved. He missed his target. Cursing savagely, he watched the car spin around, its hood now facing

Jenny, who had pushed Jamie behind her, shielding him with her body.

Mark aimed again, then lowered his gun in frustration. Jenny hovered directly in the line of fire and he didn't dare shoot, afraid that a bullet would ricochet off the metal surface. He rounded the corner of the booth, in the growing darkness stumbling over pieces of broken wood, then started running, watching helplessly as the car surged forward.

Jenny stood frozen, unable to move. There was no place to run to, no place to hide, not with her ankle throbbing and Jamie clinging to her waist. The car stopped a few feet away and the headlights came on, trapping her in their beam, blinding her. Fear leaped into her throat. There was something terrifying about the fact that she couldn't see Burke. It made him seem inhuman, indestructible.

And then she heard his voice, that hated, frightening, never-forgotten voice taunting her, "This is it, Jenny. I've caught you at last. I want you and Jamie to get into the car. Don't try to run. I have a gun pointed at your head. One wrong move and I—" Burke caught a swiftly moving shadow to his right and fired, shouting, "Drop your gun or I kill them both."

Mark flung himself to the ground and rolled over as bullets flew over his head. Fear clawed at his gut, but his voice was steady when he shouted back, "I'm a police officer. The game's over, Williams. You haven't got a chance of getting away. Every cop on Long Island is looking for you."

Burke's answer was another volley of bullets.

Behind Jenny, Jamie clutched at her sweater convulsively. "It's him. It's the monster, Mom," he cried, his scream barely audible above the noise surrounding them. "He's going to kill Mark."

"No, he won't," Jenny denied fiercely. "Burke's just a nasty man. Mark is bigger and a much better shot." God, she prayed it was true. Grabbing Jamie's hands, she pried them loose. Limping to the car, she kept her body between him and the Porsche. There was one chance, one slim chance of getting Jamie to safety, but he would have to do it on his own. "Sweetheart, you must do exactly what I tell you. When I say *now,* I want you to run straight past the rear of the car and toward the gate."

The lights just inside the fence suddenly came on, making the night on their side appear even darker. Glancing toward the booth, Jenny saw Mark dash along the fence, a swiftly moving shadow merging with the night. Relief rushed through her at the sight of him. He was all right.

"Get in," Burke suddenly snarled, flinging the passenger door open, its edge hitting Jenny's injured leg. Wincing, she twisted around, drawing Jamie past her and to the rear of the car. "Now!" she shouted, giving him a little shove, flinging herself to the ground at the same time. Frantically crawling to the rear of the car, she watched Jamie race across the lot, praying, hoping that he would make it.

With a curse Burke gave gas—the Porsche leaped forward with such power the door banged shut.

Jumping to her feet, Jenny watched Mark run to meet Jamie, grabbing him and dragging him toward the gate. Then, as fast as her ankle allowed, she ran in the opposite direction.

Mark half-dragged, half-carried Jamie past the booth. Damn it, where was the damned security guard, he wondered as he told Jamie to get into the Blazer. "Stay there. Don't come out," he ordered sharply, before whirling around, just as the Porsche charged past the gate.

This was the chance Mark had been waiting for. He aimed at the rear tires, hearing a satisfying thud. The car swerved and skidded, finally coming to a stop about twenty yards away in the middle of the lot. Moments later the car door flew open and a man rolled out, hiding behind it.

Mark ran out into the open, keeping to the right of the car to stay out of the direct line of fire, adrenaline pumping through his blood. He was finally coming eye to eye with the ghost. And this time he was going to nail the bastard, he swore grimly.

When she heard the shots, Jenny had almost reached the end of the lot. Breathless, blood drumming in her ears, she spun around. When she saw Mark race toward the car, her heart stopped. *No!* she wanted to scream. She bit down hard on her lip, watching with horror as bullets began to fly. Burke was shooting at Mark from behind the cover of the open car door, while Mark was out in the open, exposed and vulnerable. Jenny watched him veer to the right, keeping the car between himself and Burke at all times, even as he tried to get closer to it. Then Mark faltered and a cry was ripped from her throat. "No!"

Mark gasped as he felt the sharp pain. He lunged forward, hitting the ground, crawling the last three yards to the rear of the Porsche. Crouching, he glanced at the burning spot on his left shoulder where a bullet had grazed him, tearing the leather. Luckily, it wasn't serious, he thought, sliding a new ammunition clip into his gun. Then, gripping it tightly, he tried one more time to reason with the man. "Williams, do yourself a favor and give it up. Don't force me to kill you."

The easiest way to finish it, he knew, was to shoot through the door, but he wanted the bastard alive. He wanted to prove to Jenny and Jamie that the system worked. Besides, if he killed Williams, his death would always stand between him and Jenny.

Another bullet whizzed his way. "You're not getting your hands on the money and my kid. You can keep the cold bitch," Burke taunted.

Mark's mouth compressed into a thin line, controlling his rage. Cautiously, he eased around to the passenger side of the car. Out of the corner of his eye he saw Jenny running in a wide circle toward the booth, a mere shadow in the ever darkening night. He wanted to shout at her to drop to the ground, but he didn't dare draw Williams's attention to her. When he reached the passenger door, he straightened and took another blind shot at the man on the other side, intent on keeping Burke's attention fixed on himself.

Williams leaped and fired. It was the clear shot Mark had been waiting for. He fired, hitting the man in the shoulder. With a cry, Williams dropped his gun, turned and ran across the parking lot—straight toward Jenny.

For a moment Jenny froze. Dimly, she heard Mark shout. "Run, Jenny, run." But all she could think was that her running days were over. Thinking of everything this man had put her through, had done to her family, bitter anger boiled up within her. She made straight for Burke, throwing all her weight into the impact, tackling him, tossing him off-balance. He went down and Jenny landed on top of him, punching him wildly, landing blow after blow as they rolled on the gravel. At one point he was on top, reaching for her flailing arms. For a split second his terrifying green eyes were so close, they burned into her. She spit into his face, clawing at him.

Then he was suddenly jerked away from her.

Mark dragged him off Jenny, but the man wouldn't quit. He kicked, twisted, finally pulling free. Mark lunged for him, landing a few satisfying blows into his gut. Williams doubled over. Mark grabbed his hair and jerked his face up, hitting him on the jaw so hard that Williams's head swiveled to the right and he slumped to the ground in a faint.

At that moment Mark heard steps behind him. Straddling Williams, he glanced over his shoulder and saw the security guard running toward them. "I called the cops," the man shouted. "Do you need help?"

Mark got to his feet, rolled Williams over and, taking out the metal contraption in his back pocket, cuffed him. "Yeah, stay with him until the cops arrive." Straightening, he reached for Jenny and drew her into his arms, locking her tightly against him. "Are you all right?"

Jenny nodded, struggling to get out of his arms, her voice frantic. "Where did he hurt you? I saw you get shot."

Mark glanced at his shoulder, where his jacket was ripped. "It's only a scratch, but if you keep struggling, it's gonna hurt like a bitch, because there isn't a chance in hell I'm letting go of you."

He kissed her fiercely, cutting off her protest. She resisted at first, then her arms went around him tightly. She had almost lost him tonight. For the rest of her life, she would remember his dash through a hail of bullets. It would be at the back of her mind every morning when she kissed him goodbye. But she would learn to live with it, because she couldn't live without him. And if the worst happened, then she wanted to have happy memories, a whole house filled with memories that would help her go on with her life.

Her arms tightened around his neck and she kissed him feverishly, whispering, "I love you, I love you..."

Jamie came dashing across the parking lot, the music box he'd found in the car clasped in his hands. He stopped abruptly as the security guard dragged Burke to his feet none too gently. Sirens wailed in the distance, coming closer rapidly.

Jenny and Mark reached for Jamie at the same time, drawing him between them, their hands linking around him. For a moment, as the first patrol car shot down the road toward them, Burke was pinned in the beam of its lights. They could see him clearly, disheveled and bleeding, still struggling, madness foaming at his mouth.

Jamie took an unconscious step back, pressing against Jenny and Mark, his hands fumbling with the music box.

The clear sound of Brahms' Lullaby began to play. The sound made Burke lunge forward with such force that Jenny feared he would break free of the guard's hold.

Then he suddenly crumpled and fell to his knees.

It was past ten when they finally arrived back at the house. The automatic floodlights had come on. Jenny and Mark carried the metal chest inside, Jamie following them, the small carousel still clutched in his hands. He had held onto it all evening while they'd made their statements and while Mark's "shoulder scratch" had been bandaged at the local emergency room.

Burke, they'd found out, had lived near them for the last three months. Global Airlines was planning to extend flights to McArthur Airport, a mere twenty minutes drive away from Port Jefferson, and he'd been in charge of setting up operations. A brief shiver raced through Jenny when she thought of how close Burke had come to destroying their lives a second time. Putting down her half of the chest at Mark's signal, she straightened and firmly closed the door behind her son. Burke was no longer a danger.

But he was still haunting Jamie.

Mark looked from Jenny to Jamie, then walked up to the boy. "We still have to put up the mailbox," he said lightly.

Jenny wanted to protest. Mark looked so weary. They hadn't eaten since lunch; no one had particularly wanted to stop on their way home. She watched Jamie tighten his hold on the carousel. Then he walked over to the table and put it down. "What name are we going to put on it?" he asked slowly.

Mark and Jenny's eyes connected and clung.

"How about Lawton?" Mark suggested gently.

Jamie looked from his mother to Mark, a small grin crossing his face. "Lawton sounds better than Wilson," he said, his grin spreading. Together they went outside. In the beam of the Blazer's headlights, they put up the red barn. A promise of love and safety and happiness.

That promise was fulfilled several months later at Burke's trial.

The courtroom was crowded that day. On one side of the aisle sat Burke's parents, stiff with anger and bitterness.

There wasn't an empty seat on the other side of the aisle. Mark's family had come to give their support, and Alys and Ralph had flown in from Dallas. The rest of the seats were filled with fellow officers.

When it was time for Jamie to take the witness stand, Jenny's hand curled around her husband's, then she cast a glance over her shoulder. He had given her so much. Love, safety and a family that had welcomed her with open arms. She pressed her hand to her stomach, where a new life was growing. *Their child.* But her happiness wouldn't be complete until Jamie, too, was free of the past.

Mark could hardly take his eyes off Jenny. Her white suit was simple and elegant. The only jewelry she wore was a diamond wedding band. She looked confident and beautiful. Over the past few months, the last bits of nervousness had disappeared completely. She'd taken all her possessions out of storage. They'd had to add a room at the back of the house for her mother's musical instruments. Jenny herself practiced on them every day. Jamie had moved out of the master bedroom and had, over the holidays, shared his room and his toys with Tim. The two boys had become fast friends. Tim, like his father, had taken one look at Jenny and had fallen in love. His son had enjoyed his stay over Christmas so much that he was already talking about spending Easter with them. Carolyn was furious and at first had refused to allow him to come, but Jenny was wearing her down. Their phone bill these days was astronomical.

He turned back to Jamie, watching him stand up in the witness box, and his hand tightened around Jenny's. "He's going to be fine. Trust me."

Jenny nodded, smiling at him with tears shimmering in her eyes. Mark had spent hours coaching Jamie, patiently dealing with his fears. "I love you," she whispered, her heart overflowing with it. She looked at Burke, feeling only pity for the man who had terrorized her life for so many years.

He had hardly taken part in the proceedings. Even the sight of his son facing him in the witness box didn't seem to touch him, she noticed.

With her hands clasped snugly in Mark's, she watched Jamie face his father unflinchingly. The words just flowed out of him. No one interrupted him. When he finally stopped, he took a deep, shuddering breath. Then he turned to the white-haired judge and said, "I told the truth this time. Now, can I go back to my Mom and Dad? And, please, I want to change my name to Lawton. Will you help me?"

Gravely the judge nodded. "Yes, Jamie, I will."

\*    \*    \*    \*    \*

For all those readers who've been looking for something a little bit
different, a little bit spooky, let Silhouette Books take you on a
journey to the dark side of love with

# SILHOUETTE
# Shadows™

If you like your romance mixed with a hint of danger, a taste of
something eerie and wild, you'll love Shadows. This new line
will send a shiver down your spine and make your heart beat
faster. It's full of romance and more—and some of your favorite
authors will be featured right from the start. Look for our four
launch titles wherever books are sold, because you won't want to
miss a single one.

THE LAST CAVALIER—Heather Graham Pozzessere
WHO IS DEBORAH?—Elise Title
STRANGER IN THE MIST—Lee Karr
SWAMP SECRETS—Carla Cassidy

After that, look for two books every month, and prepare to
tremble with fear—and passion.

SILHOUETTE SHADOWS, coming your way in March.

Silhouette®

SHAD1

# INTIMATE MOMENTS®
## Silhouette®

### CONARD COUNTY   CONTINUES...

Come back to Conard County, Wyoming, where you'll meet men and women whose lives are as dramatic as the landscape around them. Join author Rachel Lee for the third book in her fabulous series, MISS EMMALINE AND THE ARCHANGEL (IM #482). Meet Emmaline Conard, "Miss Emma," a woman who was cruelly tormented years ago and now is being victimized again. But this time sheriff's investigator Gage Dalton—the man they call hell's own archangel—is there to protect her. But who will protect Gage from his feelings for Emma? Look for their story in March, only from Silhouette Intimate Moments.

# S SPRING FANCY

Three bachelors, footloose
and fancy-free... until now!

Spring into romance with three
fabulous fancies by three of
Silhouette's hottest authors:

## ANNETTE BROADRICK
## LASS SMALL
## KASEY MICHAELS

When spring fancy strikes, no man is immune!

Look for this exciting new short-story collection
in March at your favorite retail outlet.

Only from

where passion lives.

# AMERICAN HERO

It seems readers can't get enough of these men—and we don't blame them! When Silhouette Intimate Moments' best authors go all-out to create irresistible men, it's no wonder women everywhere are falling in love. And look what—and who!—we have in store for you early in 1993.

January brings NO RETREAT (IM #469), by Marilyn Pappano. Here's a military man who brings a whole new meaning to macho!

In February, look for IN A STRANGER'S EYES (IM #475), by Doreen Roberts. Who is he—and why does she feel she knows him?

In March, it's FIREBRAND (IM #481), by Paula Detmer Riggs. The flames of passion have never burned this hot before!

And in April, look for COLD, COLD HEART (IM #487), by Ann Williams. It takes a mother in distress and a missing child to thaw this guy, but once he melts…!

AMERICAN HEROES. YOU WON'T WANT TO MISS A SINGLE ONE—ONLY FROM

IMHERO3R

# Take 4 bestselling love stories FREE
## Plus get a FREE surprise gift!

Silhouette Books
is proud to present
our best authors,
their best books...
and the best in
your reading pleasure!

Throughout 1993, look for exciting books
by these top names in contemporary
romance:

**CATHERINE COULTER—**
*Aftershocks* in February

**FERN MICHAELS—**
*Whisper My Name* in March

**DIANA PALMER—**
*Heather's Song* in March

**ELIZABETH LOWELL—**
*Love Song for a Raven* in April

**SANDRA BROWN**
(previously published under
the pseudonym Erin St. Claire)—
*Led Astray* in April

**LINDA HOWARD—**
*All That Glitters* in May

When it comes to passion,
we wrote the book.

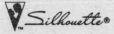